IN PROGRESS

Winner of the Eludia Award

Hidden River Arts offers the Eludia Award for a first book-length unpublished novel or collection of stories by a woman writer, age 40 or above. The Eludia Award provides $1000 and publication by Hidden River Publishing on its Sowilo Press imprint. The purpose of the prize is to support the many women writers who meet with delays and obstacles in discovering their creative selves.

Hidden River Arts is an interdisciplinary arts organization dedicated to supporting and celebrating the unserved artists among us, particularly those outside the artistic and academic mainstream.

IN PROGRESS

STORIES BY

Catharine Leggett

SOWILO PRESS
Philadelphia   *2019*

Grateful acknowledgment is made to the editors of the following publications and anthologies in which these stories have appeared, some in a slightly different form, and to CBC Radio:

Journals: *EVENT, The Antigonish Review, The New Quarterly, paperbytes* (imprint of *paperplates*), *Canadian Author Magazine, Room, Per Contra*

Anthologies: *Law and Disorder—Stories of Conflict and Crime, Best New Writing 2014, The Reading Place, Slow the Pace, Empty Nest*

CBC Radio, *The Hornby Collection*

Cover design by Miriam Seidel
Interior design and typography by P. M. Gordon Associates

Library of Congress Control Number: 2019936506
ISBN 978-0-9994915-1-5

SOWILO PRESS
An imprint of Hidden River Publishing
Philadelphia, Pennsylvania

For Rick

The author acknowledges the
support of the Canada Council
for the Arts and the Ontario
Arts Council.

L'auteur remercie le Conseil
des arts du Canada et le
Conseil des arts de l'Ontario
de leur soutien.

 Canada Council Conseil des arts
for the Arts du Canada

 ONTARIO ARTS COUNCIL
CONSEIL DES ARTS DE L'ONTARIO

an Ontario government agency
un organisme du gouvernement de l'Ontario

Acknowledgments

I wish to thank my family and friends who have been steadfast, cheering me on from the bleachers throughout this marathon, and in particular my brothers Jim, Bob, and John, sisters-in-law Shirley Leggett and Barbara Bodnar, my son-in-law Gaelan Burke, and Elyse Hogan-Wilson. I am grateful for my posse of fellow writers, Melissa Hardy, Jocelyn Cullity, and Adrienne Clarke, who weigh in with valuable advice, wisdom, and professionalism, and do so with sensitivity and kindness. Thank you to graphic designer Miriam Seidel for giving the stories "a look" and to Doug Gordon, the miracle man who turns the manuscript into a publication-ready document.

A heartfelt special thank-you goes to the editor and publisher, Debra Leigh Scott, for her dedication, devotion, and passion for the arts, and for seeing something in these stories and bringing them into the light. It is an honor to be named an Eludia Award Winner and to represent the spirit of her grandmother for whom the award is named: I hope I do it justice.

To my daughter, Courtney Burke, and my son, Bryce Jardine, my love and gratitude for your loyalty and tolerance, and for making my life oh so interesting. And to my husband, Rick Jardine, I could not have done this without your indefatigable patience, kindness, wisdom, and unflagging optimism. You keep the fire stoked.

Contents

THE 401

Once our house was in the country, beside a gravel road. But the city grew, and that changed everything.

Our road, Wilton Road, was paved, and the first commercial business to appear on Wellington Road, not far from us, was a White Rose gas station. Its sign glowed like a long, long stem growing up into the sky. The neighborhood kids hung out at its Coke machine, marveling at its clunking, and gazing in wonder when it released a bottle. We ran our hands over its round corners and traced the waves of its letters with our fingers. Summer nights, we shared pops, inhaling the scent of gasoline that splattered out onto the pavement.

Letters came from the Ontario government telling the farmers in our area that part or all their land would be purchased to make way for a four-lane superhighway called the 401. It would stretch like a band across the narrow part of southern Ontario, connecting Windsor to Toronto, and beyond to the Quebec border.

At our country church, people lingered in the shade of the maples and spoke of the changes the highway would bring. They spoke of expropriation, a word I didn't understand at the time. A few families lost so much land they had to move away, even though they'd farmed there for generations. We had a large property of four acres, but the highway would not affect us, since it would be about a mile away.

When construction began, the kids in the neighborhood watched from the White Rose. The boys knew the names of all the machines—bulldozers, loaders, graders, excavators—but they looked like yellow insects, scurrying about with their quick jerky movements and constant buzzing. They were making a cloverleaf, an interchange that would let traffic easily on and off the highway. They

1

made two hills in what was once a cornfield and connected them with a bridge, so the superhighway could flow under it like a river. I loved the name cloverleaf; it sounded so lucky.

Change came quickly to our neighborhood once the 401 was completed. The main road into London, the Wellington Road, was widened and its curves removed; a traffic light went up at the intersection with our road; Benny, an old bachelor farmer who lived in a ramshackle house, was killed on his tractor at the new intersection, a tragedy my mother had predicted; motels, restaurants, and stores began to appear along Wellington Road.

Some evenings, while sitting on our front porch, we'd watch hitchhikers, usually single men, who'd come off the highway pass by our house, and Mom would say, "Not long ago we knew everyone who walked up the road, and now we don't know who they are or where they're from, or even why they're here." In her voice, I heard regret, or melancholia.

Off in the distance, from land once holding only the whispers of corn, wheat, and rye, came the constant drone of cars and transport trucks. At night, lying in bed, I listened for the sounds of their approach, tracked them to directly behind our house, held them as long as I could before they disappeared. My dreams sped off to the cities they would pass, cities I longed to visit—Toronto, Montreal, New York, Paris.

In the summer of 1965 I was fifteen. I decided I couldn't face another year of high school with my skimpy wardrobe. I dreamed of looking like the other girls at the school in the city where I was bussed. I admired their crisp button-down-collar blouses, the long V-neck sweaters, the above-the-knee kilts, the knee-high socks, and penny loafer shoes. I had a blue mohair sweater I bought with allowance money, but it was worn thin at the elbows, and the four skirts Mom made me last year were too long, not above-the-knee skirts like the other girls wore. I rolled them up at the waist, but this would thicken my waistline. I had other clothes Mrs. Kronski, my mother's friend from church, gave me.

"They're perfectly good," she explained as she handed me a brown paper bag stuffed with clothes that smelled like freshly dug potatoes. "It would be a shame to throw them out."

"Thank you," I said, because I'd never dream of saying anything else. But I *wanted* to say: No thank you, I want my own clothes, new clothes; I want to blend in with the city girls and I don't want to wear the out-of-style clothes of a farmer's daughter five years older than me.

I watched my Mom ironing one of my Dad's work shirts from The Green Oasis nursery and told her my plan to find a summer job.

"Beth, you're young. There's plenty of time to work and make money. Money isn't everything, you know. You should enjoy your freedom while you have it."

But money was everything.

She gazed out the kitchen window, the rustle of leaves in the wind drifting in. She might have thought some extra income in the house would help, since Dad's nursery business was struggling, and my older brother Ronnie was in university at McGill. She wouldn't have to make me new clothes for the fall when she'd be busy canning and freezing vegetables from our garden.

"Well, I suppose it would be good experience," she said as if she was trying to convince herself. "A few hours to start, Beth. But if it doesn't work out, you quit. Okay?"

That afternoon, under the glaring heat of a late June sun, I walked along Wellington Road with the hot sweep of passing cars heading into the city, stopping at several of the little motels to apply for work. On the bottom where it asked what position I was applying for, I wrote, Anything.

The next day, a woman named Gail, the dining room manager and hostess from the Holiday Inn, phoned to ask if I'd be interested in starting there as a pantry girl, someone who worked in the kitchen, preparing side dishes for the waitresses—shrimp cocktails, rollmops, chocolate sundaes, pies, salads.

"I don't know what some of those things are," I said. "What's a rollmop?"

"Pickled fish. Herring. But never mind, we'll show you everything." Gail sounded reassuring, and I was relieved to hear they'd give me time to learn.

"But here's the issue," Gail said. "I need you to start immediately. Can you come in today at four? It's not much notice, but I'm short-staffed tonight and we have a full house. All you'll be doing is watching, just to get the hang of it." She sounded so friendly, so encouraging.

Sunday night and I was going to my first job. I smelled the sweet scent of freshly cut hay in the distant fields, the air filled with a soft haze. Usually I'd be with my family, sitting outside in the back yard or sprawled on the living room floor watching Ed Sullivan and *Bonanza*, all of us lazy after a roast beef dinner. Or I'd be with my friends, Pam and Carole, hanging out at the White Rose.

But here I was, walking where I'd lived all my life, walking towards the fanciest motel on Wellington Road, making my way towards the star perched on top of the Holiday Inn's green and yellow sign, overcome by a feeling of independence and being grown up now. I was walking towards a new life.

Chilled air and soft music greeted me as I stepped into the spacious lobby. I looked across the room to a stone fireplace that climbed up an entire wall. Two business men sat on the gold couches by the hearth and seemed to be bent over paperwork spread out on a coffee table. Out the back window and across a courtyard, I saw someone run and jump off a diving board into a pool, the deck lined with sunbathers on lounge chairs.

"Hi," I said to a young man in a dark suit with a red tie behind the front desk. He smelled of Aqua Velva. I knew because my brother Ronnie practically took a bath in it when he went out on dates. His gold name tag said "Alphonse, Front Desk."

"Hello, Alphonse? Excuse me," I repeated because maybe he didn't hear me.

He raised his head and looked at me with pale blue, red-rimmed eyes.

"I am supposed to meet Gail. From the dining room," I explained.

"Just a minute," he spoke briskly, picked up a phone and dialed, then slammed it down when no one answered. "I'll have to get her."

I could tell he didn't want to.

While I waited, I leafed through a pamphlet from a display case. A woman wearing a powder-blue blouse with white slacks, her tiny waist accentuated by a broad black belt, lounged on a green bedspread, leaning back on an elbow, her legs crossed at her ankles, her feet in flat black pointed-toed shoes. She smiled up at a tanned man with a big, white-toothed smile, his shirt rolled up at the sleeves, one hand raised, as if he were gesturing to her. Their eyes were locked, and I could tell they were making exciting plans. In another picture featuring the dining room, a family smiled at their untouched dinners. I'd be working for this red dining room lit with candles and white cloth dinner napkins and red tablecloths; I could hardly believe it.

Alphonse came back across the lobby. He opened the gate door, stepped behind the counter, and without looking at me said, "She's coming."

A woman with puffy platinum blonde hair, a black bow positioned just over her even roll of bangs, came out of the dining room, her red dress flowing as if caught in a gentle breeze. The loose bodice fell like a cape over the main part of the dress and gave her the appearance of floating. Her gold-laminated flat shoes made me think of the magical shoes of a princess out of a fairy tale.

"Hello," she said. "You're Beth, I take it?"

"Yes," I said, as she looked me up and down.

Closer, I could see the pencil lines of her eyebrows, arched over her brown eyes and blue eye shadow. She was older than her voice sounded on the phone, somewhere in her fifties, and she sounded harsher, less friendly.

"Well, thank goodness you're here. This has been some kind of day, I can tell you. Follow me."

We headed to the entrance of the dining room, mysterious and dark looking, as if we were entering a cave.

"We're only now getting cleaned up from lunch, and we should be all prepped for dinner," Gail said as she picked up a stack of menus at the hostess stand.

As we crossed the dining room, I saw a few diners lingering over a late lunch. I put on my very best smile and tipped my head back a bit, in case anyone was watching me. I wanted to show how at ease I was, how I belonged. I wanted to float like Gail.

One whole side of the room faced the pool, the water a stunning turquoise, and an awning shielded the dining room from bright sunlight. The diners seemed deeply engaged in conversation, as if the piped-in music and dim candlelight spread over them like a magical mist and cast a spell. A couple seated at a table along a wall must have been in love, their eyes locked as they smiled at each other, like the couple in the brochure. Now I was in the brochure, encased in the conditioned calm air of this place, not even a motel, but an inn— so much more sophisticated—racing towards my dreams.

"So that's the dining room," Gail said, after we'd zigzagged our way through the tables, some of them still covered with dishes. "Now I'll show you the kitchen, where you'll be. This is called the gangway." She led me down a short, wide hall, towards two swinging doors. "Always, always use the right door, whether you're coming in or out. Remember. Or you'll get smacked in the head."

Gail pushed open the door, and I followed her in.

The kitchen rushed at me with the force of a breaking wave. I squinted against the glare of white tiles and fluorescent lights and the white uniforms of the staff buzzing around. Noise ricocheted off the walls and floor: metal crashing, machines chugging, bells ringing, waitresses shouting, knives chopping, deep fryers hissing, griddles spitting, fans humming, an unending bewildering commotion.

Someone shouted, "Shut-up!" at the top of his lungs, and silence fell against the steady chug of a dishwasher.

A tall thin chef stepped into the center of the kitchen, mopped the sweat off his forehead with a cloth he tossed over his shoulder, and looked at the astonished kitchen workers. "That's better. Keep your voices down. We're in the shit with this banquet and yelling doesn't help! Go back to work. Quietly!"

"Come with me," Gail said. "Careful how you step on the floor; it gets greasy."

She led me to the tall chef and introduced him as Eric. "You sure you want to work in this madhouse?" he asked.

His big puffy chef's hat reminded me of one of my mom's muffins and added at least a foot to his height. He had a nice smile and an English accent.

"Welcome on board. You picked a busy day to start." Then he excused himself and went to help a waitress load a tray.

"There's a bowling banquet going on; bowlers from all over. Something like three hundred of them. I hate the game, so I don't get it." Gail pointed to another area of the kitchen, where chicken dinners were being loaded on large oval trays and taken away by waitresses out another set of swinging doors.

"Over there"—Gail pointed to a long counter, with a row of glowing orange bulbs, behind which two cooks worked—"that's the dining room and coffee shop kitchen. That pass-through you see on the other wall, that hole in the wall behind where the cooks are standing and off to the side, that's where the coffee shop girls pick up their orders. They don't come into the kitchen that much, just to get dishes from the dishwashing area."

"Over by the row of orange lights, warming lights, that's where my waitresses order and pick up their food." Gail motioned for me to follow her with her index finger as we stepped off to the side, still facing the dining room kitchen. She lowered her voice and said, "Do you see that short cook with the broad shoulders and muscular arms, the one with the five o'clock shadow?"

"Yes," I said, and saw that he was looking at me. He made a funny smile, like a sneer, and jerked his head back. He seemed to mouth something, but I couldn't tell what he was saying, or if he was even talking to me, and I looked away.

"That's Gus. I call him the mean Greek. Watch out for him. If he starts bothering you, just ignore him. The other cook is Nick, little Italian Nick we call him. He's nice, and so is Eric. But not Gus. Now, follow me, I'll take you downstairs and show you the uniform room."

After I'd changed into a white uniform dress and a yellow apron, I met Gail, who was waiting for me in the pantry area where I'd be working, across from Gus and Nick.

"Those will do for now, but you'll need something sturdier for the kitchen." She pointed to my white canvas running shoes and scowled at them.

"Okay," I said.

She didn't tell me anything about shoes on the phone.

"Here's an elastic." She plunked a red rubber band into my hand. "Pull your hair back and put it in a ponytail. It's a health regulation."

She waited for me to finish arranging my thick, wavy hair at the nape of my neck, before continuing. "Now then, this area is where you'll work. It's called the pantry."

I looked around. Mostly stainless steel and glass, with humming fridges, freezers, a milk dispenser, a milkshake machine, and stainless-steel shelves filled with big round containers and dishes. A sink, half-filled with scummy water, pie lifts, and ice cream scoops, had rags piled up around it.

Gail moved along to white containers with ladles, lined up in a row and slanting towards us. "These are for salad dressings, and you can see what a mess the waitresses make of things. They don't care, as long as they get what they want, so they can make their tips."

The whole area looked as if a small tornado had swept through.

Gail kept on with her pantry tour, opening cupboards and fridge doors and telling me far more than I could hope to remember. Her face seemed pinched into a perpetual state of frowning and I wondered if she was always like that or having a really bad day, and that's why I was there, to make her day better.

"Start by cleaning this up. Look at it. What a mess! The girls can be pigs. I've got to get back out to the dining room and get things ready for the dinner rush. Just ask someone if you need something. Ask Eric, he'll help you. You look like a smart girl, Beth. Just use your common sense."

She turned quickly and headed out of the kitchen, her dress fluttering behind her, and before I could tell her she had a piece of lettuce stuck to her heel, she disappeared out the swinging doors.

Salad dressing dripped out of containers; chunks of lettuce lay strewn across the counter; a tub of vanilla ice cream was on its way to becoming soup; a cream pitcher had tipped and a white waterfall dripped down the front of the cooler, collecting in a pool on the floor. It looked like someone had tried to beat up a blueberry pie. I didn't know where anything went or what they'd run out of, and I wondered when Gail would come back to train me, or if someone else would.

All the time I worked to make my area shiny and clean, I heard a clucking noise. I turned to see who was making it and saw Gus, his face glowing in the red heat lamps; he was watching me. Tic, tic, tic, tic—the kind of sound a person makes if beckoning a dog with a biscuit. He smiled and jerked his head back, but I ignored him, like Gail told me to.

The dining room waitresses, in their black dresses with red trimmed collars and red aprons, flew around the kitchen like a flock of red-winged blackbirds, squawking at Gus, who hammered on a little bell and shouted, "Pickup, pickup, pickup, pickup." He seemed mad all the time as he slammed their orders down. "Get it out of here, move your asses!" he shouted in an accent so thick I could hardly make out what he was saying, and some of them shouted back, "Shut up, Gus!"

Nick worked quietly beside Gus, sometimes telling him to lay off the bell, and helped the waitresses with their orders, "This yours, this yours," wiping the rims of their plates with a cloth to clean them. Not Gus; he didn't help anyone.

Then Gus went crazy on the bell, hammering it over and over, shouting a waitress's name which eventually I figured out was Janet.

"Move it, move it, move it!" he shouted. He noticed me watching and yelled at me, waving a sausage in the air.

"What you looking at, hot stuff? You like poot-sos? Poot-sos?"

I had no idea what he was talking about, and turned away, remembering what Gail said, but it was hard. I was raised to be polite to adults, and ignoring Gus went against everything I'd been taught.

Janet, a dining room waitress, came into the kitchen, her chubby hands full of orders, talking to herself. She took plates down from under the heat lamps and arranged them on a tray and was about to go back to the dining room.

Gus slammed on the bell, even though she was standing right there. "Get this out of here, move your fat ass! Twenty minute it sit here. Take. Take. Take!" He jabbed his finger into a steak.

"Like hell it's been sitting there that long!" Janet stood on her tiptoes, glaring at him. "You're full of shit. I just put that order in ten minutes ago. My table's having appetizers. I can't take it out there now. Can't you read a goddamn bill? Look," she pointed at a slip of paper. "The order says soup and salad, doesn't it? Can't you read English for chrissake?"

I snuck a peek at him then. I didn't think he would be able to read English, his Greek accent was so thick. I'd never seen anyone so angry looking, his eyes slits, his teeth bared. Then he boomed, "Move your fat ass. Get this out!"

Gail came into the kitchen, carrying a stack of menus with gold covers.

"Train your people. Hire professionals, not fat pig idiots!" Gus shouted at Gail, and I thought how terrible that was, and not even true. Janet was pudgy but not fat, and no one should be called a pig. I felt sorry for her.

"You're the idiot, Gus! Worse than a pig."

"Stop it, both of you!" Gail shouted in a voice that didn't sound anything like it had on the phone. She called out to Eric at the back of the restaurant, where he was still helping the banquet crew and the dishwasher. "Eric, get over here and settle this. I'm sick of the way Gus talks to my girls."

Eric came bounding forward with lengthy strides, his heavy black shoes so speckled with goop it looked like seagulls had perched on them.

"Gus!" he boomed into Gus's face on the other side of the amber lights. "Take that order down and don't put it up until Janet's ready for it."

Gus started to say something back.

"Don't argue with me." Eric shook his finger at Gus. "Get the orders out." He turned to Janet. "And you, Janet, get your shit together, will you?"

"Gus has it in for me. He's been on my ass all night," Janet said.

Gus shoved his face under the heat lamps. "I wouldn't get on your ass for no money."

"That's enough!" Eric scolded both of them.

I could tell Eric didn't like shouting; his face went all red. I thought he should fire Gus for what he said to Janet. Then I saw all the people running around in the kitchen—the banquet waiters and cooks, the dining room and coffee shop waitresses, the busboys, the dishwasher, the banquet cooks. It would only add to the confusion. Or maybe he was afraid of him.

All night I kept looking at my watch and thinking about what would be going on at home—Ed Sullivan, *Bonanza*—or if Pam and Carole had phoned to see if I wanted to hang out. The dining room waitresses flew in and out, calling out their orders to me—salads, pies, shrimp cocktails, pâté, and some of them showed me how to arrange the food on the plates. I tried my best and explained that I hadn't been trained yet.

Janet said, "That's how it goes around this joint. They throw you into the fire and watch you burn."

The dinner rush was slowing down, and Gus started back up with his clicking noise. Nick kept saying something to him, and I thought he was telling Gus to leave me alone. Once, I accidentally looked at Gus when Nick had gone downstairs to get supplies, and he jerked his head back as if he wanted me to go over to him.

"Poot-sos," he repeated, a word I'd never heard before, but with him waving a sausage around, I could pretty much figure it out.

Janet came into my pantry area and leaned against the ice cream cooler.

"I know Gus is bothering you. Pardon my French, but just ignore that asshole."

She poured herself a glass of milk, peering at me over the top of the rim as she drank, then swiped away her milk mustache with the back of her hand.

"What a night!" Janet's mascara was smudged under her eyes, but I don't think she cared. "I had so many bitchy customers. Miss this and miss that. Three of me couldn't keep up with it."

A tall, slim waitress joined us, her bright red lipstick freshly applied, her short grey hair neatly trimmed around her ears. She had a narrow face, a long, pointed nose, and piercing eyes that reminded me of hawks I'd seen in our yard. Her pencil-thin eyebrows made her eyes seem more severe. Her name tag said "Roberta," and she interrupted what Janet was saying to me in a clipped voice, "I need a strawberry shortcake parfait, right away." She snapped her fingers in front of my face. "What's your name, anyway?"

"Beth. I don't know how to make that. No one has shown me." She looked like my grade seven teacher Mrs. Wiley, who was strict and just as skinny.

"Oh, come on. Surely you know how. Oh, never mind, I don't have all day. I've got customers waiting. Get out of my way, Janet."

Janet stepped aside and rolled her eyes.

Roberta cut a square out of a white cake she pulled out of the fridge and shoved it into a tall parfait glass, threw back the freezer lid and leaned inside, scooping strawberry ice cream into the dish, coming up every so often to catch her breath. Then she dove inside the freezer again, her voice muffled as she talked.

"Why would they hire someone to work in a kitchen who doesn't know how to make a parfait?"

She sounded mad at me as she slapped the freezer lid closed and topped off her dish with strawberry sauce and whipped cream.

"Do we have to do everything around here?" She stuck a maraschino cherry on top of the parfait.

"I don't know," I said, and felt stupid. Maybe it wasn't a question meant to be answered.

Roberta started back to the dining room, walking so fast her white shoes squeaked on the tile floor as if she had a little dog yapping at her heels.

Janet watched her, a glass of milk still in her hand, and stuck out her tongue. I started laughing.

"Roberta's a bitch on wheels," Janet said.

I changed into my shorts and floral blouse and walked through the dining room, all the lights on now, table clothes crooked on most of the tables, napkins heaped up, and food spilled on the carpet. Gail and several waitresses sat at a big round table, doing something with their customer checks, counting money, and smoking.

"Goodnight," Gail called out. She had her shoes kicked off and rested her feet on a chair. "See you tomorrow at three. Good job!" she added and blew smoke up towards the ceiling.

As I passed through the lobby, I saw my parents sitting in the coffee shop. What were they doing here? My dad had on his khaki shorts and brown T-shirt, and my mom wore a green sweater over her housedress. If I'd known they were coming, I would have told them to dress up. I stepped into the coffee shop, closed now except for a few stragglers like my parents.

"Sit down, Beth. Want something to eat?" Mom sipped on her milkshake.

"No, I'm tired. I just want to go home."

But the truth was, I didn't want anyone to see me with my parents because of how they were dressed, like country people, not like the people who stayed in the Holiday Inn.

"How come you're here?" I asked.

"To walk you home," Mom said. "It's not safe for you to walk home alone after dark."

I didn't think I needed to be walked home; I wasn't a baby anymore, especially now that I had a job.

As we crossed the lobby, headed for the front door, Alphonse at the front desk motioned for me to come over. He probably wanted to ask me how my first night went.

"Kitchen and housekeeping staff are not allowed to walk through the lobby. You leave out the kitchen door," he said, still encased in his Aqua Velva cloud.

His fingernails looked as if they'd been manicured, and I thought of my own hands, stinking of Thousand Island dressing and shrimp, my pink nail polish chipped. I tucked them behind my back. I wasn't good enough to be in the lobby.

My job and my life became the same thing. My hours were extended because I caught on fast and didn't complain. The waitresses squabbled all the time, and often I was at the center of their fights. Beth, I asked for my pie first! Beth, I need the salads now! Beth, what about the shrimp cocktail? Beth, get a move on! I tried hard to please everyone, and I figured out that if I gave them quick service, the service to their customers improved, and so did their tips. It was all about money.

Roberta was the most demanding, and if Janet happened to be around she went after her. "Leave the kid alone, Roberta. She's not just working for you."

All summer long, Gus waited until there was no one around, or everyone was too busy working to notice him bugging me. "Hey, hot shot. Tic, tic, tic, tic. Hot shot. Poot-sos, poot-sos," and I knew if I turned and looked, he'd be waving a sausage around in the air.

Roberta towered over me, her eyes pinched and her mouth puckered as if she'd bitten into a lemon. "I'm going to give you some money," she said, her voice sharp and urgent. "But you have to work for it, and you'll only get it if you give me good service. So, when I come into the pantry asking for something, you do it fast."

She handed me two dollars and some change, and shook her finger, as if scolding me. "All Janet does is wag her lips. She talks the big talk but she's as cheap as they come. I don't take advantage of a kid."

Janet started tipping me too, though not as much as Roberta, and she got the other girls tipping, and that made Roberta mad since now she had competition from all the waitresses. It was true what Roberta said about Janet talking a lot. That's why I liked her. Some of the things she came out with really made me laugh.

"If Roberta's nose gets any sharper, she'll start pecking," and "Gail's got a pencil shoved up her ass." I'd never say these things.

At night, I took my tips home and dumped them into the center of my bed, arranging all the coins together into specific denominations. The bills came from Roberta, the pennies from Janet—she talked about how her kids cost her so much, and how she was a single parent, and when I got to be poor old Janet's age, maybe I'd understand what it was like to be broke. Roberta was right about Janet being cheap, and sometimes it bugged me, but since she joked with me and gossiped about the other waitresses, it didn't bother me to be bribed with kindness instead of money.

I'd collapse on my bed, my arms sticky with ice cream and pecan pie, too tired to take a shower. I'd fall into an exhausted sleep and dream of people yelling at me, where's my pie, I ordered a shrimp cocktail, this isn't the right kind of dressing, poot-sos, poot-sos. Sometimes I fell asleep with my money still on my bed, and when I woke up, I had coins sticking to my arms, legs, and face.

I didn't have time to take the bus downtown to go shopping for clothes. I'd fantasize about the blouses I'd buy, the above-the-knee skirts. Clothes without me in them, just garments suspended in mid-air, owning no body.

I was tired all summer long. I imagined this was how people in the work force must feel—either half-dead or half-alive. Sometimes I wondered if Mom was right, if I was too young to be working so much. I'd only been out with Pam and Carole a couple of times since starting my job. We took the shortcut through the field to the White Rose and met up with some kids they knew, new to our neighborhood. That was before they went away to camp and to their cottages, and they wouldn't be back until the end of summer.

Gail kept heaping more hours on me, and I had to cover for another pantry girl when she got sick.

"Saying no, standing up for yourself, is part of what you have to learn. Don't let them push you around and take advantage of you,"

Mom said, when I told her Gail wanted me to work on one of my days off.

The assistant innkeeper, who usually only nodded at me as he passed through the kitchen on his way to see Eric, stopped to talk to me in the pantry.

"Your name is Beth, isn't it?"

"Yes," I said, listening hard to understand him through his accent. He was German, Swiss, or Austrian, I didn't know which, but he sounded like Colonel Klink on *Hogan's Heroes*.

"You do a good job here," he said. "You keep the pantry clean and the waitresses like you."

"Thank you," I said. He was a boss; he made me nervous.

His eyes scanned my work area. It was shiny clean and well stocked, but we hadn't had dinner hour yet, and it wasn't always tidy, though I tried my best.

"What do you think about learning to waitress?"

I was so surprised I could hardly speak. "Great!"

"Good. In the coffee shop. We have a position coming up. Let's start you on counter service and see how you do. We want you to start tonight. Go to housekeeping and get fitted for a uniform. Phyllis, the head coffee shop waitress, is waiting for you. I'll let Gail know." Then he turned quickly on his shiny black shoes and headed for the dining room doors.

A waitress! I'd never dreamed it! Wait until I told Pam and Carole! And my parents. I'd get out of the kitchen, away from the stink and the slime and the heat. I'd miss working close to Nick and Eric, but I sure wouldn't miss Gus and his meanness and nasty gestures. I'd make even more money! I could have all the clothes I wanted!

Eric, who'd been watching me with the assistant manager, crossed the kitchen.

"I overheard what he was saying. Congratulations. We're going to miss you in here, kid." He smiled and patted my back.

Gail came into the pantry carrying an armful of menus.

"I've just heard the news," she snarled. "After all I've done for you, and you're leaving and going to the coffee shop. Don't expect any favors from me."

She threw the entire stack of menus on the floor and pointed down at them.

"Now you can pick them up."

She pivoted on her gold slip-on shoes, the ones she wore between meal times, and disappeared through the swing doors.

Tears welled up. I'd no idea what I'd done wrong. Why did she hate me?

"Hey, hot, hot stuff," Gus shouted at me, and laughed as I picked the menus up off the floor. "Think you something? Boss likes your ass."

"You're a jerk," I said, and couldn't believe I'd said it.

"I'll show you, hot stuff."

"Go fry an egg." I glared at him. Despite what Gail said and did, the promotion made me feel different somehow. Janet was right; she had a pencil shoved up her ass.

One night, I was getting supplies from the walk-in cooler in the basement, a room smaller than my dad's den, where he did paperwork for the nursery. I was pulling a gallon of cream off the shelf, the blast from the noisy cooler fans blowing icy air across my back. I turned around to leave, and Gus stood in front of the closed door, blocking it, his arms crossed and legs apart.

"Hi," I said, startled, pretending I wasn't frightened though my entire body trembled.

His head was down, his cook's hat had slid to the middle of his forehead, his eyes up. The white light in the cooler darkened his five o'clock shadow.

"Are you getting something from the cooler?" I managed, trying to sound like being here with him was a natural occurrence.

"What you gonna do? You call me name now? Go ahead. Come on, hot stuff. Call me name. Call me name." Then he muttered something in Greek and I had no idea what he was saying. "I got you now. You big shot now?"

"I have to get this cream upstairs. I have customers. Phyllis is waiting." My mind raced, and I wasn't sure I was making any sense.

"Leave. Come on, leave."

He motioned to the door, but he had it blocked. I didn't know what to do. How could I protect myself if he came after me? I could scream, but with the fans blasting and the heavy door closed, no one would hear me. He started across the small space towards me. I twisted the lid on the jug of cream to loosen it.

"Here, catch," I said, and tossed it at him.

He caught it and the lid flew off. Cream spilled down his front and onto the floor. I ducked around him and pushed open the cooler door with all my strength.

"You can clean it up!" I shouted over my shoulder.

I don't know what he would have done to me, but I surprised myself with my bravery and enjoyed what I thought was a victory. Mom was right, I had to speak up. But he'd frightened me too, and when I got back to the coffee shop, I sat at a counter stool and waited for my trembling to stop.

After that, Gus just glared, swore, or mumbled under his breath. Or he'd hammer on the bell. I was glad he stopped talking to me. I was glad I shut him up.

Every night someone came to meet me.

Sometimes, Dad came alone in the car to pick me up, or both Mom and Dad would drop into the coffee shop and I'd make them a milkshake with extra ice cream. As we walked across the lobby, I waved to Alphonse at the front desk, though he never waved back. Kitchen workers and waitresses were all the same to him, strictly back-door people. At the beginning of the summer I cared what he thought of me. I was so naive then.

When Ronnie came to meet me, he walked ahead, if we walked on the road, in case any of his friends saw him; it wasn't cool to be out with your little sister. Sometimes, we'd cut through the field close to the Holiday Inn, take the path that the neighborhood kids and people who worked along Wellington Road used, a shortcut to Wilton Road. A billboard had gone up announcing a Red Barn Restaurant was coming soon. Cows used to graze here when it was farmland, before Wellington Road was straightened, before expropriation and the 401.

Late one night, Mom and I sat together in the living room watching Johnny Carson talking to Dean Martin, her favorite singer. I was too tired to shower and change out of my uniform. My pockets bulged with money. I'd been doing better lately because I was happier and gave my customers better service. Gus was away on holidays, and Nick, sweet little, funny little Nick, who said "Mamma Mia" and put his hand over his heart every time he saw me, filled in for him.

The house smelled of tomatoes. Mom was in the midst of canning, making sauce, and I could hear it bubbling in a large pot on the stove. Right now she was darning socks, her usual form of relaxation. She was always doing something, always working, though she called it being productive. The front door was open to let in cooler air, but the noise of passing cars and trucks kept cutting into our conversation.

"They're working you too hard at that place, Beth," she said. "It's not fair for a girl your age. The summer's almost over and you've had no break at all. You'll have plenty more opportunities in your life to work. Youth is a time of innocence, then it's gone. You don't know that now while you're young, but it's true."

I was relieved to hear her say that, though I didn't want to admit it. Lately I felt more independent, especially as my bank account grew, and I imagined all the clothes, the jewelry, the shoes I would buy.

"I'm okay, Mom," I said. "I can handle things."

She peered at me over the top of her reading glasses. I waited for her to say something more, but she didn't. Maybe she thought I was becoming more adult, like Ronnie. Maybe she was getting used to change and had come to realize that, no matter what, we were growing up, and she couldn't stop that from happening. Maybe she thought that one day I'd be gone too, and the letting go had already begun this summer with my job.

"Summer's almost over, Mom," I said. "I'll be going back to school soon."

She nodded, her cheeks dimpling with a smile. "Yes, you will." She was relieved, too.

I finished waiting on my tables and went into the kitchen to restock dishes. On my way back to the coffee shop, carrying a tray of water glasses, I saw Gus, dressed in street clothes, talking to Nick. I wondered what he was doing there; he was still on holiday. I walked past him, pretending I hadn't seen him, but I felt his eyes on me. I wished he'd stay away forever.

I finished around eight-thirty, my hours reduced as the busy season was winding down, and I didn't have to stay until close every night. I phoned home for a ride if I was going to work late or I'd walk home along Wellington Road if it was still daylight. Now in late August, night came earlier, but I thought it was still light enough to walk.

I crossed the parking lot and headed towards the field and the shortcut to the White Rose. I'd grab a pop and see if anyone I knew was hanging out there. Carole and Pam might be back from their summer holidays. A hint of autumn chill pinched through the humid air. The crickets chirped wildly, as if they knew a killing frost was on the way, their time almost up. The ditches were overgrown with goldenrod, the grasses tall and brown.

I started along the wide path that crossed the field, towards the big billboard, the future site of the Red Barn Restaurant. I tried to guess the number of times I'd gone this way, every day to and from public school with Ronnie. Hundreds, maybe thousands of times. Or how many times I'd walked the path with Carole and Pam, on our way to the White Rose. Once the Red Barn came that would change too, like everything else.

I stopped to pluck a stem of wild wheat, chewed its sweet tip, and inhaled the sweetly scented night. A setting sun was making a dramatic exit, sending up flares of oranges and pinks and painting the clouds mauve.

As I approached the billboard, I looked up at the lights that shone down and listened to hear if any kids were hanging out behind it. All was quiet, and I walked on.

A few feet away from me a bird swooped up into the air and shrieked, flushed out of the tall grasses and weeds by my passing.

I heard something behind me and turned to look. Someone rushed at me from behind the billboard, but in the glare of the setting sun I couldn't make anyone out. I started to run, but I felt a pull on my collar, my arm pinched, and I was pushed down into the ground face first.

I tried to scream. A hand clamped over my mouth, shoved my face harder into the dirt. Brittle weeds jabbed around my eyes. I couldn't breathe. The grip over my face so tight the fingers pressed into my jawbone. A sharp pain in my neck from being yanked. My thigh being ripped at, my nylons clawed through. The zip of my nylons running up and down my legs. My body crushed by the weight of another. Absurdly, I thought of my uniform getting dirty and torn, wanted to pull my skirt down to my knees.

He grunted and gasped. I tried to heave with my shoulders and my chest. I couldn't move. I tried biting. Fingers squeezed into my face harder.

I heard a voice. Strangely calm and clear. My voice. Fight for your life. Don't give up.

I willed myself into a fit of violent heaves, wriggled back and forth over the ground, trying to find movement whenever his force weakened. His free hand burned paths over my skin. My muscles convulsed. His grip loosened from my mouth. I gulped for air, started to make a noise. He grabbed my hair and yanked my head back. His hand covered my mouth again. I bit as hard as I could. He yelped. My leg came free of his crushing weight. I raised it and with all my strength smashed my heel down hard into him, not knowing what I was kicking, but just kicking and kicking. He grunted. I wriggled and kicked over and over.

The swish of his clothes sliding off my nylon uniform. His weight lifted and I rolled away. I struggled to my feet. I ran. Sounds came out of me, a hurt animal, the sounds of terror, as if being chased by death.

My nylons hung like cobwebs around my legs. Burrs grabbed at my clothes and lost their grip on the slippery fabric. The weight of money in my pockets banged against my thighs as I ran.

He swooped down on me again like a bat. My jaw hit the ground with a crack. Pain shot through my elbow. I scrambled to get up. His hand grabbed my uniform in the middle of my back. I gave a quick heave forward. He clutched at the hem of my skirt. I flailed my arms and legs wildly, swung out against anything. I squirmed and kicked, my breath coming in short gasps. My foot connected with something, his face, I thought.

His hands lost their hold, fell away like chains. I rolled towards the billboard, scrambled to my feet. My chest felt tight and pinched.

I started running, tripped but didn't fall. Off to the side, his muscular body hunched over, motionless, his face buried in his hands.

I heard him coming up behind me, chasing me again. I raised my knees high to clear the uneven ground, just as I did when I ran along the path with my friends, but I ran faster than I ever had before.

He didn't get far. He tripped. The dull thud of his body hitting the ground. "Shit," he said. I didn't look back. I kept my eyes fixed on the glowing White Rose sign.

I ran all the way to the White Rose, never stopping, never looking back. In the far corner of the parking lot, several kids gathered around their bikes. I ducked into the women's washroom at the back of the station and steadied myself at the sink and looked at my face in the dirty mirror. I sobbed and shook; I could hardly breathe, my chest constricting with fear. Had it really happened, was I attacked? It didn't seem real. I touched the scratch on my cheek and looked down at my tattered nylons. Yes, it had happened. I did not want it to be true.

I had to slow my breathing, force myself to take even breaths, to bring myself under control and stop my trembling. I splashed water over my face and took my hair out of its ponytail, ran my pocket brush through it, to make myself appear as if nothing happened. If I kept my hair down, it covered the scratch. But why would I want to cover it up? Why should I?

I wiped dirt from my uniform with a wet paper towel. I took off my pantyhose and tossed them in the garbage, then put my shoes back on. I kept telling myself over and over, I am safe, I am okay, I have to make it home. I took more deep breaths while steadying myself at the sink until someone knocked on the door.

"You almost finished in there?"

I took a deep breath, stepped outside, and passed a woman who scowled at me.

"Teenagers," she said.

I didn't recognize any of the kids clustered at the far end of the White Rose lot, still huddled around their bikes.

As I walked along Wilton Road towards home, I fought back waves of panic and the temptation to scream at the top of my lungs with the roar of each passing truck. What would I tell my parents? It was almost dark.

They were sitting in the back yard, in the glow from the back-door light. Mom had a large bowl in her lap. Dad sat beside her and waved.

"How did you come home?" Mom shouted.

"I walked with someone from work. I'm going inside to shower and change."

"Okay," Mom called back.

I took a long shower. In my room, I threw my coffee shop uniform on the floor, kicked it into the corner of my closet, and lay down on my bed.

Later, Mom knocked on the door and said, "Beth, you okay?"

I answered, "Yes. Just tired. I'm going to sleep."

I lay awake, and tried not to think about what had happened, but when the memory was too strong and too real to ignore, I thought I smelled sausages.

Could it have been Gus? Would he come after me because I threw cream at him, because I called him a jerk? If I had just ignored him the way Gail told me to, would this have happened? I thought about going to talk with the assistant manager at the Holiday Inn. But I couldn't say for sure it was Gus. It might have been someone who came off the 401, or someone from the neighborhood. Against the glare of the setting sun, I couldn't make him out.

I would be asked what I was doing taking the shortcut through the field so close to dark. Wasn't I being reckless? Putting myself in danger? Didn't I have myself to blame? Wasn't I asking for it? I should be ashamed for being so foolish. I was lucky my carelessness didn't lead to something far worse.

I would pretend nothing had happened. Keep it to myself. Live with it. Deal with it on my own. If I did that, made myself brave, then no one else would have to be involved. I had created the situation. My parents had enough worries with Dad's nursery, and they were talking about selling off some of our property, which got my Dad worked up, and Ronnie going back to McGill meant money pressures. And Mom always busy, working all the time. They didn't need any more problems. I told no one.

I never set foot in the Holiday Inn again. Passing it one night on the way into the city with my parents, I saw something was wrong with the sign. The star on the top wasn't lit. I thought of the wide-open lobby and the piped-in music. The lobby was cold and bare and open, the music tinny. I was glad not to see Alphonse or watch him raise his nose in his superior way as he reigned over his space—the lobby king. I was going places he'd never go, places he couldn't even dream of. I could never go back into that kitchen with all its smells, the grease, dirty dishwater, frying food, bleach, garbage, without feeling sick to my stomach. Gail and her flowing red dress and gold shoes, once the outfit of a goddess, seemed cheap. I would never be able to serve customers in the coffee shop again, especially the families with children, their sweet faces looking up to me. I would want to tell them to run for their lives, that danger lurked there. But I couldn't prove anything. I could never see Gus again.

At night, as I lay in bed and listened to the hum of traffic on the 401, I imagined that every single car and truck was filled with Gusses. I willed them to keep on going and never stop. My whole body tightened as I tried to block out the noise, but I could not get those vehicles filled with evil out of my head.

All summer, I had worked to earn money to buy pretty clothes, and I hadn't bought a thing. I didn't care anymore if I looked different from the city girls, or what they thought of me. I thought of all the people I'd worked with, where they'd come from: Germany, Greece, Italy, England, France. My world had opened up and revealed itself, its dangers. I would always have to stay alert, watch for something that could leap out and grab me, take me down.

I wondered if I'd ever feel safe again. What I needed to do, what I had to concentrate very hard on, was to listen to the sounds inside my house. Listen to my parents talking about the garden, Ronnie's laughter, water rushing through pipes, listen to the usual creaks, the rocking chair runners on the front porch, the back door opening and closing, the sounds of belonging and being cared for, protected and loved. I had to train my ear to hear once again the familiar sounds of my past, focus only on them, be comforted and soothed, and hope that once again I would return to peaceful sleep.

CIVILIZED

"**Y**ou know better than to do that, Maggie," Mom said, standing at the kitchen sink, plucking what I thought were little hats off the strawberries. Dad told me strawberries wore hats to keep the sun off the tops of their heads. Mom said if I believed everything he told me I'd have a head so chuck-full of nonsense, it would spill right out my ears. I'd been kicking the wall while I stared at her brown shoes, squished down at the back, and her white socks that drooped around her ankles.

She kept plucking the bonnets off the berries and I started kicking again, killing time.

For so long, I'd been excited about my birthday, and now it was finally here. In May, I started putting ticks on my Goodchild Brothers Insurance calendar until I arrived at B-day, July 17th. Nights when I was too excited to sleep, I lay in bed and followed the shadows of trees gliding up and down my bedroom wall, etched by the back-porch light, and dreamed about what a magical day it would be. Down the hall, I heard my parents' voices and I knew they'd be whispering about my birthday present.

"Are we having whipped cream?" I asked. My mother was going to make my favorite, strawberry shortcake, especially for my birthday.

"Maggie," she sighed and turned to look at me. "For the third time, yes I will make whipped cream." She crossed her legs at her ankles, thick like mine—how I wished mine were slim, but Mom said thick ankles ran in families and there was nothing a person could do about it.

Kleenex fell from Mom's apron pocket as she crossed to the stove and picked up a spatula. I loved that apron when it was still bright blue, and the red pocket shaped like a tulip wasn't ripped. As she ran a spatula around inside the big blue canning kettle, her underarm waddled and reminded me of bread dough before it went into the oven.

Some days Mom looked pretty, but today wasn't one of them. It didn't help that she was making jam and wore her green dress with flowers so faded they looked more grey than yellow. Later, once the jam was made, she'd change into the new blue dress she made last fall, wash her hair, and it would be wavy and thick, the red in it standing out in the grey, and it wouldn't be limp the way it was right now, with the steam blasting up into her face. Standing over the kettle, she held her jaw rigid, which made her pale lips look thin and turn downwards, as if she might be thinking about something really serious and not about my birthday.

"Don't forget to leave enough berries for my cake," I said, and she seemed to wake up.

She waved her spatula at the pints of berries that filled the counter. "There are plenty, don't worry. I've got to get to them before they go off. Go outside and play. That will make the time go faster while you're waiting for Lesley Ann." Mom shoved her hair out of her eyes with the back of her hand, her fingers red and sticky from the strawberry juice.

It was blazing hot, so I decided to sit under the big maple. Lesley Ann was my new best friend, and the idea of her coming this afternoon put jumping beans in my stomach. I was proud to be turning ten. Ten was a special number; it was very different from nine; there was something magical about it. My mother told me I had lived one whole decade and in those ten years I had grown more than I ever would again in my life. I knew I wasn't a baby anymore, if that's what she meant. She asked me if I remembered my first birthday. No, I said. You'll remember your tenth, she said, because I had developed memory, and I could reason and think things through. I knew the difference between right and wrong, but sometimes I got confused.

I watched our dog Black coming across the yard, her tail waving behind her like a feather plume, snagged up with burrs, her whole body heaving with panting when she lay down beside me. I ran my hand over her side and looked across the yard.

My dad raised chickens, wretched little things called bantams that laid strong eggs which I could barely eat. Now the chickens were pecking at the rotten grass seed and left their droppings everywhere. I couldn't play outside in my bare feet or I'd get the disgusting stuff stuck between my toes. But the rooster was the worst part. Sometimes it would turn on the hens or come after me with its spurs flying around my head and shoulders. That made my father and brothers laugh. The more I screamed and cried, the more they laughed, and I ran into the house and right into my bedroom to make sure I was safe.

My mother hated the rooster too. "Howie," she'd say, "why don't you chop off that damned thing's head?"

Right now, the rooster pecked away at the ground, then raised its head, puffed out its chest and feathers, its wings flapping. "Stupid thing," I said, sitting under the tree, watching its every move, waiting for two o'clock when Lesley Ann would arrive.

Lesley Ann lived ten miles away, the closest girl to my age in the area. We had closer neighbors, but they didn't have girls, only dumb boys that my brothers played with. I was glad my brothers had gone this morning to Rawley's Creek to spear carp with their friends, but now that it was getting close to noon, I was starting to worry they'd be late for my party. Once Lesley Ann arrived, we would play for a while and then, when my father came home from his job at Northeast Lumber Supplies, we were all going to The Three Little Pigs restaurant for hot dogs, milkshakes, French fries, and ice cream. The restaurant said it was okay for my mom to bring her own cake. We could have hamburgers if we wanted to, but I would have a hot dog because I'd had one at Lesley Ann's party at The Three Little Pigs.

I loved that restaurant. There were pictures of pigs on the walls, hoof in hoof, dancing up a storm, playing flutes and drums, and in the background down a long lane, lined with lime-green trees round as lollipops, stood their house all pink and nice and snuggly. We got party hats and serviettes with birthday pictures and sometimes even balloons. The waitresses went all out to make sure that kids had fun.

Mom called to me from the kitchen window to come inside for lunch. How could I eat when I was so excited? There on the table sat one of those nasty banty eggs, all dark yellow and mean-looking, on a slice of burnt toast. I asked her if I could eat it outside, under the tree, and she said yes, as long as I remembered to bring the plate back inside.

Black was still stretched out in the shade, but when I held the plate under her nose the smell of food stirred her right out of her sleep and onto her feet, and in no time she'd wolfed it down and licked even the tiniest crumbs away.

I was lucky my birthday fell on a Wednesday, the same day my dad got home earlier from work because Northeast Lumber only made deliveries until two o'clock. Sometimes on Wednesday, he'd go out after work with friends and drink beer, but he wouldn't be doing that today. He'd be home an hour after Lesley Ann arrived, and he'd shower and shave, put on clean clothes, and I'd open my gifts (Lesley Ann would bring one, though my mother told me it was rude to count on it), and then we'd all go out.

I took my plate back inside and went into my room. It was still too early to get ready for Lesley Ann, but I couldn't wait. I opened the closet door and looked at my dresses. I didn't have many, but Mom promised to make me new ones when she ever found the time, which wouldn't be soon, not during canning season, especially with the vegetable garden ripening at a rate she struggled to keep up with. My sleeveless blue and white gingham dress fit the best, though it was tight around the arms and pinched at the waist. I didn't like how pudgy I was getting, but Mom said that was what happened to girls around my age. I'd been shooting up like a weed, she said, and my gingham dress had two faded rings around the bottom where she'd let out the hem. They reminded me of the rings in the bathtub my brothers sometimes left.

I'd probably be as tall as my mom but never as tall as I wanted to be, since height was like thick ankles and there wasn't much you could do about it. I slipped on my dress and white knee socks. The elastic had stretched out in my socks and they sank down my legs, but if I didn't move too quickly, I could keep them up. I didn't like my black patent leather shoes because of the strap, which I thought was for babies, and because they didn't have heels, not even little ones. I faced the mirror and fastened a pink bow in my hair. My hair, red like Mom's when she was a girl, had sprung with the humidity and curled up as tight as a pig's tail, which made my face look even rounder, even fatter! I didn't hate my freckles as much, since Lesley Ann had freckles too.

Lesley Ann arrived right on time, and when I heard the car I ran out to meet her. She handed me a box wrapped with fancy paper covered in balloons and with a big red bow, which we took to my room and slid under my bed, in case my brothers started snooping when they came home.

Mrs. White brought Lesley Ann in their brand-new 1961 white Chevrolet Impala, with the top down. I'd been for a ride in the car when they first got it. I had the back seat to myself and I ran my hand over the red-striped upholstery, the wind bashing at my face. Mrs. White and Lesley Ann had kerchiefs around their heads that held their hair in place and flapped in the wind, though I could tell Mrs. White used lots of hairspray and maybe didn't need a scarf. The best part was the radio, since our Ford didn't have one, and Lesley Ann and Mrs. White sang along with the song "Runaway." I hummed along, I'd only heard it a few times, and Mrs. White said Del Shannon was a real hunk, and she would know. Mrs. White had a stack of movie star magazines, and Lesley Ann and I leafed through them as we lay on her twin beds and dreamed about what our lives would be like if we became movie stars.

Mrs. White and my mother had lemonade on the back porch. I wished my mother wasn't wearing her work dress, and I wished she'd taken off her apron since it was stained even more. The strawberry juice made her stomach look like a big red bowl. Mom's fingers, curled around the sweating glass, were the same color as Mrs. White's nail polish, as if she wore pink gloves. A strand of hair kept coming loose from a bobby pin and she whisked it off her face like a pesky fly.

Mrs. White looked so stylish and cool in a sleeveless yellow shift dress, white pearls, and a matching white handbag, her platinum blonde hair turned into a French roll, like someone out of one of her movie star magazines. After the first time I met Mrs. White, I told my mother I loved the color of her hair, and my mother said she'd never get her hair color from out of a box.

Lesley Ann wore a hot-pink, store-bought dress with a broad white collar trimmed with lace, and pink knee-high socks. I wished

I'd remembered to use elastics to hold up my socks; I was getting tired of pulling them up. She had pointed-toe white shoes with heels, which I absolutely adored, and she carried a purse covered in little pink flowers, and with a white satin drawstring, which I also adored. Her chestnut hair was done in one even curl just below her chin. I could tell she had on a dab of her mother's lipstick, which I wasn't allowed. "There'll be plenty of time for that," my mother said. I also wasn't allowed to tease my hair the way Lesley Ann did sometimes, and anyway, what would happen to my curly red hair if I teased it? I wanted to be as slim as Lesley Ann, and as tall, but I'd be average, just like my mom, along with our shared thick ankles.

I patted the pink bow in my hair and decided it wasn't right for someone my age. I'd leave it there for now, to keep my hair out of my face. One day, I would have straight bangs like Lesley Ann, which skimmed the tops of her perfectly shaped eyebrows as if they knew to stop growing there. Lesley Ann was destined to become a movie star because anyone who got a bright red two-wheeler for her birthday was destined for something special. Del Shannon, the hunky singer, would hold her in his arms and sing her the "Runaway" song. The bike sparkled when she walked it out of the garage, all glittery and shiny with a red and white seat that matched the Impala seats. Red and white streamers fluttered from the handle grips, and the white basket on the handlebars would carry her lunchbox when she pedaled to school. I never dared to ask for a girl's bike. I knew better. My brothers shared a black one, and when I sneaked rides on it, I had to lift my leg high over the center bar. Lesley Ann's bike had a low swoop, a girl's bike. Her parents had more money than my parents, and they didn't have as many kids, just Lesley Ann.

Mrs. White backed out of our driveway and stopped beside the road where we'd gone to pick daisies in the ditch while our mothers drank their lemonade. Lesley Ann carried her bunch to her mother.

"Here Mommy," she said. "I picked these for you."

Mrs. White reached for them with her white-gloved hand and lay them on the seat beside a jar of my mother's jam. I was happy my mother had given her a gift, and hoped one day they'd become best friends, like Lesley Ann and me.

"I'll put these in water as soon as I get home." Mrs. White adjusted the rearview mirror and pushed at her hair, which didn't seem to shift, then spoke to Lesley Ann. "I want you to play like a little lady and stay clean and tidy. I do not want you playing with those boys. Do you hear me? They're too rough."

"Yes," Lesley Ann said. "I promise I won't."

"You girls have fun," she said as she arranged a kerchief over her hair, slipped on her black pointy sunglasses, and drove off.

Something about what she said, about playing with those boys, made me feel ashamed, and not just of my brothers, but of our house, too.

I looked at it from across the road, a yellow brick house my dad built before I was born. The yard, way bigger than Lesley Ann's, didn't look like much with its patchy grass and weeds. My dad was putting in a cement sidewalk, and he'd left two empty wheelbarrows sitting out. We used boards to walk on, especially when it rained and the yard filled with mud. My brothers had already moved into a room upstairs he'd almost finished. When all that was done, my mom wanted new kitchen cupboards. My dad was always working on our house; it seemed like it would never be finished. Lesley Ann's house was part of a subdivision and was done when they bought it. It was smaller than our house, a white clapboard bungalow with powder-blue shutters, tucked between trimmed bushes, and a small yard with thick green grass. There were two bedrooms, because there was only Lesley Ann. In the living room they had a coffee table with an enormous gold glass ashtray, end tables with lamps always on dim, shelves with horse figurines, and gold velvet cushions with big round buttons in the middle.

When I went inside their house, and saw how everything stayed in its exact place, I felt peaceful and calm. Even the air in their house seemed still. Lesley Ann and I looked through magazines and I could hear her parents talking in the kitchen, so quiet, so soft, I knew it must be romantic.

"What are they talking about?" I asked, imagining they planned a night out dancing or a trip to Hawaii.

"Search me," Lesley Ann said, shrugging her shoulders and flipping a page. "They're having their martinis."

Lesley Ann and I picked more flowers, then patted Black and smacked croquet balls around in the yard while we waited for the others to come home. My brothers were late. That figured. It was more than could be hoped for, those morons being back by two, when they were supposed to be. Now it was after three and my father was supposed to be here, too. Today of all days, how could he be late getting home from work? He wasn't even here yet, and he had to get cleaned up and changed into his good clothes, and it would take at least a half hour to drive into town to the restaurant. I wanted to eat by 5:30, the way they did at the Whites', the time normal people ate, and not like at my house when dinnertime was when we saw the food on the table, always late during canning season. I felt something in my stomach, a knot tightening up, like a fist closing, a feeling I'd had before.

My brothers and three other guys came across the fields beside our house, buzzing around each other like a swarm of flies around chicken droppings, as they passed something between them. As they neared our yard their noise settled down, and they approached in a single file. They were in close when my brother Brian broke with the line and started after Lesley Ann, holding up the ugliest, creepiest thing I'd ever seen: a brown, whiskery carp with huge bulging eyes.

Lesley Ann screamed and ran around the yard in a hot-pink flurry while I stood by helplessly, shouting at them to stop and to leave her alone. The dog barked and roared around, the other boys laughed, and the chickens scattered in all directions. Brian kept chasing Lesley Ann, his arm outstretched, running at her with the monster fish, and Norm, my other brother, laughed along with the others. The rooster, worked up by all the commotion, started after Lesley Ann, flying up around her shoulders. Norm went after it, grabbed it, and kicked it high up into the air, a ball of feathers flapping, twisting, squawking. Brian stopped dead in his tracks to watch the rooster, and I saw a way clear for Lesley Ann's escape.

"Come here, come here," I screamed, waved frantically, and jumped up and down, my socks down at my ankles. I spotted Lesley Ann's purse lying in the dirt, and the sight of those little pink flowers all crushed and dirty sickened me. I scooped it up and we charged for the back door, escaping inside.

"What on earth is going on out there? What's all the screaming about?" my mother asked as we stood in the kitchen. She had her hands sunk deep into the sink, washing mixing bowls, and I imagined she must have made my cake, and it would be in the oven now, baking. I sniffed the air but all I could smell was strawberries. She dried her hands in a tea towel and went over to the stove, her shoes shuffling across the linoleum.

Lesley Ann was hopping on one foot, holding the other in her hand and whimpering. "I think I've got a broken bone."

My mother gave the strawberries a quick stir, put down her long wooden spoon, and stepped over to Lesley Ann. "Let's see. Stand still now."

She held on to my mother's shoulder for support, and slowly lowered her foot to the floor. When it touched, her face scrunched up like an accordion, and her eyes pinched closed.

"Ouch," she said, gasping.

"Stand on it," my mother said, offering her hand for balance.

She tried it again and said, "Ouch."

"Again," my mother said, letting go of her hand.

Now Lesley Ann held on to the wall as she shifted back and forth, her face loosening up each time she tested her bad foot.

"We'll keep an eye on it, but I think it's fine." My mother went back to the sink and stuck her hands in the suds. I wished she'd sit down and rest and talk to us. She'd been up working since early in the morning when my dad left for work, but as I saw all the berries still on the counter, I knew she wasn't about to stop. "Stay away from the boys, you two. You know how they love to tease, Maggie. Go on now into your room and play for a while."

In my bedroom, we dug through some of my old toys and dolls, but they seemed as tired as the people I saw sitting on park benches outside the old folks' home in town. From the kitchen window, my mother was calling out to Norm and Brian.

"Come in here."

"Why?"

"Because I said so, that's why."

"In a minute."

"In a minute, nothing. You'll come in right now. I want to talk to you and I want you to come in and get cleaned up."

Lesley Ann sat on the edge of the bed listening. "They're going to get it for chasing me with that fish, aren't they?" she said, her face breaking into a dimpled smile.

"Yes," I said, knowing that whatever my mother said to them about chasing Lesley Ann would go in one ear and out the other, and as soon as she had her back turned, they'd exchange glances and snicker.

I heard a car pull into the driveway, and I hurried to the window. "Is that your dad?"

"Yes," I said and watched him get out of the car.

"Thank goodness, I'm starving."

She tried to join me at the window, but I turned to face her, to block her view and keep her away. "We'll be going as soon as my dad is ready."

"I'll get cramps if I don't eat soon," she said.

"He's inside now," I lied. Something was wrong, in a way I'd seen before. With some effort he closed the car door, leaned against it, opened the door once again and closed it, and staggered back a little. His arms went out straight beside him like a trapeze artist, and he started down the gravel path to the house, taking some quick steps, some slow ones, swaying as he came. He started to sing "Happy Birthday," his black lunchbox, shaped like a barn, tucked under his arm. His navy-blue work uniform, with Northeast Lumber Supplies written in gold letters on the front, was cleaner than usual, but that was because it was a shorter work day. Maybe he didn't need to shower before we went out. Maybe he only needed to change his clothes, but for sure he'd have to shave. He liked to joke about how he had more hair on his face than on his head.

From out of nowhere the rooster came flying at him. He dropped his lunchbox and grabbed at the rooster, his face tightening as he struggled with it, and then he drop-kicked it off the end of his brown work boot, clear across the yard. "That'll teach you, you goddamn miserable thing," he said, and started to laugh, a silly, high-pitched laugh I only heard when he was like this.

The back door opened, then I heard him in the kitchen, singing something, and my mother's voice raised, but I couldn't make out what she said except, "Howie."

"Why don't we play Snakes and Ladders," I said to Lesley Ann, to drown out my dad's noise, a combination of singing and shouting like he was watching a ball game.

"Is that your dad singing?" she asked. "He sounds really weird or something. Why does he sound so awful?"

"He loves to goof around with my mom and sing." Partly a lie. He made up silly songs when he got drunk. "Especially when he comes home from work."

"He does? That's weird. My dad likes his martinis when he comes home. He never sings."

She didn't believe me about my dad liking to sing. I wouldn't believe me either, and now it got even louder, something about Elly and jelly and smelly, and my mom's voice telling him to stop and to get himself straightened around. If Lesley Ann had Black's ears, they'd be pointed straight up right about now.

"Your turn to roll the dice," I told her, but she wasn't concentrating on the game at all; she had her ears glued to my parents.

I wished they'd be quiet, but instead it was getting worse, they were getting louder. I kept talking to Lesley Ann, trying to move her attention away from their racket. "What are you going to order at The Three Little Pigs?" "Will you have a strawberry or chocolate shake?" "How does that Del Shannon song go again? 'Run run run run runaway'? Let's sing it," but she was more interested in my parents and their shouting and hardly paid any attention to me.

I didn't want her, my new best friend, to hear them. She came from a house of stillness and quiet voices, with dimmed lights, where cushions stayed in place and shoes were lined up at the door, and there were no baseball bats or catcher's mitts thrown around the living room. My parents' fighting might frighten her the way it frightened me. Maybe Lesley Ann got cramps from not eating, but my stomach bunched up into something tight and all I could think was stop fighting, stop fighting, stop fighting.

Mom's voice rose as she shouted, "How could you, Howie? You know how excited Maggie is. How could you today? I've been so busy I didn't have time to make a fuss. I didn't want these berries to spoil."

"So I celebrate the birth of my youngest. So what? Can't a man go out for a few once in a while?"

It was getting impossible to distract Lesley Ann from their noise.

"They're fighting," she said.

"Not really, that's the way they talk. They're loud talkers." I wished I hadn't said that as soon as I did. No one would believe that.

"Sounds like fighting to me. My parents fight sometimes, after martinis. A big one after my dad came home with the Impala. My mom said we couldn't afford the car payments. But not as loud as your parents. What's wrong anyway?"

What was wrong? A bunch of things, so it was pretty hard for me to answer her, plus I didn't want to. It made me feel tired just thinking about it, like I was walking around carrying a bag of bricks. Their fights were always about the same things, about the work that had to be done on the house, the sidewalk to be put in, my brothers' room to finish, the vegetables rotting on the vines in the garden, never enough time or money, my mom shouting at my dad to get a higher-paying job, and to get ahead in this world he had to take risks, and my dad saying he wasn't cut out for a desk job and she knew that when she married him.

Listening to them fight was like trying to walk through the back yard after a good hard rain and more and more mud would clump onto your boots. Sometimes it went on into the night, and I'd put a pillow over my head and say, stop it, stop it, stop it, as if repeating that would somehow help. Their arguments were like Black chasing her tail, going in circles, with no beginning and no end and no way of making anything better. I was never going to get married. Not if it was like this.

"They'll stop in a minute," I told Lesley Ann, though they were still shouting. I really wanted to believe that. "These things blow over pretty quick." I sounded like my parents when they wanted me and my brothers to forget about something, and I knew it wasn't true.

Outside, my brothers were playing catch and Black was running back and forth between them, chasing the ball, her long pink tongue dangling out of her gaping mouth. My brothers were ready for The Three Little Pigs, in their clean jeans and shirts, their hair brushed, but my parents were still shouting at each other, though maybe not as loud.

Lesley Ann's party dress was wrinkled from sitting on the edge of my bed. Her white collar had a smudge of dirt from where the rooster flew up. Beside her on the bed lay her purse, the pink flowers crumpled, the satin drawstring stained with dirt. She kept looking around my room, as if searching for something to do.

"When are we going?" Lesley Ann asked in a voice that sounded bored, with not a speck of excitement.

I told her I'd go check and went to see what was going on with my parents, but when I got to the kitchen door, I stayed out of view. My dad sat at the table, still in his work clothes, a tuft of his grey hair standing straight on end. My mother's back was to me. Her dress had torn around a button, where the fabric had worn thin, and a gap showed the freckles on her back. The kitchen clock said 6:05, and no one was even thinking about going to The Three Little Pigs, or anywhere else.

They weren't screaming at each other anymore, but they were still mad. I wanted to step in and say, Let's get going, Lesley Ann is here and she eats early, and if she doesn't she'll get cramps, and it's my birthday, but their fight spiked again, and my dad said, "You're right I'm tied down. To you, the kids, this house, the yard, the garden, our debts, my job . . ."

I wondered if they'd even wanted me to be born. If they were so unhappy with their lives, why did they even have me and my brothers? They were the parents, weren't they supposed to know what they were doing? I knew what I wanted. I wanted them to get changed so we could go; we still had time. We could be at The Three Little Pigs by seven and Mom could phone Mrs. White and tell her Lesley Ann would be late, we got so carried away with all the fun we were having, and it would be no problem for us to drop her off on the way home.

I was about to step into the kitchen to tell them my plan when my mother shouted, "How was I to know you'd never amount to anything?" and I shrank back into the dining room. Who was I trying to kid? This day wasn't going to get better, and I knew it, and Lesley Ann would never forget what had happened.

On my way back to my room, I brushed tears from my eyes with the back of my hand. She could not see me crying. Her parents would never make her cry.

"I've got an idea," I said to Lesley Ann, and sat beside her on my bed. "I should open up your present." The weight I felt inside me, the bricks I carried around, had gone into my voice, and I had to raise it to make it sound lighter. I pulled the parcel from under the bed, and we sat cross-legged. I pulled on the red bow, carefully slipped the bright wrapping paper off the box, opened it, and inside I found two pairs of knee-highs, one navy blue, the other white, made of thick fabric that would stay up, a black barrette with glittery rhinestones, and a mauve book that said, My Secret Diary, with a lock and key.

"That's for your deepest darkest secrets," Lesley Ann said. "Don't forget to lock it and hide the key. That way, no one will know what you're thinking about."

I thanked her several times for everything, all so special to me, but especially the diary. I ran my hands over it, thrilled by the idea of being able to write what I wanted to and only I would know.

From the kitchen, the sound of my parents still arguing, their voices lower than before. I pulled out a puzzle, two kittens playing with a huge ball of yarn, and we worked on that until Lesley Ann said, "I don't want to go to The Three Little Pigs anymore. I want to go home. I'm phoning my mom."

"Please don't!" I said, panic rising in me, about to plead with her that we'd be going soon, but she had figured out we weren't going, just as certainly as I knew it. Along with me, she'd given up all hope, and I couldn't very well keep her locked up in my room. "Can't you just wait a bit longer?"

"No, I'm going." She slid off the bed and stepped out of my bedroom. I heard her dialing the phone in the dining room where it hung next to the kitchen, and I strained into the hallway to listen as she talked to her mom.

"Can you come get me now? . . . No. . . . No. . . . Nothing. . . . We didn't go. . . . I can't tell you now. Just come and get me, okay? . . . Now. Hurry." She hung up and I rushed back to sit down. I didn't want her to know I'd been listening. What would she tell her mom when she got home? That she had a terrible time? For sure she'd tell her she hadn't eaten anything, not even cake. Her mom probably already knew that we never went to the restaurant, and there wasn't even a party. I knew Lesley Ann must hate it here now, and, thanks to my parents, I knew she was never coming back.

As she waited in my room, we kept working on the puzzle, but neither of us was really interested. "I think you are missing some pieces," Lesley Ann said, and she was probably right, but too much had already gone wrong for me to agree with her.

I picked up her purse with the drawstring and tried to rub the dirt out of it and fluff up the little pink flowers.

"What are you doing?" she asked.

"Trying to fix this, make it look new again. It just needs washing."

"Keep it. It's wrecked."

"What will your mom say?"

"I'll tell her I lost it."

"Won't you get in trouble?"

"No, I don't think so."

I didn't want the purse, didn't want to be reminded of the whole rotten day. Maybe Lesley Ann wouldn't tell her mom about being chased by my brothers, those boys she was supposed to stay away from. Maybe we could still be friends, but I was afraid to ask her, in case she said no.

A horn blasted outside, and Lesley Ann left out the front door. She limped a little as she passed by the kitchen door, but my parents didn't even notice her go.

I followed her out, waved to Mrs. White, and sat on the front steps with Black, watching as the convertible disappeared down the gravel road and sent up boiling dust. I sat there for a long time, running my hand over Black's fur, not waiting for anything, just putting in time, while color drained out of the sky.

On my way to my room, I lingered at the kitchen door, staying hidden in the darkness of the dining room. My father said, "Everything will be fine, Elly." But it didn't look fine. My mother, still in her apron and green housedress, was crying, dabbing at her red eyes with Kleenex, looking away from him and out the open window.

In my bedroom, I took off my gingham dress and kicked it into the corner, glad to be out of it since it left red lines around my arms and waist. I'd tell my mother I couldn't wear it anymore, that it was too small for me, and what I wanted was a shift, and not something gathered at the waist. I pulled on my turquoise pedal pushers and my plaid blouse, the white socks from Lesley Ann, and my red running shoes. I slipped my new diary under the mattress, and pulled back the covers on my bed, lined up my pillows, and covered them again to make it look like I was in bed, the way I'd seen my brothers do. I turned off the light in my room and closed the door.

Black was curled up on the front porch, and I could hear my brothers playing ball in the back yard, though it was almost dark. "Come on, Black," I said, and started along the driveway, then onto the road, Black wagging her tail and bouncing along beside me. At first, I walked very slowly, but the more I thought about today, the faster I walked. By the time I got to Lesley Ann and the fish and my dad and his silly songs, and my parents' fight, I was running.

The song, run run run run runaway, my little runaway, played in my head over and over until I was panting as hard as Black, and my hair matted with sweat. I slowed to a walk and looked behind me, but I'd gone far enough that the lights from our house had been swallowed by darkness.

I walked on and on, down the long stretch of road, the song still playing in my head as if hunky Del Shannon was singing it to me and telling me what to do. Black's panting was getting louder, and my feet were getting sore. I usually went sockless with my red runners, and the thick new socks Lesley Ann gave me made my shoes pinch. I took them off, stuffed them into my pockets, and felt gravel poke up through my thin soles.

It got so dark I could barely see my hand when I held it up in front of my face. Around me, the air tasted like dust from the road, made thicker with the dew. In the distance, a bird's squawk sounded like a scream, like it was calling, help, help, help. The crickets started up, quiet at first, then chirped louder, as if they were frightened and knew something terrible was about to happen. Far off in the distance I saw the dim lights of a house. I wondered if I should go to it, knock on the door, ask to use the phone and call my dad to pick me up. I would say that I went for a walk and got lost. I hadn't been down this part of the road in a long time, but I wasn't lost. I knew where I was.

I saw the headlights of a car coming. I crept down into the ditch and Black followed me. Dew from the long grass covered my arms. Around us frogs croaked, and something lumpy moved in the grass, probably a toad. I hated toads. I caught Black around the neck, so she wouldn't try to lick it then foam at the mouth. We waited until the red tail lights went from angry glaring slits to tiny specks, then were swallowed completely by the night.

We walked on, but not nearly as fast. My back hurt, and I stopped often to rub the backs of my legs. I wanted to lie down, wanted to be home in my bed, but I kept on walking. I'd stay out all night, all the next day, stay out forever. I'd walk right away from them and their fights and towards the life Lesley Ann and I imagined if we became movie stars.

What if my parents discovered I was missing? They would have by now, they must have. They'd frantically search the house, the yard, and my brothers would go up and down the road shouting, Maggie, Maggie. They'd think I was kidnapped, or that I ran away, and they'd be terrified. They'd cry as they thought how terrible their lives would be without me. They'd talk about all the horrible things that might have happened to me. They would blame themselves. It would serve them right if they were scared out of their wits!

Soon, my father's car would come up the road. He would jump out and hug me, tell me how sorry he was.

Black kept stopping for breaks and I bent to rub her head. My feet felt heavy and pain shot up the front of my legs; I thought I couldn't take another step. I hadn't thought about what would happen once I was hungry and tired, what I'd do next. I stood in the middle of the road, the dark fields surrounding me like a large black lake. I was in the middle of the lake, and I was drowning. I tipped my head back and gazed at the Big Dipper, traced my way along the handle, and imagined myself balanced on the very tip, as if I stood on the end of a diving board. If I jumped off, where would I end up? What would it feel like to have no parents, to be a runaway with nowhere to go? What if bad people found me and tortured me? Carried me to a cabin far away in the woods. I didn't want to think about that. Or rich people might rescue me, pamper me as if I was a stray kitten. They'd give me everything I wanted, make me feel special. Notice me. Maybe it didn't even matter how rich they were, as long as they made me happy.

I turned and started back, Black falling in behind, stopping sometimes when she needed to rest, until off in the distance I saw the glow from my house. It looked like every single light was on, not like Lesley Ann's where it was always dim. I wanted to walk into a calm, soothing house, so this fist in my stomach would go away. Because I never knew what to expect, if my parents would be fighting, exhausted, and hating their lives. And me, and Brian and Norm, along with it.

I quietly opened the front door and tiptoed into the house; I could hear my brothers upstairs in their room. My parents were still in the kitchen, talking now. This was the part of their fights I waited for, when they'd spun around for so long they'd worn themselves out with their arguments and chasing their tails. Worn out—the way I felt right now. I didn't want to talk to anyone, I just wanted to go to my room. I wanted to be left alone.

The kitchen clock said ten. I'd been certain it was much later than that, at least two in the morning.

I kicked off my running shoes. Lesley Ann's ruined drawstring purse lay at the foot of my bed. I picked it up and shoved it under my mattress, along with my new diary, then I lay down on the bed, beside the lump of pillow that was meant to be me, if anyone had looked in.

Sometimes when my parents fought, my dad would say, that was it, he was leaving, and he'd go to the car, turn it on, and sit there, the fumes clouding out of the exhaust. I would watch from the window and cry, hoping he'd leave to end their fighting and the pain, but also wanting him to stay. I would miss his stupid jokes and stupid songs. If he left, who would take care of us? How would we make ends meet? My mother didn't have a paycheck. Then he'd turn off the car, and sit and smoke, and I knew he'd be thinking about how he'd change, and stop drinking, and make Mom and all of us happy, and make more money. Because what else could he be thinking? Sometimes, after he'd been sitting alone for a long time, my mom would go out and join him, her beige sweater draped over her shoulders, and they'd talk, even laugh, with the storm that had swept through them earlier spinning somewhere off in the distance. They'd sit in the car, surrounded by darkness, pretending to be going somewhere, never moving an inch.

No one had come looking for me. No one even knew I was gone. On my birthday, shouldn't everything about the day be special for me? If I told my mother that my birthday turned out to be the worst day of my life, she'd tell me to stop feeling sorry for myself and to not try to get attention the way Lesley Ann did with her injured foot. She'd say I was made of strong stuff and that the hardest lessons in life are the ones that hurt the most. What lesson had I learned—that no one cared? That I meant so little to them that they hadn't even noticed I'd gone? I could hardly wait to write in my diary. But right now, I was too tired.

"Maggie, Maggie, wake up. We're going out for something to eat." My mother was standing beside my bed, looking down. She'd changed into her blue dress, the one she wore for special, her hair combed, her lips painted with red lipstick. She didn't look as tired as before, and there was a lightness in her green eyes, though they were still rimmed red from crying. Behind her I saw my father's dark outline in the light coming from the hall. I squinted into the light and saw he wore a short-sleeved white shirt and his good pants.

"Aren't you famished?" my mother asked. "I know I am."

I rubbed my eyes with my knuckles. I didn't want to get up. My stomach still hurt and my legs ached.

"Can't I just sleep? I'm not hungry. I'm too tired."

"Come on," Dad said. "The boys are already out in the car. We've got to get going, we've got a birthday to celebrate." He used the phony voice, as he sometimes did after he and Mom had a fight and he was trying to patch things up. "You've already had lots of sleep. The boys checked in on you earlier and they said you'd gone to bed! You've been sleeping most of the night."

I tried to climb into the back seat of our two-door Ford, but Brian said, "No way, you're in the front," and kept pulling on the seat so I couldn't get in.

I didn't want to sit up front, on the hump and between my parents, but Brian kept pulling and Mom said, "Come on, Maggie, you're up here with us."

"Yeah, cuzz you're still a baby," Brian teased, using a squeaky voice meant to sound like a baby, enjoying his victory of having more space in the back, and reminding me how he was older and that made him better than me.

We backed out of the driveway and onto the road, headed for town. I sat stiff between my parents, careful not to touch them, my hands clasped together, resting on my legs.

Out on the highway, Brian and Norm were playing a game in the back seat, sticking their hands under their arms to make a fart sound, then laughing.

"Stop it," Mom said after a while. "I don't want to listen to anything so disgusting."

"I don't see why we had to come anyway," Brian said. "I was already in bed."

"Because it's your sister's birthday," Mom said. She glanced at my father, as if waiting for him to add something, but he didn't, so she said, "We need to celebrate."

"Whoopee-do," Norm said, but quietly, as if he knew he could stir things up again and get another fight going.

Dad had both hands on the steering wheel. Light from a huge moon, hanging like a big orange tiddlywink in the sky, fell on his scratched knuckles.

"The Highway Oasis has the best hamburgers in town," he said. "They're big and fat and the juice runs right down your arms. They make their own patties and they always put on a nice big slice of onion. They are way better than the burgers at The Three Little Pigs." He paused, as if he might be waiting for one of us to say something, and when no one did, he said, "They stay open until 3 a.m., just in case you get a craving." He chuckled, like he'd told a joke, but he hadn't.

"Great, Dad," Brian said, but he didn't mean it.

Brian probably knew the way I did that Dad was trying to lighten things up, because maybe he felt bad about coming home drunk and fighting with Mom on my birthday.

"Nothing better than a nice big slice of onion before going to bed," Norm said, going along with Brian's sarcasm.

"Gives you dreams with onion breath," Brian said. "To keep away the boogeyman."

"That's enough," Mom said. "I've had about as much as I can take in one day."

What about me? I thought. Wasn't this as much as I could take in one day?

After Mom said that, everyone went quiet. I turned to look back at my brothers and their heads bobbed with the sway of the car. I hadn't thought about The Three Little Pigs for a while. The excitement I felt earlier had vanished hours ago and shaped into something else—anger, fear, and shame that pulsed through my body and sent me down the road. As if running and walking would make a difference, but it hadn't. It only made me tired, numb, and disappointed.

Suddenly, I felt my mother's hand on my head, stroking it. I couldn't remember the last time she touched me so tenderly, and I knew that it had to do with my birthday and all that I'd missed out on, as if her hand could take away my hurt. I pulled my head away.

The town lights were brighter now. Mom began to tell me about the night I was born. She had worked all day doing strawberries, just like today, and then I decided to make my appearance in the world just as she was thinking about going to bed. I was born at 11:57 at night. She said right now, as we got closer to midnight, was the exact right time for us to be celebrating my birthday. "Things have a way of working out," she said, her voice so far away it was hard to know if she was talking about right now, or in the past, or some time in the future. I wasn't sure if she was even talking about me anymore.

I thought about what she said, about how things had a way of working out, as we waited for the carhop to bring our food on a tray and prop it on the window. Saying something directly, unless in the middle of a blowup, was not something my family did. Did she want me to think this midnight trip to the Highway Oasis was part of some big plan they hatched earlier, and maybe I was even the stupid one for not guessing it? Was that their plan? No, it wasn't. She took what really happened and twisted it into something else, like turning a strawberry into jam, a solid into mush. A story that was supposed to make her feel better, but I knew it was a lie. Even if I was born three minutes before midnight, who wants a three-minute birthday party? Couldn't she even hear herself?

I wanted to tell them their fight made me sad and wrecked my birthday. I wanted to be heard and felt sorry for and pitied. I wanted them to notice me and to apologize for what had happened. But my family never apologized. I couldn't say anything. Because if I did, they might start blaming each other, and around and around they'd go all over again, and the knot in my stomach would get bigger and bigger.

"This is delicious!" my dad said as he bit into his hamburger. "I've noticed that the later you come here, the better the burgers get. How's yours, Maggie? Good?"

He was doing the same thing as Mom, and I was supposed to agree with how special this all was. I knew the difference between right and wrong, truth and lies.

"Yes," I said. "It's good."

I had no appetite, could barely force down the tiny bites I took. I was going along with this whole fake family party, because if I didn't, if I pouted or acted like a crybaby, I'd be blamed for spoiling things. I could just hear Mom or Dad saying, look, we've come all the way into town to make this nice for you and now you're going to sulk? The least you can do is try to act like you enjoy it.

Except for Lesley Ann, no one had tried to make me feel good. But I wasn't about to say. The very last thing I wanted was to start my parents fighting again.

"Lesley Ann could never come out this late to eat," I said, trying to sound like eating hamburgers at midnight was grown-up and sophisticated, but I didn't mean it at all. I wanted to eat at 5:30, have calm in my house, be normal like the Whites.

"Oh well, maybe they're not civilized," my mother said, her voice suddenly light. She smiled a little and seemed to be having a private thought. "It's very stylish to eat late."

No, it wasn't. Especially not when you're ten. My mother was trying to cheer me up, pretending, just like me. But I think what she wanted was what Mrs. White had, but she wasn't going to say so, because if she did, it might open up something inside her, and I imagined her running down the road, away from our house.

Right now, I was a kid, stuck between my parents, stuck in this family, but I wouldn't always be. One day, I would grow up and move away, I would live in a house like Lesley Ann's, white, with shutters the color of the sky, cut green grass with no weeds, a trimmed hedge and red flowers. I'd have a dog like Black and there'd be no chickens. I'd ride around in my red convertible with the radio turned up loud, the sun shining down on me, and my hair, long and blonde and straight, would blow in the wind. I would walk with my head held high, every bit as high as Lesley Ann's family, the way my mom said I should, because I would be very grand, very civilized.

I took another bite of my hamburger, the meat tasteless and coarse. When no one was looking, I scrunched up the rest in the wrapper.

Next year I'd be eleven, and the more grown up I got, the closer I would be to my destiny. I thought about what I wanted for my birthday next year, in case anyone asked me. A girl's two-wheeler, pink, with long streamers and a bar that swooped down low. A fancy purse with a shoulder strap and a gold clasp. Some movie star magazines. A shift dress. With great big flowers. White shoes with heels. Lipstick.

My mother and father were talking about the vegetable garden, and Mom said she'd done up twenty-five jars of jam, enough to keep us well stocked for next year.

"Oh, Maggie," she said. "I almost forgot to tell you. After we have our hamburgers, we've got strawberry shortcake with whipped cream when we get back home."

If I ate anything more, I knew I'd throw up. I was about to say I would have mine tomorrow, when I suddenly knew what I really wanted for my birthday next year. To be happy. That's what I wanted, more than anything.

THE EXPO FEVER

Ellen's hair whipped around her eyes and face; the grit from the plastic mats needled her legs, making them itch as it spun in the air.

"Hey you guys, can you roll up the windows? We're getting blown away back here," she called out to her parents, Vera and Walt, sitting in the front seat. Every time Walt lit a smoke the windows went down like an elevator.

"Boo hoo hoo." Pete lowered his *Mad Magazine* and made a crybaby face at her.

Her brother had been sulking ever since getting in the car three hours ago, and he'd be stuck with her in the back seat of the Mercury for another six hours.

Vera rolled up her window, leaving a small gap, and wrestled with the road map that filled half the windshield. "I will be the navigator," she said to Walt. "I've mapped our route so we don't get lost. You drive, I navigate."

"It's one straight line on highway 401 until we get to the Quebec border and it changes to autoroute 20. The challenge will be in Montreal," Walt said.

Some of the boys Walt worked with at Clearview Glass, who'd already been to the World's Fair, said the roads were twisted up like a plate of spaghetti and the signs all in French so you didn't know what direction you were going in.

"I still don't see why I have to go," Pete said, his face stuck behind the magazine. "I'm old enough to stay home alone."

"I want to come home to a house still standing," Vera said.

"The only reason I'm going is because I can drink beer in Quebec legally," he said.

"Not in front of me you won't," she said.

Pete rolled his brown eyes back in his head and mumbled something Ellen couldn't make out. He wanted to stay home and be with his girlfriend, Cindy.

Pete's dark hair flopped down over his face and Ellen could make out little scratches on his cheeks. Walt said if he used a sharp razor then he wouldn't nick his zits. The cakes Vera brought home from the bakery, piled high with colorful icing flowers, wouldn't be helping his complexion.

Ellen looked at the back of Walt's salt-and-pepper hair and watched as he flicked an ash out the gap in the window. From the start, he and Pete had resisted Vera's plans to go to the World's Fair to celebrate Canada's 100th birthday.

"Can't we just go up north camping like usual?" Walt had asked. "You know I don't like crowds. When am I going to get time to go fishing?"

The whole country was going, and lots of the world too, and Vera would not be left out of such a historic event. "Haven't you been listening to the TV and radio?" she asked him. "Don't you know how important this is?"

Vera turned to the window and started speaking French as if to the sweeping hills of crops and grazing cattle. "Pouvez-vous répéter, s'il vous plaît. Je suis perdu."

She twisted in her seat to face Ellen and Pete; Pete raised the magazine higher to cover his face. "Do you know what that means?" she asked Ellen, her green eyes bright with excitement. "Je suis perdu?"

"No," Ellen said, catching her hair and twisting it at the nape of her neck.

"Well, you better learn it. You might need it. It means, 'I am lost.' It could come in handy when we get to the Expo site. It's huge. Built on two islands in the middle of the St. Lawrence River. The theme is, Man in His World."

The tip of Vera's hot-pink neckerchief touched her face, its color accenting her cheeks and her lipstick. Sunlight pouring through the car window lifted the strawberry blonde in her hair and made the grey almost disappear. Ellen couldn't remember the last time she looked so alive.

Vera turned to face the front windshield and started singing "The Centennial Song," the Canada song composed especially for Expo. "Merrily we roll along, together all the way . . . proud and free . . . it's the hundredth anniversary of confederation . . ."

"Mom, stop it please," Pete begged, his face coming out once again from behind the magazine. "That song is driving me nuts! I can't get it out of my head." He liked the Stones and Hendrix, and thought the Canada song was for babies.

Vera's passion about Expo had started about a year and a half ago, around the time Ellen wanted to redecorate her room with white daisy wallpaper. "After Expo," she said. And Pete, the Great Canadian Voyageur, wanted new paddles for his canoe. "After Expo." Walt wanted a new Coleman camping stove and tent for their annual trip up north on Georgian Bay. "Possibly after Expo." The World's Fair sat on the calendar—a wedding, a birthday, a christening, a graduation, a religious holiday—all wrapped into one.

She cut articles out of the paper, wrote away to the Quebec and Canadian governments for information, pored over glossy brochures at the kitchen table until the small hours of the morning, making notes in her travel book and updating her "must see" list.

Sometimes Ellen joined her, her elbows on the table, chin cradled in her hands, and watched. "It's just a fair, Mom. You're not actually going to see the world." There was something unsettling about Vera's enthusiasm, as if she had one thing locked in her vision—a specific blindness that prevented her from seeing anything else.

Not that she didn't deserve a break or a vacation. She worked hard, getting up early for work at the bakery, where she decorated cakes for special occasions. When she brought unclaimed cakes home, Walt would say, "Vera, you're a born artist! Look at those flowers! Nature herself doesn't make them that pretty!"

She worked late into the night at her sewing machine, creating the ensembles she'd wear at Expo, shoving the polyester fabric under the machine's drilling needle. Then she'd take a break and look dreamily across the kitchen at the dinner dishes drying in a rack and say, "A person has to have dreams, something to look forward to. Everyone needs an escape. One day I hope to have enough money to see the world: Paris is number one on my list. For now, the world is coming to our country and I am going to be there to greet it."

One night, Pete came into the kitchen, and as he watched her sew he stuffed a slice of cake in his mouth.

"What the hell is that?" He gaped at Vera's outfit, wiped icing off his cheek, and licked his fingers.

"It's called a pant-dress. It's all the rage." Vera held up a garment of yellow-green with pink and white flowers, the top and bottom attached, and wide legs that went all the way to the ankles. "Isn't it pretty?"

"We'll be able to spot you in a crowd," Pete said, with a goofy laugh that sounded like a snort.

Vera had lapsed back into humming the Canada song as she leafed through a brochure she'd pulled out of a shopping bag stuffed with Expo information at her feet. "Did you know the World's Fair originated in France?" she asked no one in particular, and no one answered.

Ellen watched Pete's yellow canoe tip bob up and down over the hood of the car like an oversized banana. Walt had made a deal with Vera. He'd go to the fair until he couldn't stand it anymore, then he and Pete would go on day trips canoeing and fishing somewhere on the St. Lawrence River. "That way," he said, "everyone will be happy."

When they got back to the Star Lite Motel, Vera had sent Ellen to the office to ask if they had a basin. She sat beside the Formica table, soaking her feet in Cow Brand baking soda and water, her white square-toed flats kicked off to the side. "I suppose I shouldn't have worn new shoes on my first day," she said. "That wasn't very smart. I've got blisters."

Walt sat opposite Vera and blew smoke up towards the ceiling, rippling the fringe on the orange swag light hanging over the table. He sipped a beer and studied a picture of a rainbow trout arcing into a perfect C, hanging in mid-air over a river, the riverbank dense with colorful autumn trees. Ellen was glad the picture was behind her, between her bed and Pete's, because the fish looked scary with its mouth hanging open, and big enough to swallow a person whole.

"I'm bushed," Walt said. "Can't take another step." He wriggled his toes in his white ankle socks, his black canvas slip-ons shoved off to the side. His short-sleeve sports shirt was unbuttoned all the way, putting his grey and black chest hairs on full display.

Ellen and Pete lay on their twin beds watching images flicker on the TV. Vera said it was okay to have it on but no volume; she wanted to review their first day.

Through the open window, cars hummed along the highway about a half mile away. Some of the traffic would be headed for the Expo site, twenty-two miles from the Star Lite. It was cheaper staying here, and there was no problem with parking—Vera made sure to point that out when they arrived last night, after getting lost in Montreal for over an hour. Vera and Walt yelled at each other as they grabbed at the map unfolded between them until some guy who spoke English stuck his head in the window and asked if he could help.

Vera raised the pantlegs of her blue pantsuit and leaned back, her head resting against the orange curtains bunched at her head, and closed her eyes. "I think you should bring the canoe into one of our rooms. Someone could steal it."

Walt ran his hand over his chest, his dark eyebrows pinching together. "No one's going to steal that, Vera. You can't just walk off with a big yellow canoe."

She opened her eyes and steadied her gaze on him, then shook her head, too tired to argue. "What a day!" she said, her voice lifting with renewed energy. "So interesting. What do the rest of you think?"

"Yeah, quite a day," Ellen said, so tired she could barely speak. Vera had gotten them all up at 6:30 that morning so they could join the lineup at the site by 8:30, and go through the gates as soon as they opened at 9:30. "I liked the geodesic dome, the United States pavilion. It made me think of a glass cabbage," Ellen said, and Walt added, "Can you imagine installing all that glass? If Clearview Glass got that contract, we'd be set for life."

Stepping through the gates, they entered into a mishmash of shapes, like landing on another planet. Buildings shaped like a giant ski jump, a Chinese hat, a bonfire spire, cubes stacked higgledy-piggledy, an airplane wing, a cluster of tents, a tower on top of boxes.

Ellen pointed out the Canadian Pavilion to Pete.

"Yeah, so someone took a pyramid and turned it upside down. So what?" Pete was still sulking about leaving Cindy behind.

"Pete," Vera said, swishing her feet around in the basin. "What was your favorite pavilion today?"

A lock of dark hair cascaded down Pete's forehead and half covered his eyes. "Ma, I'm too tired to talk. I'll give you a report tomorrow. I'll write an essay if you want."

Vera sighed but she let it pass. All day she'd been telling Pete to show some interest, but trying to connect with any of them right now was like trying to talk to pieces of limp lettuce.

"Walt?" Vera said. "What was your favorite pavilion?"

Walt stretched his legs out straight and leaned back, his sunburned face glowing in the swag light. "Ah, let me see." He stroked his chin and turned to face her. "To tell you the truth, Vera, I couldn't say. It's one big mix-up of a memory."

She pulled her feet out of the basin and rubbed them dry in a towel.

Pete got up and turned up the volume on the TV.

"Well," Vera said. "I can see I'm not going to squeeze water out of a stone no matter how hard I try." She leafed through her Expo passport and read aloud her stamps, verifications that she'd visited the pavilions. "Chile, West Germany, England, Spain, Australia, Japan. I believe I enjoyed Mexico the most, but I'll have to think about it," talking over the TV, the way she did at home.

"Do you remember the couple I was talking to in the Australia line?" Vera asked Walt.

"Vaguely," he said, bending to massage his foot.

"The man was wearing a powder-blue leisure suit. Well, they said that the France Pavilion is spectacular."

Walt took a sip of beer. "Oh yeah," he said, placing the bottle back on the table.

Pete got up to turn the TV up louder. "Ma, I'm trying to hear Johnny Carson," he said, stripping down to his plaid boxer shorts before jumping back on the bed.

Vera continued as if he hadn't said anything. "But that makes sense, since France was the country that came up with the whole idea of a World's Fair. It's wonderful how so many countries have come together to communicate and share their culture to further their understanding of each other."

Walt nodded and said, "Uh huh. Pretty great."

Sometimes at home, Vera tried to engage Walt with topics beyond his interests. Ellen thought that living in a small town, decorating cakes for a living, wasn't how Vera had imagined her life would go. Once, she dreamed of becoming a painter, a real painter, and learning from the masters by going to see the work of the French Impressionists. "True visionaries," she said. But ever since she began her job at the bakery, her sketchbook sat on the bottom shelf of an end table in the living room, underneath a stack of old magazines.

"Your cakes are works of art, Vera," Walt would say to encourage her, but Vera might have heard it another way, as if he were saying, "Be happy for what you have, because this is it." Ellen had heard her tell Walt that for someone who installed glass, he had a pretty cloudy view of life. He didn't have her restlessness or curiosity about the world; he didn't care about the Paris art galleries she dreamed of visiting one day. He'd rather go fishing or camping. "I can't help it if I like nature," he said.

"Well, there's no use trying to talk to a bunch of zombies." Vera picked up the basin of water, and on her way to their adjoining room she said, "I'm going to bed," then closed the door behind her.

The next morning, Vera strode into Pete and Ellen's room, dressed in a white top and yellow bell bottoms, yanked the curtains open, flooding the room with morning light, and threw the door wide open, so that the Merc-canoe practically looked parked inside. "Come on, let's go. There's lots of fair to see today."

"Why can't we just sleep in?" Pete sounded like he was trying to talk through a mouthful of pancakes.

"You two get up. I'll meet you in the restaurant. I've decided to collect every stamp from every pavilion while I am here. Every last one! Then I can say I've seen the world!" She stood with her hands on her hips, her feet apart, chin up, as if she were Jacques Cartier discovering Montreal and laying claim to it.

"From all the pavilions?" Pete asked, his head still mostly buried under the pillow. "You flipped or something?" But Vera was already gone.

"I'd say she has," Walt said as he stepped into their room, dressed in seersucker Bermuda shorts, a sports shirt, and carrying his slip-on running shoes. He slumped into a tub chair, lit up a smoke, and wrestled a foot into a shoe. "You two get up. Your mother is waiting. She had some vision in the night, apparently, and now she wants to see it all."

He sat with one shoe on and looked across at them. "I'll go along with it for so long, then I'm going fishing. Next year it's back to camping, and I don't give a damn if all of France is coming to town."

Ellen knew Walt was letting off steam, and if she weren't in the room he'd say a lot more to Pete. He'd say he didn't understand what made their mother tick. Sometimes it felt like it was the boys against the girls. She even had her mother's red-blonde hair and thin nose, while her dad and Pete had dark hair and pudgy noses. As if they were on sides, but she wasn't.

Sitting in the crowded outdoor Bavarian café, Walt said, "That's it, I'm done. I've had three full days, enough's enough." He set his stein of beer down with a thud beside the straw fedora he'd bought to protect his peeling forehead from a worse burn.

Ellen was surprised he'd lasted this long, though he and Pete sat out for a few pavilions yesterday and most of today, arranging times and places to meet them. He would feel less guilty if Vera had someone to see the fair with, and that meant her, because it sure wasn't going to be Pete.

Vera got so involved with displays, and Ellen had to keep reminding her of the time. "Mom, we have to meet Dad and Pete." There was always something more she wanted to see, and sometimes they were over an hour late.

"We can't be tied down to specific times," Vera said, when Walt grumbled about how long they'd waited. "This kind of situation calls for flexibility."

"On both our parts," Walt said.

The waiter approached in his brown leather shorts with gold and red embroidery and a bib-like front, and asked, in a strong French accent, if they would like anything else.

"Another beer," Walt said.

The waiter's cap, a triangular wedge adorned with a white feather, reminded Ellen of Peter Pan's hat. He picked up Walt's empty stein and crossed to another table.

"Lovely lederhosen," Vera said. She sipped her lemonade, her eyes roaming the crowds of tourists passing outside the café. "The authentic clothes we've seen here have been so impressive."

"I think the outfits look fake." Pete drew a pack of Export "A"s out of his shirt pocket. He sneaked cigarettes at home and reeked of smoke, but now that he was here Ellen thought he was making his own rules, confusing this new open display of bad habits with being worldly.

Vera rolled her eyes and shook her head but stayed quiet. She might think she was fighting a losing battle—back at home Pete was talking about moving to Toronto soon, breaking out of Willitsburg, and what kind of control would she have then?

Walt sat sideways, his legs and arms crossed, and scowled at the crowds. "After a while, it feels like cattle pouring down a chute," he said, raising his stein.

Vera squinted in the same direction as Walt, towards the broad walkway. "If you almost close your eyes and make everything blurry, it looks like an Impressionist painting," she said, then opened her eyes wide. "I'm not sure you'd understand."

"You have to admit after three days you start to feel like one of the herd," Walt said.

"After three days, I realize there is so much more I want to see! I feel like I've hardly begun!" She opened her white purse, removed a powder compact, and examined herself in the mirror.

"Well, I guess I'm the opposite." Walt bit into his Wiener schnitzel on a bun and chewed slowly. "After a while, everything looks the same to me. It's nothing but a glorified fair. Half the exhibits I couldn't get near because of the crowds."

Vera looked out towards the St. Lawrence River, its rapids tipped with white caps—disappointment in her face. Or anger.

The waiter came back with Walt's beer and saw his half-eaten schnitzel abandoned on a white plate. "Monsieur? Tout va bien? Every ting okay?" he asked.

Loud oom-pah band music blared from the loudspeakers, and some of the other diners hoisted their steins in rhythm.

"Dandy," Walt said.

"Voudriez-vous le ketchup. I get for you ketchup?" the waiter asked, his forehead greasy with sweat, the white feather in his hat bent.

"No thanks," Walt said, and the waiter moved away to another table. "He's definitely light in his loafers. He's enjoying that costume way too much." He frowned at his schnitzel and Pete made his snort-laugh. "It would take more than ketchup to improve that piece of cardboard. If that's what they call authentic food, I never want to eat in Germany," Walt said.

Vera's mouth turned downwards in disgust. "I can see you're determined not to enjoy yourself." As she sipped her lemonade, her chin quivered, and Ellen couldn't tell if she was about to cry or shout at him.

"My enjoyment has run out. My feet hurt, my left knee is acting up. After Pete and I drop you and Ellen off at the fair tomorrow, we'll go fishing, and we'll pick you up at night, and we'll both come back for the last day. Part of it, anyway."

Obviously, they'd planned this as they waited for Vera and Ellen, as if they'd formed a team. But if Ellen was on any side right now, it was theirs.

The pavilions and their exhibits made her think of the places she'd never go. All the information coming at her like a tidal wave, reminding her of her infinite ignorance. At times she found the fair alienating, a word she'd used ever since its introduction in an English class, because she didn't feel like she fit in anywhere. She liked the films in some of the exhibits, the sculptures and the paintings, but after three full days, her interest was waning.

More than anything, she wanted to stretch out in the shade somewhere and finish her *Valley of the Dolls* novel, another world she didn't fit into: drugs and sex and men and women fighting each other, trying to escape their unhappiness with pills. She'd had cramps all day too, which meant her period was on the way. But at least they were leaving earlier tonight, well before dark, and she had Midol back at the motel.

"Drink up," Vera said. "We've got time to see a few more pavilions."

"Vera," Walt said. "Weren't you listening? I'm done. For the rest of today and the next two."

The waiter came back to their table and reached for Vera's plate. "Avez-vous fini, Madame? Fini?" he asked, his Peter Pan cap sliding down on his forehead.

"Oui. Merci."

"Veux-tu un dessert? We 'ave Black Forest Cake. The real ting."

"Non, merci. J'ai vu assez de gâteau pour toute la vie." The waiter laughed, but Ellen could tell he was confused by her comment and Vera wasn't smiling at all.

"What did you say, Mom?" Ellen asked after the waiter had gone.

"I told him I'd seen enough cake to last a lifetime." Vera took a small headscarf out of her purse, pulled it over her head, tied it under her chin, and slipped on her black-frame sunglasses. "We've come all this way for you to sit and drink beer, have we?" she asked Walt.

"We had an agreement, Vera. Remember?" Walt said.

Vera sipped her lemonade, her jaw set firm as she looked off into the crowd. "What about you, Pete? Are you going to see more?" she asked, her lips taut.

"Nope," Pete said. "I'm with Dad."

Pete kept tapping his cigarette on the side of the ashtray as if he was saying, Hey, look at me, smoking in front of you, I am a man in his world.

"Naturally," Vera said, and turned to face Ellen. "Ellen?"

"Mom, I can't. I'm too tired, and not feeling great. I've got a headache." No way would she talk about her cramps in front of Pete and Walt. And it was true about the headache.

"Everyone has an excuse. Well, not me." Vera stood up, her shoulders back and squared, chin up, and her purse hanging in the crook of her elbow. "I'm going to see more. I've only so much time left."

She turned once again to Ellen. "You sure you're not coming with me?"

The idea of her mother going off alone, surrounded by a sea of strangers, saddened her. She was about to give in, but her cramps were worsening, and she'd feel better tomorrow. "I'm going with them." She nodded towards her father and Pete.

"Fine with me. The rest of you do what you want. Don't worry about me."

Ellen knew she didn't mean that. She meant exactly the opposite, that they should worry about her, and it would serve them right if something terrible happened. She was punishing them for not sharing her enthusiasm, for not being as involved or interested. She'd immersed them in the world to fire them up but they'd failed miserably. They were not like her, and she was stuck with them in her small, cake-decorating life.

But Vera was wrong. Ellen wasn't like Walt and Pete either. She didn't know who she was; she wasn't on a team. Je suis perdu, she thought.

Vera walked towards the exit of the Bavarian café, about to be washed away in the stream of humanity flowing past.

"Hold on a minute," Walt called after her. "We're leaving, Vera. How you getting back?" Vera knew better than anyone there was no public transportation out to the motel.

Already at the café gate, she turned to say, "Who knows? I'll find my own way back. Don't count on me at any particular time, either." She gave her head a haughty jerk and stepped out, her floral dress merging with the crowd, and disappeared as if absorbed into a vast garden, one flower blurred into all the others.

"Dad, go get her," Ellen said, frightened by the idea of just leaving her.

"How? Look. She's already gone," Walt said, waving towards the throngs of people, Vera nowhere in sight.

He raised his hand and waved to summon the waiter back. "Bring us two beers," he said. "One for me, one for my son. And another Coke for my daughter."

"No, Dad," Ellen said. "I want to go." She winced with a cramp.

The waiter looked from Ellen to Walt, not certain whom to listen to. "Two beers and a Coke," Walt repeated, because he was the parent now, and Vera wouldn't let Pete drink in front of her, even if he was of legal age in Quebec.

At the motel, they sat in Ellen and Pete's room and tried to watch a baseball game. "Who's winning?" Walt asked, and Pete said, "No idea," even though he was staring straight at the screen. No one was concentrating on anything, just putting in time and wondering when Vera would be back.

Walt said, "Your mother's getting back at me for leaving early. And for going fishing tomorrow. She wants me to be upset."

Pete said, "It's like she caught some kind of fever. The Expo fever. And also because she's bananas." Pete crossed his legs at his ankles, his running shoes still on, as he leaned against the vinyl headboard and took a sip of beer. Vera would tell him no shoes on the bed, and he wouldn't be drinking beer either.

"It's that temperament of hers. Artistic. She goes at things full blast and expects us to do the same. I don't know why." Walt paused. "I think she might be going through the change." He pulled back the curtain, but out towards the highway it was pitch black.

Ellen didn't believe their lack of enthusiasm was the whole story for Vera's going off on her own, but she wasn't sure what was. Every few minutes she went to the door to peer out, anticipating seeing her mother come striding across the parking lot, swinging her purse and her Expo tote bag full of today's catch of brochures, as if she'd conquered a small country. At 10:00 p.m. they opened the door—left it open, tired of getting up to check all the time, and turned off the lights to cut down on the bugs, sending shivers of television blue cascading down the walls.

The fair had been closed for an hour. "Maybe she went to La Ronde," Ellen said. "The amusement park is open late."

"Your mother hates rides, but nothing would surprise me," Walt said, pacing the room in his white socks, then stopped in front of the picture of the leaping rainbow trout.

At 11:00, Walt said he was going out on the highway, in case he saw her walking along it. "I don't know what else to do," he said, his dark eyes filled with anxiety, and told Ellen and Pete to stay put, "in case she comes back or phones the motel."

At midnight, he came back to the room and threw his hands up in the air. "Search me where she is. I'll give it one more hour, then I'm calling the cops."

"Where the hell have you been?" Walt said, when Vera stepped into the motel room at 12:30, a broad smile on her face, her hair alive with humidity.

"Mom, we've been worried about you all night." Ellen jumped off the bed and stood beside her mother, relieved to have her back. She thought to give her a hug, but Vera was never a hugger, never one to touch.

"I've been at the World's Fair. I think that's why we're here." She tossed her shoes on the floor and pulled some brochures out of the bag. "I've seen all but eighteen pavilions. I will do the rest in the time we have left."

Walt stood in front of her, his hands in his pockets. "How did you get home?"

"I hitchhiked."

"You did not! I don't believe you! Who gave you a ride?"

"A trucker."

"You could have called the motel and sent a message for me to pick you up. I would have gone to get you."

Vera bent down to pick up her shoes, her cheeks flushed. "It's too bad the bunch of you fretted about me, but you should know I can manage on my own. And now I am going to bed. There's only two days left, and I want an early start tomorrow. I've decided to save the France Pavilion for the absolute last. It will be my grand exit. The icing on the cake!" She swept through the door to the adjoining room and closed it.

The next day, during a crêpe lunch at the Café Paris, after a morning full of exhibits, Ellen asked Vera the question that had bothered her since last night. "How come you stayed at the fair and hitchhiked back to the motel?"

Vera leaned on her elbows and bent in closer to Ellen, her eyes narrowing, and asked, "Why would you ask me such a thing?"

"Because it's a strange thing to do." The question seemed perfectly obvious. She noticed Vera's mouth twitch. "I worried about you. I was frightened."

Vera's eyes flashed. "When will this family ever understand I am perfectly capable?" Ellen knew that; it wasn't what she meant. "And if any of you really cared, you would have gone with me! Instead of ganging up on me." Vera pushed back in her chair and crossed her arms, the freckles on her tanned arms in full bloom.

Vera had said Expo was important because countries came together from all over the world to communicate and to show each other who they were. So why couldn't she communicate with Ellen right now? "We were worried," Ellen said, her voice catching as her heart raced. "Isn't that how families are supposed to be?"

"You have no business telling me, a mother, how families are supposed to be. All any of you had to do was come to the world's fair and be interested. And did you? No! That was all I wanted."

"But we did! We came! We're here! And we're interested, but in our own way," Ellen said, exasperated and confused.

"Well, not the way you're supposed to be."

Walt threw open the door of Pete and Ellen's room and said, "Thank God today's the last day and we're going back home tomorrow." He leaned against the door frame and lit up a smoke.

Ellen flipped over on her side to face her father. She was glad to be leaving, too.

Suddenly, Walt threw down his cigarette and said, "Oh for Christ's sakes! Someone's pinched the canoe!"

Pete sat up in his bed, his dark hair a tangled bird's nest, and said, "What?"

Vera appeared just then wearing the gold-green floral pant-dress she'd been saving for the last day, the legs rippling with her strides. Now she twirled like a model and said, "Ta dum," her hands upraised, and saw Walt staring at the empty roof of the Mercury.

Pete heaved his pillow across the room and shouted, "Fuck!"—a word Vera never allowed, "How am I ever going to go fishing again?"

Vera said, "I told you, but who ever listens to me?"

The afternoon heat had reached its wilting peak and Walt, Pete, and Ellen sprawled and slumped around the table at Café le Déjeuner, having a late lunch. Walt wanted ordinary food and not "mystery on a plate" from another country.

Vera sat up straight, her eyes on the France Pavilion across the crowded pedestrian lane. "Once I've seen that, I will have seen every pavilion here! All ninety!" she said triumphantly. "I've saved the best for last!"

"Ever since that guy in the Australian line told you about it, you've been obsessed," Pete said. "I'd never trust anyone wearing a powder-blue, polyester leisure suit." He sipped his beer, another fla-grant graduation into adult habits.

"Who's coming with me to France?" she asked, looking around the table.

"I'll only hold you back." Walt skimmed the beer from his upper lip, the brim of his fedora casting a shadow over his eyes.

"Well?" she asked first Pete, then Ellen. "Do I have any takers at all?"

"I'm with Dad," Pete said. "And yeah, I'd be like a big anchor tied around your leg."

Vera sighed and looked disgusted. "I would have thought, since we are leaving tomorrow, all of you might see this as your last chance. That's how I see it." She turned to Ellen, her mouth pinched in a way that dimpled her cheeks, but not in a smile. "Ellen? You coming with me?"

Ellen met her mother's gaze. "No," Ellen said. "I'm not coming. I want to finish my book and I am too tired. I cannot do one more exhibit. I can live without seeing France."

"Well, I might have known you'd join the others," Vera said.

"We're not on teams, Mom! I just want to read my book," Ellen said, and Walt said, "No teams, Vera, just family."

Yesterday, after the crêpe lunch at Café Paris, she'd barely talked to Vera except to say, "Yeah, that's interesting," or "Yeah, that's nice," as Vera exclaimed over something, or said, "Ellen come and see this, Ellen come and see that," exhausting her with her insistence.

Vera bit into her grilled cheese, put the remains down, and angled her chair to face away from them and towards the France Pavilion. She practically had her back to Ellen.

Pete had a big smirk on his face as he looked at the pavilion. "That building looks like a porcupine that's been hit on the road."

"Joke all you want. I'm past the point of caring," Vera said.

Ellen felt a pang of sadness. Maybe it did feel like her family had turned on Vera, but hadn't she been angling for it, and why not just go along with Pete's joke? It did look sort of like a dead porcu-pine, spikes sticking up here and there, in no order, and squashed in places. A building that didn't know what it wanted to be.

Walt threw down his hamburger. "Well, that's another piece of cardboard."

"I'll finish that if you don't want the rest," Pete said and reached across to Walt's plate.

"Ma," he said as he squirted ketchup onto the half puck of meat. "You sure you didn't leave something out? Isn't there something else to see?"

Vera ignored him, reached into her tote, and pulled out the matching headscarf for her pant-dress. She leafed through her passbook. "I will be the only one in this family to have seen all the pavilions!" She squared her shoulders, her chin held high, proud of her achievement.

"Yeah?" Pete said, chewing his hamburger. "I fail to see the significance of this."

"That doesn't surprise me," Vera said.

Ellen wondered if the exhibits really did excite her the way she let on, or did she feel she had to be enthusiastic because the whole country was worked up and she had to join in? Couldn't she be honest and admit that some of the displays and exhibits weren't all that interesting?

"You know, Pete," Vera said. "Maybe it is time for you to move to Toronto. You've become such an independent little man."

"I've been talking to him about getting a job at Clearview," Walt said. "I think it would be a good move for him."

"I don't agree. I think he needs to experience the world. Instead of doing what's easy and following along in your footsteps," she said.

"We'll talk when we get home," Walt said.

She stood up, tightened the cloth belt around her waist, and grabbed her Expo tote bag. "Okay," she said, "I am off. I am going to join the line." She started away from the table.

"Vera, hold on. When are we meeting up?" Walt called out.

"In four hours. But give me some flexibility."

"Where?" Walt said.

"Here?" she asked, gesturing with her hand. "It's as good a place as any." She crossed the lane leading to the France Pavilion, blended with the crowd, reappeared at the end of the line, and looked back at them. Walt raised his hand and turned it in a slight by-your-leave wave.

"Thank God." Walt's tone changed as if speaking to her directly.

"Get in there and stay in there a good long time. Give the rest of us a break. Get it out of your system. Whatever it is."

Ellen left to find a washroom, and took her time getting back to Walt and Pete, standing by the St. Lawrence to catch a cooler breeze, stopping to admire an elaborate fountain. When she returned to the café, Vera was about to go inside the pavilion. She turned, just before disappearing, and gave a victorious wave, her kerchief in hand as if waving a flag—she'd finally made it!—and then she was gone.

On the highway, headed west, back to Willitsburg, Ellen stared at Vera's empty place in the front seat, going over the events of the last two days of never-ending waiting for her mother to return, waiting for a phone message to come through the Star Lite office with news. That whole first day they only ate once. Pete took the Mercury and drove for burgers and shakes, since the motel restaurant was closed, and brought them back to the room. He didn't have his full license and shouldn't be driving, but Walt said he was too distracted to drive and wouldn't know where he was going.

The police came, knocking hard on the door so that Ellen's heart jumped, and she imagined them bringing terrible news. After they completed a missing person's report, one of the officers said to Walt, "You might as well go back home. We will contact you once we know anything."

Walt spoke as if in a trance. "We have to. I have to go back to work. The money's running out."

Before they got in the car, Walt had asked Ellen why she didn't want to sit up front with him, and a panic rose in her. Usually she would, but she felt like she might be replacing her mother, and the thought of it terrified her.

Ever since she'd gone missing, the three of them moved uncomfortably together, awkward without her, silent, no longer knowing how to be with each other or who they were. Pete and Walt quit their usual banter about their guy stuff, and Pete's sarcasm shut down completely.

Walt scanned the countryside as he drove, as though he expected to see her tromping through one of the fields. Since Vera left, he'd had a constant look of befuddlement or confusion—a perpetual state of being lost. Last night, sitting at the little table in his white socks, a toe poking through the toe, he said, "I don't know what to make of anything!" and threw up his hands.

"Are you giving up, Dad?" Ellen asked. He looked defeated, and she didn't know exactly what she meant.

"I wonder now if I ever got started," he said.

She thought of Vera sitting at the kitchen table, sewing her outfits, filled with excitement and a curiosity about the world she hoped to see. Had she seen all she'd ever thought she would at Expo?

Ellen ran her hands over her pedal pushers and watched the countryside flow past. They'd come this way before but nothing looked familiar, as if they'd entered into another alien world. She'd turned down her mother's invitation to stay with her at the site the day she hitchhiked home and turned her down again to go with her to the France Pavilion. Was she the reason Vera had left? Did Vera want her to feel bad and guilty? Or was it all of them?

Had desperation taken over when she realized it was the last pavilion, on the last day of their visit to discover Man and His World, Expo 67? The world would close up for her and she would go back to her life in Willitsburg, a desert of day-to-day monotony and no escape, the little icing flowers she created for special cakes draining every ounce of creative energy she had.

Had she decided to step out into the world alone, to go to Paris, to study the Impressionists? She was the navigator, but what direction was she going? Was she running away from them or towards herself?

SOMEWHERE

Kara walked between Blue and Colm, their feet scraping over the pavement, the sounds of a winter's night piling up around them. For a long time, no one said anything. Kara guessed they were all thinking the same thing, how it was Luke left them here.

"Do you think he's getting some kind of morbid satisfaction, dumping us here, in the middle of nowhere?" Blue asked.

"We know where we are." It wouldn't help if Blue started freaking; she'd only use up energy, and who knew how long they'd be out here? At least Kara was dressed for it in jeans and a long coat, a recent score from Value Village, but Blue's waist jacket, short skirt, and leotards wouldn't keep her warm, not for long anyway. Her feet would stay warm in her mukluks, which looked ridiculous in the mall, but made sense here.

"I feel like we're going in circles." Colm tipped his head and stuck out his tongue to catch snowflakes.

They might be. They'd been walking for nearly two hours and still no sign of the park gate. "If only the snow would let up a bit," Kara said. "At least then we'd be able to see where we've been." It was getting harder to make out the narrow road.

"We're going to freeze to death," Blue said. "Figures. You ever noticed how the most horrible tragedies happen at Christmas?"

Just like Blue to predict the worst possible outcome. The tsunami of life always overpowered her, washed away her control and options. At least Kara tried. Today for instance. How many resumes did she hand out? Thirty? Thirty-five? "We're not going to freeze to death. Colm and I will turn you into a sandwich. You're the filling, we're the bread. I read about these dudes who saved some guy on a mountain that way."

"Gee, thanks. That makes me feel a whole lot better," Blue said, sarcasm her native tongue. "Here's what I think. If you hadn't gone into Beach Bunnies with your resume, Luke would never have done what he did with the mannequins and then we wouldn't be here."

"Don't blame me for what happened. I never asked him to follow me in there." Kara wasn't so much mad at Blue as she was tired; she didn't want to go into a whole rehashing of events and the blame thing. Not out loud anyway. What difference would it make? They were here, weren't they? Wandering around in darkness in the provincial park, closed for the season.

The wind picked up, shook the trees, rattled and creaked the branches, sent the snow into a flurry of spins and swirls, then just as quickly died, letting the snow settle once again into a dense cascade.

Blue was wrong to say this wouldn't have happened if Kara hadn't gone into Beach Bunnies to apply for a job. If she'd gone to her biology class today at the Adult Education Centre, if she'd just stayed on the bus and gone to school, none of them would be here right now. And the crazy part was, somehow getting ninety-eight percent on the exam had something to do with not wanting to go. As if she were frightened by doing so well.

"I knew there was a light on in your attic. I knew it was on a dimmer switch," the instructor said, the tip of his finger resting on the grade.

She could barely make out Colm and Blue, as if she walked alone, the sounds of their footsteps absorbed now by the snow, the wind wild at the tree tops.

"Luke had a point about the mannequins in the window. He even named them David and Pamela," Colm said. "He said they were like fish out of water."

Luke's exact explanation was more poetic: their eyes were filled with hopelessness from being stuck in the window, under the hot spotlights, dressed in their bathing suits, standing in sand, longing for water, for something they could never have. Poor David and Pamela.

While Kara talked to Sales Associate Cindy about job prospects— "I'll work part-time, weekends, nights, days, once I've finished my school courses, I'm extremely flexible," and Cindy, looking up from the bikini she strung on a hanger to give her a look that said, you've got a big heap of loser-itis—Luke hoisted David and Pamela out of the store window.

On the way out of the mall, Kara saw a number of shoppers gathered around a fountain. There in front of a waterfall flowing down over fake rocks, surrounded by tropical plants, stood David and Pamela, up to their knees in water. Crazy as it sounded, they looked happier.

Luke was at the mall exit in a van, waiting for her, along with Colm and Blue. He rolled down the window and shouted, "Hop in; we're going on an adventure."

This was an adventure all right, walking, lost, with Blue and Colm, their shapes almost merged with darkness, more motion than solid objects. None of them knew the direction they were headed.

The rise and fall of the wind, whipping the night up around them, took the place of talking, kept them alert.

"This place is creepy," Blue said.

When they cleared the city, snow swizzled into the windshield, the great downy flakes instantly obliterated by the heat. They started singing "Jingle Bells." Luke knew all along where he was taking them. He sat up tall at the steering wheel and gave "The Little Drummer Boy" everything he had, taking charge of the pa-rum-pum-pum-pum. Kara stretched out on a foamy alongside some boxes and listened to the hum of the miles peeling away under them.

Luke turned north on Highway 21 and picked up speed. Partway through "White Christmas," as he looked out the rearview mirror, he said, "Shit," and tromped on the gas.

Out the back window, Kara saw red flashing lights. "You weren't speeding," Kara said. "What's the problem?"

Up front in the passenger seat, Colm turned to face Kara and Blue and repeated what Luke had just told him.

"You stole the van? Jesus, what the hell have you done?" Blue shouted.

"Not so much stolen as borrowed," Luke said, his eyes still on the rearview mirror.

"Who from?" Blue said.

"An anonymous donor. I didn't exactly ask for it, but I will return it. Let me emphasize that right now."

"You idiot! The cops won't care!" Blue leaned to look out the back window.

Kara reached into a box, removed wads of tissue paper, and pulled out a porcelain doll dressed in a red velvet robe with fake fur trim, hands stuck inside a muffler, brunette ringlets spilling out under a bonnet. She put the doll back in the box, stuffed the paper back in.

Luke was having a blast, alert at the wheel, leaning into the van's motion, angling for a way to get them out of their fix. "Hold on, kids! Here we go!"

He turned off the van's lights and sped down the highway in darkness, put distance between themselves and the flashing cruiser, then he eased off the gas and took a sharp turn into Pinery Provincial Park, without touching the brakes.

They drove past the closed-for-the-season park office, over a hill, around a curve and deeper into the park.

Luke switched on the dims and said the cop would have gone past the park by now. The headlights carved a faint tunnel through the trees lining either side of the narrow road. Kara looked out into the forest, at the black spaces the shapes of spruce, the headlights catching rake-like outlines of oaks and maples. It was snowing hard.

"Wait a minute," Colm said. "We've been here before."

"How do you know?" Blue's teeth chattered, her arms wrapped around her waist, her shoulders hunched.

"It looks familiar."

"Is it that tree over there you recognize? The one you can almost see?" Blue pointed towards the woods, to no tree in particular. "We're lost and you guys know it! Just say so!"

"I told you, we know where we are," Kara said. "We just don't know where in the park we are. So we're not lost. There's a difference."

"I don't think so," Blue said. "Not if we die!"

"We're finding our way." She didn't want to hear Blue's great big heap of how they'd never get out of here, how their frozen remains would be chewed by bears. She unwound her scarf and handed it to Blue. "Here, use this like a shawl. It will help warm you."

What was he thinking, pinching a van, Colm asked Luke as they drove deeper into the park. "I don't know, man," Luke said. "It was by the door, running and everything. It felt like an invitation. Or a sign. And then I had this urge to come here, right here. Let's just say I felt the call of the wild; the city was getting to me. Looking for work, scrounging for money. It's so pure here or something. It's elemental."

"Next time you get the call of the wild, let it go to voicemail," Blue said.

He drove deep into the park then stopped, turned off the motor, and ordered them out and to the back of the van. He told them to be still and listen. "Can you hear it?"

"Hear what?" Kara didn't hear anything.

"Do you hear cars?"

"No."

"Do you hear people?"

"No."

Luke said, "Precisely the point. There are no human sounds." He told them to listen harder and Kara said they couldn't if there was nothing to listen to. "It's not exactly nothing, just something different," Luke said.

Kara examined him more closely, saw his long hair and Cowichan Indian sweater in a different way. Maybe he wasn't a back-to-the-earther, a peace-lovin' displaced hippie, a greener. Maybe he was something else. A criminal. Crazy. What did she know about him? Only what she knew from the mall.

Luke said it was rare and precious to be away from all human sounds and if they listened hard they could hear how silence made a lot of noise. "It's kind of like hearing, really hearing, your own thoughts. We don't listen to our own thoughts. If we did, we'd be surprised by what we think." He said he had an idea and they needed to walk with him a ways. "Stand here in the center of the road, in a group, close your eyes, and concentrate very hard on what you are hearing."

Blue was the first to say she thought the whole thing silly, and

Luke told her to hush, then repeated the instructions for them all to close their eyes. "This is food for the soul," he said.

Kara listened hard, searching for the silence, and heard the moody rise and fall of wind, branches smashing together, heard a dull and constant roar, the ceaseless tumble of waves along the lake shore. The night in agitation, motion, breathing, alive. Luke was right; silence was noisy.

Luke whispered they were listening to the sound of the universe talking, and Colm said, "Whatever, dude." Luke said everyone needed to be more connected and figure out their place in the universe. "Keep your eyes closed," he whispered. "Listen, really listen."

Around them the night roared; cold flakes pecked their cheeks. The van started up. Kara opened her eyes in time to see the brake lights flicker like two blinking eyes and disappear into the night.

"What the fuck is he doing now?" Blue screamed and started running after the van, but gave up when she realized the uselessness.

They stood in the center of the road, surrounded by darkness. In a while, Kara suggested they walk so they might feel as if they were getting somewhere and to stop the cold from setting in.

"How far do you think we've come?" Kara asked Colm.

"Hard to say. Several miles. We've been walking a long time."

"Maybe he's coming back for us," Blue said, teeth still chattering, her hands planted deep in her jacket pockets, her neck sunk into her fake fur collar.

Kara could barely make out Colm in this light; he appeared like a shadow. Snow fell on her face in cold, numbing pinpricks. Clouds snuffed out the moon and stars. She raised her arm and straightened it, wriggled her fingers, but it was so dark she couldn't see her hand. She touched her nose with her fingertip by concentrating very hard on hitting the mark. Body and mind seemed no longer one. Kara's feet, touching ahead into the void, did the work of her eyes.

They came to a fork and gambled the path they chose would lead them back to the highway and not deeper into the park. The wind blew harder, ached through frozen limbs, thrashed through the tree tops. Something crashed in the bush—a large branch falling. Blue screamed and grabbed Colm's arm.

Kara forgot about trying to find the highway. She floated in the sound of wind. Air swam over her face, fingering her hair, and the pings of snow brought blood to the surface of her cheeks, gave the sensation of being hot and cold and alive. She drew in deep breaths. Frigid, sharp air sank to the bottom of her lungs, filled her chest, and spread through her veins. And always, the intricate interweaving of sounds against the backdrop of Lake Huron, the endless wash of water.

Blue said he'd left them there to die, precisely his intentions, and this would turn out to be their last night on earth. "I'll never find out what I got for Christmas."

Somehow, Kara didn't think so, and all Colm said was, "Come on, Blue. Enough of the crap."

They walked until they heard something in the distance, a low and muffled drone. A car passing on the highway. Blue cheered and spun in a circle, Colm smiled, and Kara said nothing. She'd miss something, a feeling of being involved and alert. Completely alive. They strode to where the sound came from and the sensation of lightness left her. Back to her life, her former life of closed doors and dead ends. Ninety-eight percent. Why had it frightened her? She thought she'd never be able to score so high again.

Over a hill they saw the glow of lights, captured by the downward chaos of hard-driving snow. They passed the park office and the highway came into view. Headlights shone in the distance, burned stronger as cars approached, and set the reflectors at the edge of the road on fire.

Something moved in the woods. The backs of several deer rippled in the sweep of passing headlights, unperturbed by human presence. Some lowered their heads to graze on the dead grasses puncturing the snow, raised them again to chew and watch as the three people passed, while others stood, heads held high, ready and still. Not restless or agitated, they seemed willing to stay on one side of some invisible line, held there by something deep inside, an instinct keeping them safe. They knew their place in the universe.

Kara felt like running but didn't want to alarm the deer or disturb their trust. Once past, she quickened her pace, smiled when Blue shouted, "What's the rush?"

SPACE

Sally thought about the question Mrs. Crawley had just asked her as she watched the old woman pour hot water into a teapot. Why had she stayed away so long? "I didn't come back after my first visit because I thought you didn't like me." Blunt, but Sally had an idea Mrs. Crawley might value directness.

Mrs. Crawley guided two teacups across the spacious farm kitchen, her head down, pink scalp visible through thinning white hair. She concentrated on the chattering teacups.

"Whatever gave you such an idea?" she asked, after she placed one cup in front of Sally, the other before the adjacent chair.

Sally's eyes settled on a geranium in the window, its fiery-red blossom fisted at spring's tepidness on the other side of the pane, and searched for a way to make her first impressions of her old neighbor sound less harsh. "You might not remember; it was a long time ago." It didn't seem that long, but it had to be—Phillip had been gone six years. "I brought you a plate of cookies when we moved into the neighborhood. As a goodwill gesture."

Mrs. Crawley returned to the table with a third teacup, which she set in front of an empty chair, and placed the teapot on the table, seated herself next to Sally, and sighed, as if from exertion. She shoved her white hair away from her face, her hand curved into a question mark by arthritis—"My hair's like a weed these days"—then twisted abruptly in her chair to face Sally full on. "I do remember you coming with cookies. Yes, I do." Her voice conveyed a sudden jolt of memory tucked away for so long its leap into the present seemed to startle her. She patted her knee, obviously pleased by the sudden revelation. She caught Sally's quick glance at the third teacup. "I'm easily sidetracked in my thoughts—you've no doubt noticed—so I'll explain that later. Right now I want to know what I did that scared you away for so long."

The intensity of her blue eyes forced Sally to look away to the large antique hutch across the room, as if she might find a simple answer buried beneath its cluttered surface. Her past, since her first meeting with Mrs. Crawley, was a pile of wreckage that revealed no clarity, no truth, only speculation fired by hurt and anger. Then, there was the business of the neighborhood children labeling Mrs. Crawley a witch. "Creepy Crawley, Creepy Crawley," they chanted as they passed her house.

If Sally were honest, completely honest, shame brought her there that day, but she wasn't about to tell Mrs. Crawley that.

The old woman raised her cup and took a sip, the tea swishing about inside the delicate porcelain, her unsteady hand returning the cup to its floral saucer. Her wispy eyebrows pinched over her intelligent blue eyes. "Let me see now. Didn't you tell me you have two boys? I think I remember you saying."

Good, Sally thought, she's forgotten the question about why I stayed away so long. Being alone so much would have the old woman skip from one topic to another, with no one around insisting on logical progressions or continuity. Sally understood; she spent so much time alone she often wondered if she made any sense at all when talking to people. "Yes I do," Sally said, surprised the old woman remembered the boys. "They're grown now. Both are away at school."

"And your husband?" Mrs. Crawley leaned forward as if expecting to hear something remarkable.

"That's another story. We're no longer together." This was as much information as she cared to give anyone about the end of her marriage to Phillip.

"I'm sorry to hear. I understand more people divorce now than stay married." Mrs. Crawley shook her head, apparently resigned to the notion of unstoppable change.

Sally couldn't imagine she once thought Mrs. Crawley was a cranky old woman. If anything, her translucent white skin and soft-pink housecoat gave her the appearance of delicateness and vulnerability.

"Do you know today was the first time in three years I walked all around my yard?"

She sounded pleased as a mother recounting a child's first steps.

"Really? Good for you!" Earlier, Sally watched her from her living room window, not quite believing her eyes, as if she might be seeing an apparition in a housecoat and bedroom slippers, cradling a lilac blossom in her palm, her wind-wild hair snowy in the sunlight. In all the time she'd lived here, today was the first time she'd seen Mrs. Crawley outside. She'd decided to visit a second time, while she was out in her yard, and risk the same kind of reception she got when they moved into their new house built on what once was Mrs. Crawley's farmland.

That first visit, she'd barely thanked Sally for the cookies, told her in a voice filled with resentment that the sale of her land was out of necessity, not choice. She said her arthritis was flaring up, then practically slammed the door in Sally's face. But this time, on this second visit, and Sally with no offer of cookies and uncertain what to expect, Mrs. Crawley invited her in for tea.

"How is your health? I remember you telling me you had arthritis."

"I'm on new medication. It helps me get around much better."

"Good. I hope you continue to show improvement, Mrs. Crawley."

"Pardon me?" Her hand went to her ear and fiddled with her hearing aid. "I doubt I'll ever get used to this. My nephew Edgar—he lives in Florida—insisted I get one of these things. I'd no idea how deaf I was getting." She seemed to assess Sally, size her up, and looked pleased by what she saw, as if Sally had just appeared before her and hadn't been sitting here, sharing a cup of tea. "Call me Edna."

Sally sipped her tea and looked out the window, past Edna's driveway and the row of tall spruce trees to the house being built next door, a large house with a turret front. Edna still had the largest lot, about two acres, all that remained of her farm, a sudden, surprising oasis, the kind children stumble upon in fairy tales, in the center of suburbia. "Finally, the last houses are being built," Sally said. "You must be glad."

"Yes. If I didn't get old and sick, I would have hung on to my whole farm, but it was not to be. It's not been easy watching it go, bit by bit, sliced up like a pie and served out."

"How did you farm in the early days?" Sally never once saw a Mr. Crawley.

"Oh, my husband did." She pointed out the window. "You see across the street?"

"To my house, you mean?"

"Yes, I suppose so. Now, go down a ways from your house to where the road curves, and all that was our land. My husband planted it in soybeans. He was a good man, a good farmer." She was lost for a minute, gone with remembering, then she continued, her voice softened. "During harvest, if the light was right and the conditions good, he stayed out 'til well past dusk to take off a crop. But one night he was especially late coming in from the fields." She pulled a tissue from her housecoat pocket and clutched it in her hand. "I went looking for him. I found him near where the road curves, far back in the field, pinned under his tractor."

"How terrible." All the awful stories that went around about Edna, old Creepy Crawley, as the kids called her, including Sally's own boys—stories about her being a witch and you better not go near her house or she'd cast an evil spell, all those mean-spirited rumors, and not one about this tragic incident, nothing remotely connected to truth. "Was he killed instantly?"

"Oh no, he was alive, and conscious. We talked. I told him I was going for help. He said he'd wait right there, right where he was, and continue to gaze at the stars. He had quite a sense of humor, you know, even in that state. I called an ambulance, and the police, and they brought in a truck to pull the tractor off. He talked the entire time, gave pointers on how to get the machine off him. When they finally pulled the tractor away, I went to him, gathered his head in my lap, and watched life fade out of him. Internal hemorrhaging, bleeding from the inside, not visible from the outside."

"I'm so sorry."

Edna pressed her lips together to control her trembling chin. "Can you imagine being trapped, able to look up at the sky, at all that space, and being unable to get up and walk away?" She shook her head, the crumpled tissue passing from one hand to the other until she regained her composure. "It was a long time ago. I've adjusted, but I never got over it. You never do. I surely do miss him." She examined the teacup sitting before the empty chair. "That's his tea. We have it together every day and I talk to him." Then, she shifted in her spindle chair, sat straight, shoulders pinched, chin thrust out. "All those houses, yours included, are built on sacred ground. It holds my husband's blood." Her tone changed from sadness of loss to one of emphasis.

"Mrs. Crawley, I . . ." Sally searched for something to say, a comment of consolation.

"I would have lost the land eventually, what with the city growing so fast. This whole area's been rezoned for houses, with sky-high taxes, far more than a crippled old widow could afford. I held on as long as I could." Defeat and resignation returned to her voice as she settled back into her chair and smoothed the pink housecoat over her knees.

Mrs. Crawley still owned most of her land when Sally moved here. Her cat, Karma, used to mouse in Mrs. Crawley's fields and would go missing, and Phillip or the boys had to go looking for her. One night, Adam and Cliff came home triumphant, Karma draped in Adam's arms. He said the cat came out of Mrs. Crawley's basement. Sally asked how the cat managed to get inside her house. Adam said she'd crawled in through a broken pane in a basement window. Phillip knew about the broken window and complained that Mrs. Crawley should have it fixed. "The cat could get hurt, even killed," he said. "I found Karma there once, too."

Sally examined Edna's hazy profile against the late afternoon light. The story about her husband seemed to have exhausted her, but she'd also be accustomed to silence. "You must be very excited about getting outside again?"

"Oh yes!" The question brought her back from somewhere. "I loved to work outside before I got sick. I imagine you've seen the man who mows my lawn and clears my driveway and sidewalks in the winter. If it weren't for Frank, I couldn't stay here. But he's no good at gardening, so I'm afraid my yard has slipped. I shouldn't complain. He's seventy-five and, well, neither of us is getting any younger. I'm eighty-two and, to be honest, I'm surprised I've lived this long. There've been plenty of times when I wished I hadn't, but this new medication has given me a new lease on life. I can hear, too, thanks to my nephew, my only relative. Sometimes this buzzes. Drives me crazy." She pointed to the flesh-colored instrument in her ear. "Edgar phones every Friday at six o'clock, unless he has business or something comes up. I don't always hear the phone, especially if

I'm not sitting right by it, waiting for it to ring. Then he thinks I've died or fallen, and sends around the police. Twice it's happened." She clapped her hands and gave a hearty laugh. "Edgar's had as much drama as he can stand from me. When he came to visit last year—maybe you saw the car with the Florida plates?—he said, that's it, you're getting a hearing aid."

Edna leaned in so close Sally saw patches of lines at the corners of her eyes, like the finest leather, and the horizon of pink scalp cresting her head. "Promise you won't tell Edgar?" she whispered, her eyes glinting with renewed mischief. "I hardly ever wear it. I never seem to get it set right. It sounds like there's a flock of birds flying right through my head. I've gotten used to silence. So, I wear it on Friday when I know he's going to call." She pressed her hand against her mouth to conceal a smile. "I wore it today, in case I met someone outside. And I did!" She gave a little jolt in her seat, and appeared startled. "Oh my goodness! Here I've been doing all the talking and I already know about me. Let's talk about you."

"My story's not very exciting, I'm afraid." As Sally had listened to Mrs. Crawley, she asked herself why she hadn't crossed the street to visit before now. "I live a very ordinary life." Edna's crippling disease kept her shut in, but Sally had no such excuse. Unless you counted fear. And anger. Mostly anger.

After Phillip left, she plunged into her work and raising the boys, shoved her social life so far aside it disappeared. It didn't take long for their old friends, mostly couples, to give up on her. Exactly what she wanted, to rid herself of anything connected with him, sweep him away with the ease of removing the teacups from this table with one definitive sweep of the arm, leaving an uncluttered tabletop. She constructed the walls of her life so thick with work and childcare and home maintenance and excuses, plenty of excuses, they were impenetrable; no one could ever hurt her again.

"Edna, would you mind if I come to visit you more often?"

Edna's hands rose up out of her lap in a flutter of excitement, then clasped together as if capturing Sally's question, as if she held something sacred, an opportunity for renewal. "That would be lovely!"

Good, Sally thought. She'd been alone long enough, and the two of them, despite their age difference, had much in common. Edna could offer safe friendship, one that didn't need to go snooping into the past. Yet Edna's humbling and childlike excitement, nakedly joyous, made Sally uneasy, almost embarrassed. She steered the conversation in another direction. "It must have been very hard for you to watch your land disappear bit by bit to the housing development?"

"Terribly hard. I had so much space for so long, I got used to it. But I had to let it go." Edna straightened in her chair and pointed across the room to the hutch. "Frank moved that there for security."

"Security?"

"Yes. It's blocking a door, and a set of stairs that lead to the landing and an outside door to the house. Frank comes and goes out that side door. He keeps his tools in the basement. But that hutch stays put!" Edna jabbed a gnarled finger at the hutch. "Shall I tell you the story of how it came to be there?"

Sally nodded. It would be pointless to say no.

"Frank used to pick the fruit from the orchard and bring it to me. In late summer and early fall I preserved and canned. I'm a farm wife; it's in my blood. I used to have a fruit cellar full of preserves, jams, jellies, what-have-you. Not anymore, not for a long time."

"Good for you." Sally respected self-sufficiency, especially in another single woman.

"Now listen to this. This will surprise you. My fruit cellar was really a bomb shelter my husband built." She leaned closer, as if sharing a secret, her eyes lit by the fun of sharing it. "I thought he'd flipped his lid when he told me what he was up to. It was at the time of the Cuban missile crisis. Tense days, those, I can tell you. He liked to tinker, especially when he had nothing to do over the winter, so he dug this bunker at the front of the house, accessible by the basement, and we used it for a fruit room. You should see it, all cement, no windows so the Communists couldn't see in. I used to joke about how the Commies were hiding out there in the soybeans and creeping up on us." She threw her head back and squawked at the thought of teasing her husband. "He didn't appreciate my humor, but I couldn't help it, the whole project seemed utterly ridiculous. He wasn't the only one doing this. People were so frightened about being invaded by the Commies that all around they were building bomb shelters. While he was building it he rambled on explaining all the whys and wherefores, the bolt latches he put outside and inside the door from the basement. The outside latch made it look like a fruit cellar and the inside one would keep the Commies out so they wouldn't get to us."

Edna turned to the third teacup. "Well, you made an excellent fruit cellar. No better spot for storing potatoes," she told it.

How opposite they were. Edna talked to Mr. Crawley every day, while Sally pushed away even the most fleeting thoughts of Phillip.

"After a while I had problems going downstairs. I took my flash-light because my arthritis was bad enough that I couldn't reach up to pull the string on the ceiling light. My canning stock dwindled to almost nothing, since I couldn't do it any longer. I kept reminding myself to ask Frank to go and bring up the rest, then I'd forget. This poor old brain of mine doesn't always work right." Edna tapped the side of her head.

"One night I went down, opened the big bolt on the fruit cel-lar, shone my flashlight around, got a jar of pears, the very last one, and as I was leaving, I saw someone in the shadows in the basement. I called out, who is it? How ridiculous that was, I can't hear very well, and anyway, what was a crippled old lady going to do if I found someone? Wrestle them to the ground? Beat them up? With these?" She raised her twisted hands for Sally to see. "I shone the flashlight over by the furnace and went to see if someone was hiding behind it. I snooped around a bit more, amidst the clutter, the stacked chairs, old bedframes, baskets and tools, and found no one. Eventually I went back to the fruit cellar and latched the door. On my way back upstairs I found the side door open, not wide, but a bit. Sometimes Frank forgets to lock it—I remind him every time and still he forgets. That's how the intruder got in, and since it was still open, I realized that's how he got out, too. It was one of those horrid developers that broke into my house to snoop, to see what the place was worth. They gave me nothing but pressure and grief. Forever making me offers to push me out of here."

Sally tried not to smile, knowing how unlikely it would be that someone after her land would be snooping in her basement. Better Edna think that than the possibility of it being a robber, or worse. Or else, Edna saw things that weren't there.

She remembered how Adam and Cliff told her, the night they came home with Karma, how she left her door unlocked. Sally asked them how they knew.

"Adam dared me to check it to see if it was open," Cliff said, wide-eyed with excitement.

"What for? What would he give you for doing it?"

"Five bucks," Cliff grinned.

Adam always did have a bullying streak, and Cliff was the willing daredevil. Cliff said he'd opened the door, quickly closed it, and ran like hell. She told them to never, ever do that again; it was trespassing. After Phillip left and it became the boys' job to go looking for the wayward cat, she reminded them to be careful at Mrs. Crawley's. They could call Karma through the broken window, but no more door shenanigans.

Edna pointed at the hutch across the room. "Do you see that?" she asked.

"Yes, I've been admiring it."

"After I figured out the developer had been in my house, I didn't sleep a wink all night. The next morning, I had Frank push the hutch over the door leading to the basement. I sleep like a baby."

"That's what I call a functional piece of furniture," Sally said.

"How's that?" Edna fidgeted with her hearing aid.

"It's good it makes you feel safe," Sally raised her voice. Edna seemed to be tiring, her eyes a little droopy, less bright. "This has been really lovely, but I think I should be going."

"Oh no, not yet." Edna appeared alarmed and Sally knew she'd misjudged her strength. "It wouldn't be fair. You haven't told me anything about yourself. I haven't given you a chance."

"There's not much to tell. I have a quiet life."

"Now, you mentioned your boys. Did you raise them or did your husband or did you share?"

"No, I did."

"Your husband didn't want to help with two fine boys?"

"Apparently not."

"Such a shame. You'd think he'd be proud."

"You'd think so. I was bitter for a long time, but I'm over it. I realize I'm far better off without him." If that were completely true, she wouldn't feel the plug of anger stirring in her stomach as she spoke of him.

Edna leaned in close and Sally detected the faint scent of baby powder. "So, he didn't turn out to be the man you thought he was?"

"That's true." Sally traced the gold edge of the saucer with her finger and thought about telling Edna everything. She'd never told anyone the whole truth, not her boys or her sister, and certainly not the friends they'd had when they were a couple. Maybe it was time to flick away the last of her bitterness. "We had some problems shortly after we moved here." The details of the story, so long dormant, sidelined by the practical matters of earning a living and raising the boys and her refusal to speak of it, rose stubbornly as she tried to present a clear story. "We had financial problems. I worked at home as an accountant. Phillip, my husband, was a VP for a company. Then he got downsized, fired, really."

"I know they have funny names for it these days. It all amounts to the same thing."

"One night we got into a terrible argument about money, about whether or not to sell the house or re-mortgage, the kind of thing couples usually argue about, or so I thought."

"Oh yes," Edna assured her. "My husband and I had many heated debates on how to stretch a dollar. We didn't always see eye to eye, you know."

"Just before we were going to bed, separate rooms, I should add, he'd been calling our cat, Karma. She'd run off again, didn't come home. He put on his jacket and grabbed his flashlight off the hall table. We were so angry with each other we just glared, both of us too stubborn to break the silence. Pretty childish, isn't it?"

"Well yes, but we all do stupid things in the heat of an argument."

"Anyway, he went outside to look for Karma, at least that's what I thought he was doing, since the cat hadn't come home and he'd been calling her. He walked out the front door and he never came back."

"That's an awful shock!" Edna's shoulders sagged, and she sank deeper in her chair. "How do you know something didn't happen to him?"

That's what the police'd asked when they came around, after she reported him missing, though she knew what had happened. Once they heard what she was about to tell Edna, they settled on "domestic issue." To everyone else, she explained how he needed his space and privacy, made it sound like a mutual split to protect the boys against the truth and the ugly gossip it would surely ignite.

"Edna, I've never told anyone this. Only the police. When we were fighting, he said he'd met someone and he was leaving me. They were going sailing in Malaysia for at least a year. The woman owned a boat. He had it all planned. He said he wanted his life to be something more than two kids, a wife, and a home in suburbia. He wanted his life to be less of a cliché, his words. I, we, the kids and I were not creative enough for him. So, he left." There, she'd done it, finally, let go of it, dropped it like an untethered anchor. The shame of it.

"Oh dear! He sounds like a real scoundrel. Well, he obviously wasn't deserving of you."

She could not have picked anyone better than Edna to share her secret with. "Thank you. That was the conclusion I finally came to."

Edna raised her teacup. "Here's to good-bye and good riddance. You're better off without him!"

"That's right! Here's to it."

They drank in silence. Outside, the sun was descending behind the tall spruces. Edna's mouth slackened and her empty teacup sat in her lap, the saucer on the table, as if she lacked the energy to unite the two. "Edna, I am so glad I saw you in your yard. I can't tell you what this visit's done for me. Let's promise each other we'll have many more."

"I would like that very much." She sounded tired.

"I really must be going. I'll clean up these cups before I go."

"No, no." Edna gestured for her to ignore the dishes. "Leave them. And anyway, I want to talk to my husband about our lovely visit."

Outside, white clouds banked high in the sky, striking against the pink streaks of sunset. Birds chattered, a spring breeze sniffed over Sally's skin, every inch of her alive. Letting go of the truth about Phillip, locked for so long in her heart, burning a hole through it like acid, made her feel lighter, less burdened, free. What had holding it back accomplished? What had it done for her? She had spared Phillip's reputation, kept her boys from being hurt. Tongues would have wagged once word got out that he'd run off with some slut, abandoning her and their beautiful boys.

Such a huge step she'd taken today, with Edna, of all people.

In the shower, Sally lathered shampoo in her hair and thought, despite her promise and good intentions to pay regular visits to

Edna, how she hadn't managed one since their tea social a month before. She had to work to overcome social habits she'd so fiercely developed, accepting invitations knowing she wouldn't show up, telling people she'd call them when she had no such intention, rolling herself up in a blanket to watch TV, alone. But it was different with Edna: she really did want to see her again. Suds slid down the drain between her feet and she decided that today, a Saturday, a day off, she would drop in on Edna. No more excuses or putting it off, and besides, she could look forward to a cup of tea and a chat.

Wrapped in a bath towel, Sally peered out the living room window. Two police cruisers sat in Edna's driveway.

Her nephew must have phoned from Florida and she didn't hear the phone. This was Saturday. He would have notified the police when she didn't answer. She didn't always bother with the hearing aid.

Sally dressed quickly, her hair still dripping, and crossed the street, curious why two policemen would hang around outside Edna's.

She introduced herself as Edna's neighbor and friend, and asked the officers if they were there at Edna's nephew's request, relieved to hear that was indeed why they were there.

Sally started up the sidewalk to knock on Edna's door, but one of the policemen stopped her.

"Ma'am, I'm sorry to tell you that Mrs. Crawley died in her sleep. Peacefully, it seems."

"When?"

"We don't really know. Perhaps a few days ago."

"Oh, that's so sad. I only recently got to know her." She should have visited her as she'd promised. She might have found her still alive; something might have been done.

The policeman opened his notebook. "Could I have your full name, please?"

She didn't see why he needed it. "Sally Rutherford."

He wrote it down and looked at the other officer. "Mrs. Rutherford, do you mind if I accompany you home?"

As they crossed the street Sally said, "There's no need to take me home. I'm fine. It's sad about Edna, but she was old. She lived a long time. I'm afraid we weren't really close." It was regrettable, but true.

Settled in her living room, the clean-shaven young officer studied her, then spoke. "Your husband, Phillip Rutherford, disappeared, didn't he?"

"He didn't disappear; he left me." She gave him a few of the unsavory details. "We had an argument and during the argument he told me he had plans to leave with someone else. Long story short, they ran off together, to the other side of the world. I'm fully recovered. Time heals. Edna helped, too." Why was she telling him all this? This was her business, no one else's.

"Well, let me ask you something. Do you remember your husband ever having any run-ins with your neighbor, Edna Crawley?"

"Heavens no! He didn't even know her. None of us did. I only met her twice, once when I first moved in, then again just recently. That's when I realized I'd jumped to the wrong conclusions about her. She was a really nice old lady. The only connection Phillip had with her was when our crazy cat Karma used to hunt in Edna's fields, and sometimes the cat would sneak into her house, slip through a broken window into her basement . . ."

Sally stopped, a sudden storm of recall causing a quick lightheadedness.

Karma. The broken window. Edna's trip to the basement. To the fruit cellar. She saw someone in her basement who escaped. That was what she said, wasn't it? Phillip? Going out the door, a flashlight in his hand, still pissed off from their fight, slamming the door behind him and never coming back. Surely not, it couldn't be. He ran out the side door. Edna looked around the basement, then locked the fruit cellar. It was the bomb shelter. She would have heard . . . no, she might not have; she was close to deaf. The cement bomb shelter, no windows. Way at the front of the house. Like a bunker. Her antique hutch across the door. She never went down there . . . never again.

Sally clutched a cushion and drew it to her chest, bent around it, her hands seeking something to steady her and crush a wave of nausea as she struggled to gather bits of information, link them together into a line of sense.

"Did you find . . ."—she couldn't say his name, as if saying his name would make it more likely to be true—". . . someone?"

RUTHIE AND
THE BIG BLUE SKY

Nothing but Jumblers so far today. Everything pitched on the conveyor any old which way. Cleaners, root vegetables, feminine hygiene products, munchies, dairy items, heaped together in one big pile. The Jumblers didn't talk much, just hello or something about the weather, too wrapped up in their messy lives to manage conversation, taking no notice of Ruthie—just another body doing another job—a human robot, ringing through their mountain of stuff.

Ron pushed his cart up to Ruthie's checkout, waiting until she'd finished bagging the customer ahead of him before calling out hello.

From all the way over here she smelled tar fumes. Not exactly a Jumbler, definitely not an Orderly, Ron qualified more as a Weirdy, along with Winny, though much lower on the scale. Weirdies tended to be likeable—they talked, and that added a pinch of zing to Ruthie's day.

"Another day at the coal mines, eh Ruthie?" Ron said, digging into his wallet with his filthy hands, readying himself for the damage. "How goes the battle with you?"

That started a conversation about weather, government cutbacks, the price of bananas. She wanted to tell him about the Ivory hand soap, on sale today, but lost her nerve. His hands could use a darn good scrubbing, and while he was at it, he could clean his fingernails and comb his hair. A less bulky jacket would help matters, one that wasn't covered in dirt. He had the potential for being a good-looking man if he'd spruce himself up.

Late every Thursday afternoon, she rang in his order: three or four large sirloin steaks, several cans of corn, peas, and carrots, a large tray of butter tarts, five pounds of onions, two large boxes of instant oatmeal, a large jar of instant coffee, and twenty pounds of dog food; it seldom varied. All that meat would give him strong b.o., full of protein and acid. He'd never get a woman if he smelled bad, and he should trade in that jacket for something stylish. She thought about telling him, but never did; she avoided getting too personal with any of her customers. An innocent little remark could bring about an invitation to go out for a beer, and once his tongue got loosened his emotions would rise out of him like beer foam. She knew the type. Lonely.

"See you next week," he said. "Have a good evening."

Ruthie watched him head for the automatic doors, thumping along in his big clumpy boots, then wiped the beef blood off the conveyor with a spray cleaner and rag.

You could tell a lot about people by their groceries. Another form of palm reading, more accurate.

Someone said hi. Melissa, looking as tall and elegant as ever in her well-tailored business suit, gave Ruthie a magazine smile. Ruthie smiled back, her lips pressed firmly together. Melissa's teeth made her conscious of her own—coffee-stained with more silver than a tea service, uneven as a rickety fence. "How are you today?"

"Fine, thank you. It's a beautiful day." Melissa's long fingers curved gracefully around a bag of McCain spicy fries.

"We couldn't ask for better. Not this time of year."

Melissa placed her groceries in Orderly fashion, standing her boxes on end, never laying them flat, the way a tall, thin woman would interpret the world. Her grocery order changed from one to week to another, alternating from instant rice and pasta dinners, frozen meals, cookies, fruit snacks, chicken fingers, pogo dogs, and drink boxes, to dinners for one, single portions of chicken Cordon Bleu and deli salad. Why? Ruthie knew. She read the clues; week after week they streamed by right under her nose. Melissa did that time-sharing thing with her kids and her ex. Think about it—could you picture well-heeled Melissa sitting down for a pogo dog supper or some other kind of quick-fix kid's chow? Not in your wildest, right?

Melissa watched the prices flash by on the terminal, her shoulders held back so that she looked even taller. A pleasant customer, very efficient; a rare combination, surprising for an Orderly—they kept to themselves, didn't exchange pleasantries. Ruthie wondered if she was happy. The idea of happiness might be too imprecise for her, as shapeless as that goopy stuff the kids buy that slithers all over your hand when you take it out of the package, for sale over there by the magazines.

"Let's hope this weather stays," Ruthie said, and Melissa rewarded her with another wide pearly, told her she'd see her next time and left.

Ruthie really hoped she'd find another man, couldn't imagine what kind of scoundrel would want to dump a girl like that.

More customers came, Jumblers all, their groceries sweeping by in long flowing streams of mayhem and confusion, as readable as the open pages of a diary.

Here came Winny. Ruthie hadn't seen her for a while, had just this morning wondered what she might be doing and if she'd been away. "Winny!" She watched as the old woman angled her bundle buggy up to the end of the conveyor. "Where have you been?"

"Oh, l had a little trip," Winny's soft voice, lightly buffed with an accent. Ruthie had asked her once if she came from the U.K. Winny smiled, looked as if she didn't hear or didn't quite understand the question. She told Ruthie she didn't like to talk about herself, found it a very dull topic.

She always smelled a certain way—not offensive like Ron with tarry fumes clinging to his clothes—musty, like cedar and moss, with a hint of wood smoke. Her clothes sagged loosely around her tiny frame. She was one of those environmental naturalist outdoor types, probably used that oil that they wore, musk oil or whatever.

"Where did you go?" Just once Ruthie hoped to find out something.

"Not far." Winny put several packages of pine-scented room deodorizers on the conveyor, on sale for the week or while quantities lasted. "A person doesn't have to go far to see a great deal. Real travel is a matter of keeping the eyes and brain open." She sounded educated. She pulled more deodorizer packets from her bundle buggy and piled them on the moving belt.

Ruthie looked at her terminal; she'd already rung in fourteen. "You must have a big house."

"Huge," she said simply. "I like to take advantage of a sale. It's surprising how much money can be saved."

"Do you live alone?" Sticking her nose deep into private property, coming dangerously close to breaking her own rule about keeping her distance from her customers.

"Every room is full."

She'd done it again, revealed nothing, while at the same time expanding the mystery of herself. Nothing added up: She lived in a large house, full of other people, but counted her pennies. People could get a little funny about money, once they got on in years. Saving, clipping coupons, shopping only on seniors' day, eating at McDonald's, buying green-tinted meat, spoiled vegetables, and stale baking off the reduced rack: it all got to be a kind of sport, another way of earning, a way to stay independent and in control.

Brenda, Ruthie's daughter, phoned every Sunday from Edmonton to remind her that she had to count her coins—as if she didn't know—and that it might be time to sell the condo and move into a one-bedroom. Where would Charlie's tools go if they went into an apartment? Easy for Brenda to come up with all the answers in her big new house in the suburbs, while her husband made heaps of money. Those kinds of salaries threw the whole economy. She didn't blame Brenda. Smart cookie, really. But Ruthie kept telling her, it's a long life, you don't know what lies ahead, strawberries and chocolate one minute, vinegar and blackstrap molasses the next.

As for her son Roger, not a penny to his name, bouncing around the globe like some kind of explorer, last heard from, months ago, heading off to Korea. Young people do that to find themselves, her best friend Maria told her. A troubling notion. If you went somewhere to find yourself, it meant that you'd already been there and gotten lost, didn't it? Roger had never been to Korea. Ruthie remembered when it didn't take the whole globe to go looking for yourself. It seemed to her like a dog chasing its tail.

"Beautiful day, isn't it?" Ruthie said to Winny as she bagged the last of her purchases. "Cold weather's just around the corner."

"I look forward to it." Winny smiled. "I love the change of seasons. Wakes us all up. It's a whole new challenge."

"I don't call shovelling the walk a challenge. I call it a pain in the back. I'd like to go to Florida this year, but I can't. My husband can't travel anymore, and I can't leave him."

"You'll be fine right here."

The way she said that, so self-assured, her tone as crisp as lettuce. How did she know?

Winny hummed to herself as she dropped the rest of her deodorizers into her bundle buggy. Ruthie pictured her walking from one scented room to another, the fireplaces in her large house glowing, saying hello to this one and that. A life of gentility.

That night, Ruthie met Maria at the Highway Bingo Hall. Maria called Thursday night her salvation, God-sent, a night when she could get away from Louis and all his aches and pains, a night when she hoped she got home too late to rub him down with cocoa-butter cream. "He doesn't need it. He's such a baby. My hands get tired from doing it. He says his back hurts. What about my hands? I can feel the arthritis creeping into them. Pretty soon I won't be able to get my fingers around the bingo dabbers."

Maria and Louis had an aches-and-pains tug-of-war that usually ended up in the doctor's office, settled with prescriptions. The bingo caller's voice snatched their attention back to the cards for another game.

Maria got a bingo. On the way home on the bus she listed the ways she'd spend it, her list exceeding her winnings by several thousand dollars. They looked out the window at the rows of houses. Maria chuckled. "I sure know how to spend money."

Ruthie felt chilled when she got home, decided to go straight to bed and not to bother with the local news. The sheets felt brittle as thin slabs of ice. She thought about a hot bath, too lazy to do anything about it. When she won the bingo, she'd buy a five-inch-thick goose-down comforter. Listen to her, getting as bad as Maria, spending money she didn't have. She stuck her foot over into the other part of the bed, thought about Charlie in a motel room, reading *Reader's Digest*, watching the news, bathrobe draped over the back of the chair, tomorrow's shoes polished, clothes pressed and ready to go, then turning in for the night. He always did things the same way, at the same time.

When they first married she had trouble adjusting to a predictable life. She had a spontaneous, spur-of-the-moment nature, but she'd made herself get over it. Two people under one roof ought to head off in the same direction or there'd be trouble and disappointment. Being organized meant you didn't have to go searching from one minute, hour, day to the next, looking for something to do. A second stayed a second, slipped by unnoticed, didn't get any longer than that.

In the corner of her room she imagined Charlie's robe draped over the back of the chair, his slippers tucked in beside it, his body warm next to her.

She asked Larry, the store manager, for more hours. "You're already working 35 a week, Ruthie." He looked at her a minute. He liked her; they joked together a lot. "Too much time on your hands?"

"I like working. I like being with people. What can I say?" she shrugged.

"Here's what I'll do. If someone phones in sick, I'll phone you first. You can be our number-one call girl."

"Watch your tongue," she called after him. "I'm old enough to be your mother, grandmother maybe."

"Hey, wait a minute," he turned and came back to her checkout. "I've got an idea. I do have a few more hours for you, but not until next weekend. We're having a special event in the parking lot, a fall fair. There'll be free apples and hot cider, a band, pony rides for the kids, barbecued sausages, a roulette wheel, a petting zoo, all sorts of things. And a hot-air balloon. It'll be tethered, but we'll let it up a hundred feet or so. Anyway, I need someone to ride in the basket with the operator to let go of coupons, let them fall down on people, like a peanut scramble. Some of the coupons will be for $150 worth of free groceries. How would you like to ride in the basket and toss the coupons?"

"Me?" Up there? Floating around in the clouds. "I've never even been in a plane. I'm scared to fly. Charlie and I always drove down to our trailer in Florida."

"Here's your chance to get up and away. That's a yes, I take it. Good," and off he went, a man in a hurry, already down at the personal hygiene aisle. "Next Saturday," he called back. "Blast off. Wear warm clothes."

An assortment of sweets advanced along her conveyor. A problem with her next customer, bad food craving it looked like. Severe depression. "How are you today?" She thought she'd work in a bit of conversation, see if that might help.

"Fine, thanks."

A mumbling Jumbler. Distracted. Shy.

"Pie looks nice. Great price," pushing it over the laser eye, then a coffee cake, chocolate cupcakes, a bag of Smarties. Nothing but sweets.

"Maybe I'll pick up another one. Could you wait a minute?"

Ruthie watched her go to the back of the store, her big hips swaying, stomach jiggling, her clothes a hodgepodge of clashing colors, nothing tucked in all the way around but bunched in places, hanging in others. Neglect of personal appearance—another sign of depression. Ruthie wanted to reach out and give her a great big hug, assure her that things would get better.

She brought back two more pies, a coconut cream and a cherry, looked up from under a wedge of unruly grey hair that dangled over her eyes like an awning. "Too good to pass up."

Maybe a little chat would help brighten her. "Next weekend we're having a special event in the parking lot." Ruthie put the last pie in a bag. "Careful how you carry these." She placed it in the cart. "There'll be a barbecue, free drinks, rides for the kids, a hot-air balloon. We're going to give away coupons for free groceries. You might think about dropping by. It'll be fun."

"Sounds interesting," she said unconvincingly. "Thanks."

"I just hope the weather holds. If it's anything like today, we'll be made in the shade"—a funny little expression she'd picked up from her grandson during last summer's visit. She had a little flash just then of missing him and his little sister, quickly swept it aside. Her sweet-tooth customer seemed unamused, too depressed to find anything funny.

Winny showed up late in the morning, her bundle buggy loaded with light bulbs, at least a hundred packages, Ruthie calculated at a glance. "Taking advantage of another sale, I see," Ruthie grinned. Winny really went in for the household products, seldom ever bought any food; not surprising for a Weirdy. The people she lived with got the groceries. They must, she had to eat something. They probably did the cooking, too. No wonder she looked so happy all the time. Built-in servants. Who wouldn't be happy?

"It's a glorious day." Winny smiled, taking a few minutes from stacking the bulbs. "One of the last beauties before a killing frost and snow."

That turned on a light for Ruthie. "I must remember to bring in my geraniums. Do you garden?"

"Oh yes." Winny looked surprised by Ruthie's question. "A huge garden. My pride and joy."

It fit with the whole English impression of her, down on her hands and knees snipping away at things, pressing her palms into the dirt, putting slips into a quaint little basket with a carry handle. Winny obviously lived a charmed life, though she didn't carry herself as if a cut above the likes of Ruthie and the working stiffs of the world. And you certainly couldn't detect superiority in her dress.

After the light bulbs had all been rung through, Winny put ten large packages of garbage bags down on the conveyor. "Couldn't pass these up. Not with winter coming. I wasn't sure if they'd go on sale again before then."

"What do you use them for?"

"Everything."

"Gardening? Garbage?"

"Everything. Quite literally." Then she walked across the aisle to the end of the row to look at the cereal special, her face up close to the box to read it. "Oh, the stuff they put in things."

She fingered her money, to make sure it hadn't stuck together, before pressing it into Ruthie's palm. She snapped elastic bands back over her wallet and slipped it into a cloth bag, looked up at Ruthie who had followed her motions of routine with enjoyment. "You look like you need fresh air," she said. "You'd feel better."

Later, in the staff washroom, Ruthie lingered at the mirror, surprised to see how much she'd let herself go. She hadn't noticed. Her skin looked pale and grey, like someone recovering from a nasty flu. She'd stopped plucking her eyebrows and the hair had grown back coarse and thick. Charlie pointed these things out to her, would line up vitamins beside her breakfast plate, tell her to use a little more blush. When he wasn't home, it was like losing a mirror.

Her last customer turned out to be Melissa. She seemed relaxed;

Ruthie assumed her ex must have the kids this week. She leafed through the latest issue of *People* while Ruthie rang through her Thai spring rolls, Greek salad, Tylenol, and fabric softener. "Isn't it a beautiful day?" Not very original, but something at least.

"Beautiful," a wide pearly, then eyes back down to the magazine.

"If my grandchildren lived near me I'd take them to the park tonight." Digging, trying to find out something about her.

"Yes. It would be a lovely night for that," handing the money over. "Have a good one." Not unfriendly, but not encouraging. Probably had a busy day, perhaps a little headachy. None of this surprising for an Orderly.

"We're having an event out in the parking lot a week this Saturday. Should be lots of fun."

"I'll keep it mind," she smiled, nodded, stepped briskly towards the automatic doors.

She'd follow Winny's advice and get some air. She left out the back door, cut across the parking lot to the street. At the light, her cotton jacket slung over her arm, she felt the pulse of exhaust and heat against her skin. She turned left at the corner, took the sidewalk to where the footpath came out, and took it into the ravine woodlot, frequently used by the tenants behind the high-rise complex.

The air, feathered with the smell of dry leaves and heat, put her in mind of baking, the smell of summer's doneness—not at all unpleasant. She thought of Charlie, raking up the leaves in the tiny condo enclosure, bagging them into huge plastic bags, twist-tying the tops, his slow methodical steps typical of his quiet nature and ploddingness. A jay's screech tore across the calm fabric of sparrow twitters and leaf rustlings, the light pat of her feet upon the path, the compliant distraction of memory.

Up ahead, and to the right of the path, she saw someone. Tension gathered in her neck and switched on all her senses. A person had to be wary in such a place. She never told Charlie when she walked home. He didn't approve.

Relief when she saw that it was Winny. "I hardly recognized you without your bundle buggy. Are you out for a walk?"

"I'm gathering things." Winny opened her hand. Ruthie looked beyond several small pine cones to dark lines deeply ingrained in her palm, the results, she imagined, of all her gardening work. "I use it in potpourri."

"That's a nice idea."

"Would you like a cup of tea?"

She saw pine needles in Winny's hair, the smoky trace of a collar ring on her turtleneck shirt. "I really should be going home. I've just finished work." By the time she walked back to Winny's house—among the larger houses in this neighborhood back in the direction from which she just came—turned around and came back again, it would be quite late. She'd planned to hand-wash some of her delicates tonight.

"Take time for a cup of tea at least. You people who can't slow down for a minute; it won't do you any good in the end. Where are you going in such a hurry, you should ask yourself."

She supposed it wouldn't do any harm, and if she was too tired to walk home after, she'd take the bus or phone for a taxi. "Okay, then. Why not?"—turning to start back down the path.

"Where you going? I live this way." Winny pointed into the bush.

"I didn't know there were houses in here."

"Follow me."

They took a path, faintly etched in the dirt, back through bushes they pushed aside to avoid having their faces scratched. "Watch out," Winny said, whenever she went to let a branch go, so it wouldn't slap Ruthie's face.

Up ahead two straight rows of something on the ground, about two feet apart. When Ruthie got closer she saw, alternately spaced, room deodorizer and lightbulbs; the lightbulbs had been screwed into the ground. "Winny, what is this?"

"My walk. The room deodorizers keep away skunks. I used to have a terrible time with them spraying, but they stay away from me now. They don't like the pine scent. And the light bulbs keep away other kinds of vermin, the sort with two legs. Mind you don't step on any. I don't want you getting cut."

They came to a tent in a small clearing, with a couple of stumps set up beside a Coleman stove on a table made of crates and various pieces of wood. At first Ruthie thought they'd found a fort some kids had made. Winny sat on one of the stumps. "Sit down," she said, pointing to the other one. "I'll boil some water."

"Is this where you live, Winny?" She looked all around, no sign of civilization anywhere, as if they'd gone ten miles into the bush. She couldn't even hear cars.

"Isn't it lovely?"

"Yes. Do you stay here in the winter too?" Some of Winny's clothes hung on a line between two small trees.

"Of course not. I'm not crazy. I find something else then, or I go where it's warmer."

"I thought you said you lived in a big house, with lots of people in it."

"What do you call this? Look." Her hand swept over the clearing, took in the sky. "My ceiling, my skylight, my walls. It's huge," her brown eyes appreciatively taking in the abundance of her household. "As for living with people, you weren't listening very carefully. I said my rooms are full. And they are. Trees, birds, insects, animals. Every now and then a homo sapiens, such as yourself, will stroll through for a visit." She put her hands on her knees and continued to look all around, like a farmer standing at the edge of his field, admiring a bumper crop.

Ruthie waited until the bus ride home, Thursday night after bingo, to tell Maria about tea with Winny. "She lives in the woods?" Maria kept repeating. "I can't believe it."

"Believe it," Ruthie finally said. "It was quite pleasant, too. I surprise myself by saying so."

"She's kooky." Maria looked out the window, to the strip mall they'd pulled up in front of, waiting for the driver to come back out of the convenience store that had been robbed about a month ago.

"Maybe. She doesn't seem the least crazy. Not to me, anyway, not after I got over the shock of where she lives. We had tea and I can't remember when I enjoyed a more peaceful time. She talked about the birds and everything growing around her. She said nothing about why she was living there. I got the impression that she's there by choice. She's very happy."

Before Maria's stop, Ruthie told her about the fall fair. Maria loved the idea of the grocery coupons, but Ruthie didn't mention the hot-air balloon, leaving that part as a surprise. When she'd told Winny about the fair and the balloon ride, how she had a fear of flying, Winny had said, "Well, it's high time you got up there. I'll be there. I never miss a party."

Ruthie made a hot chocolate for herself when she got home. She felt restless; she'd noticed it at bingo, could only concentrate on ten cards, instead of the usual sixteen. She picked up the remote, stabbed away at the black panel until her index finger ached, watched snatches of talk shows, couldn't settle on anything, and finally decided to call it a night. In bed, she couldn't get comfortable, tumbled around on worry cycle until the wee small hours. Silly worry, too, nothing that would appear significant in the light of day. When sleep finally came, it took on the pouncing shapes and twisted logic of the hideous, the kind of dreams that left you worn out, stole away with part of you: Charlie's slippers, his robe draped over a chair in the motel room. Someone knocking on the door. Slowly, then urgently. A key turning in the door, several people rushing in. Charlie, lying on the bed, the covers drawn smoothly over him. Sleeping? they asked.

She woke up in a chilly sweat. Still early, but she might as well get up, waste time on a second cup of coffee, maybe walk to work. She waited for the water to run through the coffee maker, looked at Roger's last postcard from Korea. Korea: more a word than a place, floating around out there somewhere like a piece of dust, with Roger strapped on it.

Ruthie looked out the patio door into the small enclosure where the impatiens sprawled on the ground like giant spiders, their bright orange flowers and leaves shrivelled, expired, the geraniums frozen to watery stocks. She'd gone to bed before news and weather, otherwise she would have known to cover them. A hard, killing frost, early this year. No time to clean up the mess now. Today she would fly.

She put the second half of her piece of toast aside, too nervous to finish it, gave her wrist a quick flick, readying herself for the tossing of the coupons. She chuckled out loud—as if she actually needed to rehearse that! She pressed her hand into her stomach; it hurt a little. High acidity. Nerves. She'd told her manager she'd show up early to get a good look at the balloon, before her maiden flight. How, she wondered as she dabbed on lipstick at the hall mirror, stopping to notice the lines in her face and how tired she looked, did she manage to get herself talked into this one?

Cold this morning; she just about suffocated on the bus, dressed in all these clothes. Lots of people had already gathered in the parking lot, a number of them huddled around the hot apple cider booth, waiting for a free cup of warmth. The Scrambler spun a pattern of chaos for a few squealing riders, and a couple of children embraced the cold plastic shapes of the carousel horses. At the far end of the parking lot the hot-air balloon, tethered to the ground, swayed and bobbed like a giant jellyfish, its flame making fiery gasps. Her stomach danced nervously. She looked up inside it, a hollow silken cave, so flimsy, depending on something as elemental as fire. And what if some of the fabric touched the flame while she was up there? The idea of it spun the ground she stood on.

At the other end of the parking lot a number of men worked on a huge metal arch. She had no idea what it was to be used for. On her way over to examine it, she saw Ron, the road crew worker, with a very attractive woman clasped to one hand, two children strung together on his other. "Hi, Ruthie," he called out. "Want you to meet my wife, Heather."

"Hi." Ruthie managed a smile. She almost didn't recognize him, all scrubbed and shiny and combed, decked out in an expensive leather jacket and a cable-knit sweater. "These are my kids," he said, his face beaming. "Howie and Lisa."

Stunned, she kept on smiling, stilled her tongue from blabbing, I thought you weren't married. You cook like a bachelor. All that red meat you buy. You sweat it out your pores. In her mind, he was paired with dogs, only dogs. No kids. No beautiful wife. "Did you leave your dogs at home?"

"Dogs?" He looked at her, not understanding at first. "Oh, you're thinking of the food I buy. Oh no, that's for my neighbor. He's handicapped. I pick it up for him. Along with his groceries. I help feed the dogs, too."

Ruthie didn't know what to say to this new Ron; it was the other one she knew, and he wasn't here right now. "Nice to meet you," Heather said, and the four of them, strung together like paper dolls, headed towards the carousel and its tinny music.

"See you Thursday," Ron said.

"Ruthie, Ruthie," she heard someone call and, turning, saw Maria and Louis coming towards her through the dozy crowd. Louis looked a little stormy around the eyes, probably not enjoying the event one bit, would want to get home to his La-Z-Boy chair. "Did you hear?" Maria asked, her eyes wild and excited.

"Hear what?"

"They found that lady."

"What lady?"

Maria talked fast, her voice rising, causing several people to look at her. "That lady who made you tea. They found her this morning, in her tent. Dead. Froze to death."

A killing frost, Ruthie remembered Winny's words. "I don't believe it. Not Winny."

"It's true. We were out early this morning and saw an ambulance and police car on the path that goes into the ravine. Then we heard it on the radio. It's so sad." Maria's eyes on her, watching.

Ruthie started walking, moving along with many other people towards the big silver arch. She wanted to let the shocking news settle over her without Maria's questioning and speculations. She'd only known Winny as a customer, apart from the one cup of tea, but this horrible news made her feel strangely dislocated.

Four guys worked at either side of the arch. A stage stood between the arch's two columns. Cables, wires, and long ropes hung from various points. An area had been fenced off to keep people back from the structure. The sun gleamed off its peak; the shape of it made Ruthie think of the front door of a large cathedral.

Ruthie saw Larry, her manager, talking to a couple of people a few feet away. "I'll be right back," she told Maria and Louis.

"Hey," Ruthie said, tapping his arm.

"Ruthie! I've been looking for you. It's too cold for the balloon to go up. It has to stay on the ground."

It should have come as a relief, but she'd grown accustomed to the fist of fear she'd felt in her stomach.

"We're having reverse bungee jumping instead. It kind of leaves you out, Ruthie, for the coupon thing. Maybe you'd like to pass some out in the crowd." He took a big pile from a pouch he carried and handed it to her.

Walking around handing these out wouldn't be the same, not even close.

"Make sure the regulars get some. Oh, by the way," Larry's tone turned serious. "Have you heard about the bag lady?"

"Winny?"

"I never knew her name. That funny old English lady. Did you hear?"

"Yes." Bag lady? She'd never thought of her like that. She walked back to Maria and Louis, handed them some coupons. "I'm going to look around a bit," she said.

Maria said they'd stay to watch some bungee jumping, once it got going.

The news of Winny made her blood slouch through her veins. At the petting zoo, children timidly ran their hands over pigs and goats, squealing when the animals' wet noses came up to nudge their hands. She wandered to the maple syrup booth, a couple of craft booths, admired the work of a woodcarver and a T-shirt designer. She went into the store to talk to the other cashiers. She told them she wouldn't be going up in the balloon.

"Oh, Ruthie," Mavis, the cashier she usually worked beside, sighed. "It had you pumped up, didn't it? I know you were scared shitless, but I think you were enjoying it."

Ruthie said yes, she supposed so, in some curious way, she guessed she had. They talked about Winny, the words of her death just hanging in the air around them, senseless and awkward and stupid. Outside, swarms of people filled the parking lot; the morning sun had burned off night's chill. Suddenly, something shot past the window and up into the sky. The crowd whistled, clapped, and cheered. A body. Shot from the arch, on the reverse bungee. Launched skyward on long rubber cords, then reaching the end of the rope, snapping back down towards the ground with rocket speed, then bouncing up again. Yo-yo person. Up, down, up, down, up, down, bouncing, bouncing, bouncing, until the cables gradually lowered the person to the ground. Ruthie felt the bowl of nervous excitement in the center of her stomach. "I think I'll go out and watch," she said to Mavis.

She watched for a while as bodies shot up into the sky, into the heavens. Each time someone went up her palms moistened, her heart thumped wildly. What would it feel like to fly?

No one took any notice of her there in the line. They were all too busy looking up, down, up, down, vicariously enjoying the thrill, their thoughts on how it must feel. When Ruthie stood next in line to jump, she lost her invisibility.

"This line's for jumpers," the young guy said, adjusting his ball cap.

"I know. I'm next." Hard to say with her voice trembling so.

"I don't know. No offense or anything, but you might be a little old."

"I'm going up. You can't discriminate."

"Do you have any medical problems, a heart condition, high blood pressure?"

"Clean as a whistle."

He went over to talk it over with another guy and came back. "Okay, but we want you to sign a waiver. Just a precaution."

On the platform they hooked and harnessed her, while the guy at the microphone talked to the crowd. Ruthie saw several people she knew. Oh, they looked surprised to see her standing there, getting ready to fly. They weren't the only ones. Ruthie couldn't remember when her heart had kicked up such a fuss, when she'd felt it so. She saw Maria and Louis, Maria with her hand over her mouth; she didn't look well. She saw Melissa, leading a pack of Girl Guides; they all stopped to watch. Had she been wrong about her too? A Girl Guide Leader; it hadn't even entered her head. Ron and his family stood over by the petting zoo. And over there, the depressed woman with all the sweets, watching and smiling.

The announcer said she should prepare for takeoff. Then a huge pull around her groin and under her armpits and ZIP. Wind rushing at her, whistling by her ears, her mouth smeared over her face, tears squeezing out of the corners of her eyes, her organs flattened on the bottom of her stomach. Up, up, up, a porpoise streaking through the sea, a jet plane tearing across the sky, a bullet fired from a gun. Through the narrow openings of her eyes she saw two clouds drift apart to open up a seam of big blue sky. "Charlie!" she shouted and raised her arm up above her head and let the coupons go. "Charlie!" Alone with him, held in complete suspension by the hands of God; she walked on air. A sudden, tremendous pull at the groin and shoulders, then down she plummeted, her organs flying up through her body to her throat, a sea of astonished faces looking up, then WHOOSH, back up into the sky. "Charlie!" Down again, up, down, bouncing, bouncing, sky, faces, sky, faces, swimming, air outlining her body, each time the bounces getting shorter until she touched the earth with the tip of her shoe.

People rushed up to her, patted her on the back, spoke to her all at once, their voices a mat of excitement while her ears still exploded with the rush of wind, her body quivering with the experience of out-of-control freedom, still bouncing, the ground rushing under her feet—she had no idea what anyone was saying to her.

Somehow, she managed to get herself back into the store and headed straight to the washroom. She grabbed both sides of the smooth, cold ceramic sink and shook. She threw up. She looked into the mirror and began to recognize herself. Her eyes, blazing, adventure-filled, happy, and changed. Hair, totally sprung, a wild hedge protecting its garden of crimson burning face. A cavern of huge smile out of which poured an avalanche of laughter. Tears oozed from her eyes. Alive! Oh yes, she thought, I'm certainly that.

She walked home later, took the path that went through the ravine. She found Winny's clearing and laid a bouquet of mums on the ground, near where they'd had tea.

The rest of her walk home she thought of Charlie. Tomorrow she would start packing up his things. Time to move on. She'd gotten close to him today. He was with her, always. And then, well, she would book a flight to Calgary, surprise those young grandkids of hers, take them to the park on an autumn night, push them on the swings, let them feel the roar of wind against their ears, dangle their feet in the world of possibility. And after, who knows, maybe a flight to Korea, to float like a particle of dust with her son. And after that? Perhaps a tent in a clearing.

IN THE HOLE

Ronnie adapted quickly to her new job, which surprised her; she'd been out of the work force for so long. She fell into easy chitchat with the customers, and after being at Forever Doughnuts for only a month, she knew the names of all the regulars and the way they liked their coffee.

Two priests, the grocery store crew, the cyclists, the lesbian couple, workers from the Addiction Research Center. Leonard, a street person who shouted at the racks of doughnuts, "There's no center. There has to be a center." And of course a lot of cops, since the station was right across the street.

She quickly overcame her fear of not being able to learn anything new, of not keeping up with the physical demands of the job. Her co-workers had their doubts at first, but now she got a "You go, girl!" followed by a high five at least once a day, and mostly from the younger ones. They would see her as the motherly sort, the kindly older woman you could trust.

She wasn't ancient, didn't feel that way, though at 62, she had to be honest, she was getting up there.

Darcy, the oldest cop, always sat at the back and let the other cops do the talking. His quietness, his tendency to remain the observer, made her want to pry something out of him. "I heard you turned down a desk job," she said as she wiped the table beside his.

"That's true." His faded grey hair and trimmed salt-and-pepper mustache seemed to brighten his blue eyes.

"Wouldn't it be easier than being on the street?"

"Probably. I wasn't cut out for desk work."

He looked at her as if amused by something she'd said. What was it that put that spark in his eyes, or made him tilt his head as if sizing her up?

"What's the worst situation you've ever had to handle on the beat?" She surprised herself with her directness. Not at all like her.

He raised his coffee cup, took a sip, stared, set it down, and seemed in no hurry to answer her question. "It's hard to say." A line had formed at the counter; she couldn't wait for his answer.

Another day, she asked him, "Is it tough on the streets?"

"I was undercover with the drug division for a long time. I got pulled and asked to go back into uniform. You can only go under-cover for so long. If you do it long enough you forget who you are, end up becoming the person you are pretending to be. That's when it's time to go. Some cops go right over to the other side."

"That would be hard, wouldn't it, balancing two lives, one real, one phony?"

"Not as difficult as you think. And, correction, both are real."

One lunchtime in October, Sylvia and June, wives of William's col-leagues at the university, came in. They made brief eye contact with Ronnie, but they didn't seem to recognize her. Of course, she was wearing a uniform and her visor cap, and she was out of any envi-ronment they might expect to find her in, the department Christ-mas party or the one or two other socials held throughout the year, and they never saw her without William. She wouldn't say hello, not now when there was a line all the way to the door. Customers had no time to wait during lunch hour.

Ronnie overheard their conversation as they moved forward in the line beside hers.

"We'll find out this afternoon what the charges are," Sylvia said.

"Did he have much on him?"

"Enough."

"Marijuana? Wouldn't there be a fine for that? Surely not jail time?" June said.

"No, no, the other. Crack cocaine. He doesn't do it himself. He just sold it. We've got an excellent lawyer."

Leonard came charging through the door, head down, mutter-ing, his hair wild and spiked into upraised hackles. He stomped up to an overblown poster of the new Chocolate Craze doughnut and screamed at it, "What's in the hole? Can't be empty, can't be empty!" He shook his wiry head of hair and stormed off to the washroom.

"Oh my God," Sylvia gasped. "That scared me. I never come this far east."

Late that afternoon, on her long bus ride home from work from the east end of the city to the west end, Ronnie thought about what she'd overheard between Sylvia and June. Had one of Sylvia's kids been caught with drugs? She'd said they had an excellent lawyer. Ronnie hadn't seen Sylvia for a while, not for several months, not since the cocktail party held in honor of a department visitor from Scotland.

She recalled being unsettled by a conversation with Sylvia and June, though she couldn't say why. Hard to believe she'd known them for over—how long?—twenty years? Not that she knew them well, or anyone from the Philosophy Department for that matter. She was an accessory, an attachment that came with William, without academic connections, publications, or conferences to report on. Among department members, conversation seldom strayed towards the personal even though they'd had their share of messy marriage breakups, partner swaps, and predatory office temps searching for a mate, including the already married. Weren't they all pretending that scandal happened somewhere else? To other people?

But what had unsettled her when she talked to June and Sylvia? Ronnie had been standing by herself in the corner, sipping a glass of white wine, looking into the dining room and the people gathered around the table loaded with cheese, crackers, fruits, and pâtés, when June sidled up beside her. "Hi, Veronica!" June said—the name William's colleagues and spouses used for Ronnie. June seemed very happy to see her, delighted, that was how she remembered it, as if they were long-lost friends. Had she, June wanted to know, travelled during the summer?

"We rented a cottage for a couple of weeks. It was very relaxing," Ronnie said.

It just so happened, Ronnie learned when she returned the question, that June had just come back from a grand trip visiting her children. "All of them scattered about on the face of the earth." She flung her hand into the air and fluttered her fingers. But now she was back to work in her position in nuclear medicine. She couldn't believe what Veronica was telling her; she and William, empty nesters for four years?

"My heavens! I lose track." June clutched her silk scarf. "Forgive me. I barely keep track of my own children, and now with grandchildren, I'm hopeless." Her dark hair gleamed over the shoulders of her bright yellow tunic top. Her children were busy building careers—two doctors and a dentist, and all with families, she didn't know how they managed it, but somehow, she shrugged her shoulders, they did.

June glanced around the room, then she placed her cool hand around Ronnie's wrist and squeezed. "Please excuse me, but I see someone I absolutely must talk to. Don't go away, I'll be back soon."

Of course she didn't come back. It didn't matter. What more did they have to say? Later that evening Ronnie talked to Sylvia about their children, a kind of inventory of what they were all doing.

Ronnie watched an old woman board the bus, struggling with the bags she carried. A young man jumped up from his seat to help her. The bus started up again, merging into traffic.

It was shortly after that department party with the visitor from Scotland that she started to change and became overcome with restlessness and an overwhelming feeling of being left out.

For many years she'd stayed close to her comfortable, older suburban neighborhood, not venturing far, raising three kids, with never enough time for what she had to do in a day, never mind go exploring. But now she left the Prius in the garage and took the local busses to investigate the city she'd lived in for so long. The bus gave her the opportunity to discover again the city she neither knew nor felt connected with anymore.

On her very first excursion, she visited a new mall. A beautician in a white lab coat stood outside a store and waved a sniff strip, luring Ronnie to a chair in front of an array of liners, blushes, foundation creams, concealers, and shadows. Foreign tools to Ronnie, who used only a light application of mascara, blush, and lipstick. The clerk, a young girl with tired eyes and sweeping eyelashes, gave her a lengthy spiel about the makeup line, what it would do for her skin, and how it would hide blemishes and signs of aging. "No one needs to see the real us."

Something in her sad eyes, and not her promises of enhanced beauty or a new look, "a new you," had Ronnie consent to a free makeover. By the end of the treatment the beautician was almost whispering. She had to take this job out of desperation, after a nasty divorce, in order to make ends meet. "Plus, I'm going to night school to upgrade myself. I'm raising my son alone. He's seven."

She handed Ronnie a mirror, but Ronnie looked past her own image to the young woman behind her, saw the droop in her shoulders, the worry settled on her face, her chin set hard with a look of determination. She was a good mother, Ronnie decided. Ronnie bought the promotional special, which included free perfume and a cosmetic bag. Somehow, mistakenly she knew, she felt the girl's future and the future of her little boy depended on her.

At home, she examined herself in the bathroom mirror and couldn't believe whom she saw. No one she recognized. A stranger. She washed off the new imposter and sent her down the drain.

At dinner she told William about her bus excursion to the new stores, how she planned to sightsee the whole city as if she were a tourist. "Mission re-acquaintance," she called it.

"Sounds creative."

Should she tell him about the makeover? He'd be amused, might think it odd, though he wouldn't be critical. He never went so far as criticism, preferring instead to keep their discourse on an even keel, away from any violent rocking. He would say she was fine the way she was; just fine.

He sliced his pork chop and told her they couldn't duck hosting the next department get-together before the holiday season since no one else was volunteering. "It's our turn, Veronica."

Ronnie had been gazing out the window, barely aware of what she was seeing, and almost missed her stop in front of the community center, three blocks from her house. She reached for the bell, gave the cord a tug, and the bus came to a lurching stop.

Late November, and the city was getting its first heavy snowfall. A long lineup of regulars had formed in front of Ronnie at Forever Doughnuts. One by one they approached. "Hey, Ronnie, what's up?" or, "You pour the quickest double-double east of Adelaide," or, "You're looking more beautiful every day."

"Liars over there," she pointed. Or, "cut back on the sugar," or, "how about switching to decaf? I'm just saying, you could use more sleep." The quick retorts surprised even her, seemed to leap off her tongue with a mind of their own. The regulars relied on her witty comebacks. "You rock, Ronnie. We love you."

"Can I help you?" She looked up from her cash and saw June, scanning the menu board. Behind her, Sylvia. She'd been too busy to notice them before.

"My friend and I don't have much time." June's face pinched with concentration as she read. "How long will it take to make a bagel with light cream cheese? Toasted." Now she scanned the rows of doughnuts behind Ronnie. "Do I get one of those with a meal deal?"

Ronnie pointed to the menu overhead and explained what was clearly written, her voice struggling to control a tremor. Should she say, it's me, Ronnie, or Veronica as you call me, William's wife—you know, he's a member of the Philosophy Department.

June ordered then and from behind Sylvia said, "I'll have the same. But we are in a hurry."

Ronnie poured their coffee and overheard Sylvia say to June, "If older people keep taking the jobs, what chance will young people have?"

Ronnie apologized for the small spill of coffee on the counter and filled their cups back to the top.

"You'll bring us the bagels when they're done, will you?" June asked.

Ronnie pointed to the end of the counter and explained they would have to wait there, until they were ready.

"I don't see why they can't serve us at the table," June said.

The lunch rush now over, Ronnie went from table to table, gathering the dirty dishes and putting them in a bucket, staying clear of June and Sylvia's table, where they leaned towards each other, deep in conversation. She carried the bucket into the kitchen, placed it on the counter.

Hillary, the kitchen helper, was bent over a large sink filled with sudsy water. She looked up at Ronnie, tears dribbling down her cheeks. "Larry and I haven't had sex in over a year. Last night I heard on Oprah that means a marriage might be on the rocks, but I love my husband and he loves me. We've been together thirty-three years. We cuddle a lot, does that count? I thought we were happy. How do you know if you're happy?" She sniffed, and wiped tears with her hand, leaving a clump of soap suds on her face. "What is happiness anyway?"

Ronnie slipped her arm around Hillary's fleshy shoulders and gave her a hug. "It's a really good question. It makes beautiful sense to ask it."

Back out front, Sylvia and June had gone.

That night, on her bus ride home, she wondered why they had come into the doughnut shop. Something to do with the conversation she'd overheard before, about the drugs, perhaps? Maybe one of Sylvia's kids had gotten mixed up with the wrong crowd, took a bad turn. Maybe he was charged today. How very sad that would be. How many sleepless nights had Ronnie put in while raising her own kids? They got into so many situations—irate parents, jail, police visits to the house, calls from other kids saying one of them was in bad shape, could she come? How many times had she paid off their Visa balances? Heard their anguished stories about suicidal friends? Always some drama unfolding as life bubbled up around them—and somehow, they made it through. No dramas now.

After the kids moved out, she threw herself into house projects, de-cluttering every cupboard, every drawer and corner, painting, tending to tasks pushed aside year after year. It was then, after all the projects were done and she'd started her bus tours around the city, that she saw the Help Wanted sign at Forever Doughnuts.

She had no intention of applying for the job. But the idea came to her after her second city tour when she stopped at a new store to admire the long red hair on a mannequin. A sales associate noticed her lingering in front of the window. "Would you like to try one on?" she called.

"I'm just admiring. I wanted long red hair once, but that was a silly fantasy."

"We make hair fantasies come true."

Ronnie looked up at the sign, Wigs Only. She laughed, "No, no. I'm just looking."

"I can picture you with red hair," the clerk said.

Ronnie walked closer to her. "You could?" She'd had red hair when she was younger, but never long. She used to think about dying it red again, and letting it grow, but she could never work up the nerve.

"Can you tell I'm wearing a wig?" the clerk asked.

Ronnie had to admit she couldn't.

"Come on in. Try one on." The young woman clasped her hands together as if praying. "Please. To tell you the truth, I'm so bored I desperately need someone to come in and try one on. You don't have to buy anything. I shouldn't tell you this, I know it's not professional, but my mom had emergency heart surgery last night and I'm pretty upset. She lives far away, in Nova Scotia. I'm nothing but a bag of jitters today."

How could Ronnie turn her down? "I must be half crazy, but okay."

"We'll go for the red wig in the window, the one that caught your eye. We'll indulge your fantasy," said the clerk—Shelley the Wig Therapist, according to her name tag.

Ronnie sat in a high swivel chair in front of a mirror, and Shelley got to work. She brushed Ronnie's short grey hair back from her forehead and face and lacquered it down with hair spray as she told the story of her mother. "Stressh killsh," Shelley said through bobby pins clenched in her teeth, sliding them into Ronnie's hair one by one. Shelley's mother was taking care of her own mother, who was completely crippled. "To tell you the truth, she's not the nicest grandmother. In fact she's a real bitch, if you'll pardon the French. She's always criticizing my mom. Never has a nice word for anyone. Plus, as if that wasn't enough, my little sister had a baby, so mom's helping raise him until my sister's done high school."

She stood in front of Ronnie, raised the wig high in the air, and slowly lowered it into place, tucking hair in under the cap, styling it as she continued her life's history. Her father left when she was so young she barely remembered him. Her mother drank too much, but with three kids to raise on her own, who could blame her if she overdid it once in a while? Well, maybe more often than that, to be completely honest. "So this isn't a good day for me. You're really helping me out. This keeps me busy, takes my mind off things."

"Close your eyes," Shelley said and swung Ronnie's chair to face away from the mirror. "No sneak previews."

She must prepare herself, Shelley declared, because she was about to become a new woman. This was what was really meant by "born again." Once all the fitting had been done, and the brush run through it for the last time, she spun the chair to the mirror and stepped aside for Ronnie to see.

A younger woman with greener eyes, milkier skin, a contoured jaw, a look of intelligent alertness, stared back at her. "It doesn't look like me."

"I know. Totally. Isn't it cool? It'll take a while to get used to, but it's you all right, it's another you."

She looked—dare she say?—sexy.

"You should treat yourself." Shelley's brows arched high, enticing her, inviting her to take that one little step that would make all the difference.

"Oh, no. No, I couldn't." This whole business had progressed much further than it ought to have.

"You know, a lot of people resist. But why? It's fun. It's harmless. Slip this on Saturday night, put on some makeup, get yourself some new lingerie, and I guarantee you your husband will go crazy." She swivelled Ronnie's chair to offer a profile view. "You know what I sense about you? There's a tiger in you waiting to leap out."

A tiger? Hardly. A mouse, more like. The woman with the long, luxurious red hair smiling at her from the mirror seemed to say go ahead, live on the edge, try something kinky. "I'll take it." What had she let herself get talked into?

After Ronnie left the wig shop, she headed to Titles Bookstore, bought a casserole cookbook, ducked into the washroom, took the wig out of the Wigs Only bag and put it in the Titles Bookstore bag, stuffed the Wigs Only bag into a garbage can, and caught the bus home. She stashed her new purchase in the bottom drawer of her dresser, next to the makeup.

The next morning, she watched William back out of the drive on his way to the university. She showered, put on panties and a bra, applied the new makeup, slipped on her wig, and did her morning chores dressed only in her underwear. She cranked up the rock and roll on the CD player, danced and sang as she emptied the dishwasher and swept. She felt the swish of red hair across her bare back and paused at the mirror to admire the stranger.

On the day she took the bus to Forever Doughnuts to apply for the job, the Help Wanted sign still posted in the window, she got off at a nearby library, went into the handicapped washroom where there was only one toilet and a door she could lock, came out wearing the wig and makeup, and went into the doughnut shop.

Ronnie arranged to get off work early on the day of the department's Christmas wine-and-cheese social. William would be a little later getting home today after the colloquium, and he'd bring the speaker with him.

By seven, she had the food ready. Not much to it really. Some fruit, dips and crackers, a small assortment of warm appetizers, blue-veined cheeses, and a selection of wine. If anything, hadn't she become more efficient since her Forever Doughnuts job?

She dressed in black pants and a powder-blue blouse, brushed on a little mascara, a trace of blush. She roamed the empty house and waited for the guests to arrive, her stomach knotted into familiar nervousness. She made minor adjustments to the food arrangement and raised wine glasses to the light to check for water spots.

After William arrived home, and the social was in full swing, she circulated through the room with tiny quiches and mushroom puffs still warm from the oven. "Would you care for one of these?" she asked, moving from person to person.

"Oh, don't they look lovely? Did you make these? All that work." No, she repeated, she wasn't nearly so talented—the finger treats, like the weather, little points of interest around which the conversations spun.

Ronnie passed the plate in front of Sylvia and June. They were talking about their families. "Oh thank you," Sylvia said. "These look delicious, Veronica. And I imagine you made them?"

Ronnie would appear to have all the time in the world to spend on life's frills, an easy assumption to make, but before she could say no, Sylvia rushed ahead with a question. "Are your children coming home for Christmas?" She gave a pinched, expectant smile.

"I don't know yet."

"Oh." Sylvia sounded alarmed. Her family had declared months ago they were coming home, and she anticipated utter pandemonium. "Utter." Her eyebrows pinched together as if she might be experiencing pain. "But it will be such fun. Delicious fun! I've already begun my baking. The children insist I make shortbreads shaped like trees, as I always have. They simply refuse to grow up, but they've told me it's not Christmas without the shortbreads shaped like trees. They've threatened not to come home if I don't bake them. Can you imagine?"

No, Ronnie could not imagine. "I haven't talked to my kids about Christmas," she said. "They'll be home; I'm certain of it."

"Oh, Christmas is a very big deal at our house." Sylvia's tone registered somewhere between disbelief and disapproval. "My kids phone all the time to talk about it, they're so excited. It's a real family time. But we're unusually close. We're unique in that way." She held the quiche up to examine it, then took a bite. "I should get your recipe; these are delicious."

Ronnie looked into Sylvia's eyes. "My kids will come home, they'll spend a few minutes with William and me, then they'll be on the phone, planning their get-togethers with friends. I'll visit with them when they straggle in at all hours, that is, if I manage to stay awake."

"That sounds so sad." Sylvia sounded sympathetic. "How could you have them home and not visit with them?"

"I think it's sad, too," June, quiet until now, said, and nibbled on a mushroom puff.

"Not sad," Ronnie said. "Just realistic. They have their own lives. We'll visit, but they won't give up their activities for me. And I wouldn't expect them to."

Sylvia and June looked taken aback, as if Ronnie had said something terribly wrong, so outlandish they couldn't find words to react.

The doorbell rang. Ronnie motioned to William she'd get it. Two policemen stood on the front steps. One was Darcy, the other she'd seen at Forever Doughnuts, but less often, and they'd never spoken. The other one made the introductions. "I'm Constable Pearce, and this is Constable Freed." He motioned to Darcy. There had been a break-in at a neighbor's house across the street this evening, and several things had been taken. "Have you seen or heard anything?"

"No," she said, avoiding eye contact with Darcy.

"Would you mind asking your guests?" Constable Pearce looked inside to the crowded rooms. "We'll wait."

Ronnie went from one person to another asking if anyone had noticed suspicious activity across the street, and returned to Darcy and the other cop to tell them no, no one saw anything out of the ordinary. Constable Pearce gave her his card and Darcy's. "Phone us if you hear something."

She leaned against the closed door. Darcy didn't seem to recognize her, not without her wig and makeup, and the other cop didn't appear to either.

When she was partway down the hall, the doorbell rang again. Darcy stood alone this time. "Would you mind stepping outside, please?" The other policeman sat in the cruiser parked at the curb, his head down, as if he might be writing something. She closed the door behind her.

He looked up at the cloudless sky, the stars bright. "You look better without the wig and the makeup. I always thought you would."

She had the sensation of being stark naked, exposed. And of being lost. Naked and lost on her own front porch, at her own house where she'd raised three kids, in the neighborhood she'd lived in for thirty years, and yet somehow it seemed strangely foreign.

She felt him staring at her. "Are you all right?" he asked.

"Yes," she managed.

He started down the sidewalk, then stopped. "I've known from the start, you know. I used to be the master of disguise. It can be a dangerous business. It's possible to lose yourself."

Lose herself? Was that it?

After the cruiser disappeared around the corner, she went back inside, pausing at the dining room door to find William in the crowd. He stood with a large group of people, laughing, talking, thoroughly enjoying himself, by the look of it, here with his people, in a room filled with a thick, steady buzz, the way Forever Doughnuts sounded at noon. The gorgeous lull of belonging. She started towards the partly filled tray of quiches she'd placed on the table with the intention of restocking it, but stopped, and headed upstairs to the bedroom.

She pulled the Titles Bookstore bag out of the drawer, removed the wig, and slipped it on. She applied her makeup—she was becoming quite expert at her transformation.

She descended the stairs slowly, one step at a time. She would introduce them all to Ronnie, let them hear her wisecracks, let them get to know her, find out who she really was. So what if she made a spectacle of herself? They might not even realize it was her. And after all the guests had gone, she'd ask William if he wanted to go out for a doughnut and a coffee, introduce him to the gang, let him get to know the other side of town.

IN PROGRESS

Tree branches scraped the sides of the trailer. Connie tightened her grip around her seat. It would take Dennis a while to get used to hauling it and parking it in tight spots.

Linda jumped up from a chaise lounge set in the sun in the site next door, came running over, paperback in hand, and directed them. Her arms made wide sweeps through the air.

"I see you, I see you," Dennis said. Linda wouldn't hear with the windows rolled up.

Connie hadn't seen her sister-in-law in almost five years, but watching her motion wildly and dart back and forth to check for clearance on either side made her remember how Connie's family had always called her a take-charge type. Connie rolled down the window and smiled, her fingers fluttering in a wave.

"Keith, they're here," Linda shouted over to her site, to Connie's older brother, then called out to Dennis, "You're too close to those trees. Stop." She thrust both palms into the air. "You're cutting it too close. Back up. Approach again."

Dennis inched the trailer straight ahead, tilted his head from one side to the other to check the mirrors mounted on both sides of the van. "Those branches won't hurt anything," he said. The branches screamed against the sides of the trailer.

Dennis stopped, turned off the motor, and Connie slid from the seat into Linda's embrace. "We expected you earlier. We've been watching since noon." Linda released Connie and stepped back. "Hope the branches didn't leave scratches."

"Heavy traffic," Connie said, then looked up to the top of the trailer. "I don't think so."

Linda had put on about twenty pounds, perhaps because of the hysterectomy, though during phone conversations she'd claimed there were no side effects, just no more periods, and that not a side effect but a blessing.

Keith came down the short path between the two sites and stepped in behind Linda. "Hi there." He smiled and raised his hands, together open-book style and full of fishing lures, oblong shapes of bright red, green, yellow, orange, pretty enough to be pieces of jewelry. "My hands are tied." His way of saying he'd have to forgo a hug from Connie and a handshake from Dennis. "You made it, I see. How did it handle?" Keith meant the trailer. "You got enough power in that?" He nodded to their van. He pulled his trailer with a half-ton.

"Seemed to," Dennis said.

"No problem with overheating?"

"Maybe a little on hills. Nothing serious."

"That's good." Keith hadn't stopped smiling. Connie remembered how that was a sign of his nervousness. "Let's get it unhitched and positioned, get the legs dropped." Keith looked at the lures in his hands, then headed to the picnic table. "I'll go put these down."

"I've got eggs boiling," Linda said to Connie. "Come on over to our place and we'll have a drink while the guys are setting up."

In the trailer, Linda said, "Have a look inside there." She grabbed a bottle of white wine and held the refrigerator door open for Connie to take a peek. A mountainous macaroni salad occupied most of the middle shelf, and a bowl of coleslaw and a pan of squares filled the shelf below. "I've got burgers for tonight, enough for Mark and Sheila, too, but I've got bad news about them." She turned around to look up at Connie, her face flushed from bending and rearranging the fridge, her grey hair shining in its light. "They won't be here until tomorrow."

"Why not?" They were all to be here today, her two brothers and sisters-in-law; the family reunion had been planned for months.

"Their motor home broke down on the highway. It's a rental. It won't be fixed until tomorrow. I've got enough food here to feed an army."

Food. Say reunion to Linda and Keith and immediately they started to talk about food.

"Oh well, we'll have to eat plenty. It won't keep for long." Linda popped the cork on the wine bottle.

After dinner, after the cleaning up, they sat around Keith and Linda's campfire and sipped Scotch.

Keith answered Connie's question about this year's fishing expeditions with one of his own. "Did I tell you about my Quebec fishing trip?"

He might have. She might have forgotten. "No."

"No? Back in February? The week of the twelfth. Was it, Linda? Or was it the fifth? Oh, never mind, it doesn't matter. I think it was the twelfth. It was a Saturday, anyway. Sure I didn't tell you?"

"I'll stop you if you have."

A couple of times Connie thought the story sounded familiar. He'd gone with a bunch of guys to a lake deep in Northern Quebec. "You have to understand, when I say remote, I mean it."

"I understand."

"The fishing shack was two hours out from the nearest town, which was already far away from a city of any size, then we took snowmobiles the rest of the way, about thirty kilometers back on trails. I mean remote." First he described the guys who went on the trip, then the lake.

Connie watched the fire's light splash over his face. They had camped together as children and every night they gathered around the campfire and told stories. She tried to remember as many of the details as she could—how old they'd been, what they wore, her mother, her father, what they did for entertainment out in the bush. She'd been doing this lately, attempting to fill in the blanks of her past, search for a more complete picture. Many times she couldn't remember herself in the pictures, as if she hadn't been present in her own childhood.

Keith's voice changed. He was giving details, of no consequence to the story, but which made him smile.

Connie nodded and said, "Uh-huh." She'd been doing this all along, to show that she listened, when of course she hadn't been.

"One of the guys got sick. Chest pains. Scared the hell out of us. Another fellow and I decided to go and get a doctor; the guy was too sick to move. So we went back and picked up the doctor, and we started back to the cabin and, on the way back, the other guy's snow-mobile broke down."

"Really?" This, then, was the crux of the matter, what he'd been angling for, the central point on which the rest of the story depended. Connie thought how her "really?" might have sounded adolescent, possibly insincere. What should she say? Early on, Keith had singled her out as the audience. Linda would have heard the story many times before, and Dennis kept poking the fire with a long stick, which made the flames spit sparks into the night. Keith could strike up a conversation with just about anyone, but not with Dennis, a man of few words, certainly fewer than Keith, and with different interests, an enigma as far as Keith was concerned.

"Yes, really. We tried to get it going again, but we couldn't. And it was snowing, coming down hard, not quite a blizzard, would have been if there'd been any wind at all. A bad one, too. I rode the rest of the way to the cabin with the doctor and left the other guy."

Keith halted the story to ask himself what the other guy's name was. He listed a few and settled on one. "Walter. That's what it was. No, wait a minute. Wilfred. No, no, Walter. Something that started with W. Jesus, my memory's bad. No, it was Walter. I'm sure of it."

Connie wondered if, as a little girl camping with her family, she had told campfire stories. Probably not. She was the youngest. And a girl. Girl stories were boring, lacked adventure.

Keith was telling how the doctor medicated the sick man, who had turned blue by the time they got back, and who would have died if the doctor hadn't come. Keith went back to collect Walter-Wilfred in the near-blinding blizzard, in the pitch-black of night, and on their way back to the cabin, they almost got lost several times, a harrowing story in itself. The rest of the trip was uneventful, except they caught a lot of fish. Later, he heard the blue man had a quadruple bypass and now golfed eighteen holes, no problem.

"I'm going to bed. I'm beat. I got up early today," Dennis said, shortly after Keith finished. He stood, adjusted his pants and shirt, and looked at Connie. "You coming?"

"I'll be along soon. You go ahead."

"I'll bring you a flashlight."

Dennis disappeared down the path through the trees and came back with the flashlight.

"Fishing tomorrow?" Keith asked him.

"We'll see."

The worst thing Dennis could have said, so unenthusiastic, non-committal, parental sounding. Keith looked disappointed, almost sullen. Or was it disgust? He wanted Dennis to speculate about what might be biting, and what kind of lures they'd use. He wanted to haul out his tackle box right now, take it to an empty picnic table, huddle with Dennis under the glow of the Coleman lamp to rummage through and select their bait. Keith held out some kind of last-ditch hope that Dennis might experience a spiritual breakthrough and become a fisherman, better still, a fishing partner. Keith could stop hoping: Dennis would rather be out on the highway driving to some place he'd never been before, the van eating up mile after mile of roads. Sometimes, Connie wished Dennis would go along with Keith to make him happy, instead of the way he looked right now, disappointed that his brother-in-law was such a wuss.

Dennis said goodnight again and left. Keith poked away at the huge bed of burning embers, coaxed more flames out of it, then tossed on a couple of more logs. He gathered up the glasses and returned with another round of Scotches.

"You know, after that incident in the bush with the guy who had the heart attack and everything, I took stock of my own life. It's a real wake-up call, I can tell you." He and Linda, Connie might be surprised to hear, had taken up walking every night for an hour. Their doctor told them both they had to get their weight under control or risk serious health problems.

"Yes," Linda said. "We've become a pair of regular old farts."

Keith and Linda talked about their health, the health of their friends, listing the surgeries, the illnesses, the divorces, the deaths, the grandchildren. They sounded much older than Connie, but it was only six years in Keith's case, four in Linda's.

She heard a whip-poor-will in the distance. It brought a memory of early camping days, loosened by her daydreaming earlier. She walked with her mother on their way to the outhouse. Her mother swung the flashlight and Connie watched as the circle of light skated over the gravel road. Beyond that light, total darkness, thick and impenetrable, as if it were a wall. "Listen," her mother said. "A whip-poor-will. Hear it?" They stopped. Her mother turned off the flashlight. The bird's call echoed through the night. "Some people think it means bad luck is on the way, or that there will be a death soon. I think it's beautiful."

Now, the whip-poor-will's song rippled from an increasing distance.

Dew had fallen, the fire had collapsed to an orange-red puddle. Connie's belly burned with Scotch. Too much Scotch, she'd think tomorrow. She said goodnight and picked her way along the pitch-black path to the trailer without using the flashlight Dennis had brought her.

Mark and Sheila pulled in around noon the next day. An adjoining site had been reserved for them on the other side of Linda and Keith. The original plan had been for the guys to get up early to go fishing, but since Mark and Sheila hadn't shown up on the day they were supposed to, and since they arrived in the early afternoon, the original plan had been, as Keith had put it at mid-morning, shot to hell. "I might as well have stayed in the city." He slammed his trailer door. Dennis carried his coffee back to their trailer, where he sat and read the paper. He'd walked to the box out on the highway, early this morning, while everyone else still slept.

Mark's arrival set off a group of crows, high atop a spruce, into a squawking frenzy. "Isn't anyone going to offer me a beer?" he asked, once the greetings were over.

Mark had a way of energizing people, making them enjoy themselves. Without him, the rest of them were putting in time, waiting for him to officially kick things off, bring on the excitement and the party. Sheila stood behind him and smiled. Mark had acquired a slight paunch. A blue vein bubbled down Sheila's leg. They'd both aged a little but looked well.

Mark waved at the motor home he'd rented. "The only good thing about this piece of shit is that it has a queen-size bed. Sorry we're late. There was this awful grinding noise coming out of it, and I didn't know what the hell it was, so we pulled off at a service center to have it looked at and guess what? I bumped into an old buddy from the west coast. Can you believe that?" He looked around at the others.

"No shit," Keith said, impressed.

"For heaven's sakes," Linda said.

"When was the last time you saw him?" Connie asked.

"About twenty years ago. So, while the mechanics were figuring out the rattle, we had coffee with this guy, Brad, his wife's Susan, a bit of a looker, too." Sheila rolled her eyes. "He tells us he's a lodge owner on a place called Shywind Lake, not too far from there. He asked us if we wanted to be his overnight guests while the motor home was being fixed. At first we said no, but the trailer wasn't done and who knew when it might be, and he kept upping the ante, said he'd had some lobsters flown in from the east coast, we could join them in a lobster feast. He offered us a room with a Jacuzzi overlooking the lake and promised me a round of golf. So," Mark shrugged his shoulders and threw his arms open, "it got impossible to say no. Hope you guys didn't mind. By the time the motor home got fixed we would have been really late getting here last night. I thought it would give you all a chance to get caught up. Plus I thought, what the hell, one night won't hurt."

"I thought it wasn't going to be fixed until today," Linda said.

"No, yesterday, but late."

"Hell," Keith said. "You should have stayed with them two nights."

Keith meant that as a kind of self-punishment. He'd been stuck here with the women, and Dennis, who might as well have been another woman for all the fishing he'd talk about or do, while Mark was out there having an adventure. Worse, Keith had lost a fishing trip on account of Mark.

How Mark loved excess, though he could be critical of it in others if it crossed over into tackiness.

Connie, Linda, and Sheila went to Linda's camp site to catch up on family news, mostly about kids and grandchildren, while the men set up Mark's rig. Sheila and Mark had both been married before, had only been together for seven years. Sheila talked about her kids from her other marriage. It was as if she talked about strangers.

Keith came to ask Linda where she'd put the crescent wrench. Sweat poured down his flushed face.

"I haven't seen it," she said.

He raised his hands and looked off into the bush, made a huffing noise, then turned back to her. "If you'd just leave things where I put

them, then I wouldn't have to waste all this time looking for them."
He stomped off to the pickup truck.

"I didn't touch your fucking tools," Linda shouted after him.
She looked first at Sheila, then at Connie. "You can see he hasn't
changed. Same old disgusting habits. Blaming everyone else when
he lost it. You see what I have to go through all the time?"

Years ago Connie would have been sympathetic. You poor thing.
It's not fair. Not anymore.

After dinner, seated around the campfire, Mark filled everyone in
on his work.

"It sounds like a very glamorous life," Connie said, and wondered
if she might have sounded a little sarcastic.

"I guess it is. I get to travel, I meet interesting people, I'm making money. Pretty good money." Mark put his hand on Sheila's knee
and rubbed it.

The great thing about Mark's work was that he never knew what
to expect. He had a life of surprises. For instance, back in the spring,
he had crossed paths in an airport—he couldn't even tell them which
one, he did so much travelling—with an old pal of his, from university days. This guy, Cam, owned a white-water rafting company in
Utah. He invited Mark to come down and take a trip on the river, be
his guest. "It was early in the season, see." Mark sipped his Scotch,
took a moment to savor it. "Too early for tourists." He didn't know
when he agreed to meet up with Cam that he was going on the test
ride, to see if the river was ready for the public.

Connie looked up at the sky streaked with a dramatic sunset while Mark told about suiting up, then hopping on a raft large
enough for twenty, but which carried only four on this day. There
he was, swept along in a brisk moving river, more than brisk, really,
but nothing too serious, not yet anyway, and Cam kept saying, just
wait, just wait.

Connie knew the raft would spill.

"We came around a high cliff, and there was a stretch of rapids
that went on and on and on as far down the river as I could see. We
hit a huge patch of standing waves. Boom! We flew, we were air-
borne! Cam was working that oar, trying to steer the thing, and then
it was game over."

"What do you mean, game over?" Linda sounded irritated.

"I mean, game over." Mark turned to Keith. "The raft flipped."

"I've been rafting when that's happened," Linda said.

"Not like this, you haven't," Mark replied.

"Let him tell his goddamn story," Keith said.

"Didn't know I needed permission to speak."

"Next thing I knew, I was in the water. The waves just snapped my head back. My eyelids were opened by the force of the water. It was so cold I pissed myself. My helmet shifted when I hit. My head smashed against the boulders. I had absolutely no control. There was nothing I could do. At first, I tried to fight the river and then I gave up and let the river carry me. I floated with my feet pointed downstream, steered clear of the rock faces. And all the time I was floating, and out of control, you know what I kept thinking? I kept thinking that if I survived this, I'd buy tech stocks. Take a chance. Weird, eh?"

Keith laughed. "You bullshitter."

"No, I'm serious."

"So, what happened after that?" Connie thought he must be close to the end of the story.

"About fifteen miles along, the water slowed enough so I could swim to the bank. It was all I could do to crawl out. I had no energy. I just lay on the bank and wondered how it was I managed to come out alive. In about a half hour, Cam came along in the raft. Bastard. He laughed like hell when he saw me." Mark looked up at the stars that had poked through the hood of night. "I was his goddamn guinea pig. I could have been killed. I should have sued his sorry ass. He's an idiot."

"He looked like he was made up of purple patches, more bruises than skin. I'm not kidding." Sheila rubbed Mark's shoulder.

Keith threw more wood on the fire, then told Mark and Sheila his Quebec fishing story. "It's not as exciting as yours," he started, "but it's kind of interesting."

From Quebec the stories went to Chile, which Mark had visited during one of his business trips, then the conversation shifted to practical matters, the next day's plans, the fishing expedition.

"I'm going to pass," Dennis said. Mark and Keith looked at him.

"You're coming," Mark said. "Come on, man, we're going to catch fish. Lots of fish."

"I'm going to drive into town and buy some repair stuff for the trailer," Dennis said. He'd been puttering around on it ever since they arrived, his big Lego construction set. Connie wouldn't mind going fishing, but, along with Sheila and Linda, she hadn't been asked. Didn't matter. If she really wanted to go, she'd rent her own stuff and go for an afternoon. Nothing as ambitious as Keith and Mark had planned, a dawn-to-dusk excursion, fishing with a capital F.

Noise outside the trailer at six awakened Connie. Voices spoke in low tones. Dennis snored lightly beside her. She pulled aside curtains to peek out the window and saw Mark and Keith, walking around Keith's camp site with their fishing gear. Linda stood on the steps of her trailer, her arms folded across her dressing gown. A large cooler sat at the bottom of the steps. Linda would have made enough provisions to last for days.

Later, Dennis went to town for fix-it things. Connie, Sheila, and Linda visited throughout the day as they prepared food, did up dishes, swept out their trailers. They walked to the camp office to see if there were any messages on the bulletin board from their families and to make a couple of calls home, but the phone was out of order. With their three trailers in a row, they were neighbors. They laughed about being womenfolk, banding together to do women chores and share their lives, form a sisterhood, while the menfolk caught fish and repaired a shelter.

Linda, saying she'd had trouble falling back asleep after the guys left, went for an afternoon nap. Sheila and Connie thought that sounded like a good idea, and Sheila thought she might treat herself to a pedicure. In the fullest heat of the afternoon, Connie went to lie down and read. She listened to the wind, and beyond that to the water; its rush blended with the wind. The campground so still.

Sheila and Linda joined Connie and Dennis for coffee, which Dennis had made after he came back from town. The caffeine cut through their nap drowsiness. They decided to go into town for dinner, since no one felt like cooking. Keith and Mark would have scoffed at such a plan. Didn't we just leave the city? Isn't that what this is all about?

Long after dark they returned and looked over at Keith and Linda's site. No fire. No Mark or Keith.

"The vehicles are here," Linda said.

"They're probably down at the beach, doing something with the boat." Sheila turned in the direction of the lake.

They grabbed flashlights and headed down the narrow paths carved through the trees and bushes, streams of darkness which led them to the water. Cottage lights flickered from distant islands, and behind them, campfires poked through the bush. Otherwise, pitch black.

"Fish must have been biting. Prepare to clean fish, girls," Linda said.

Connie swept her flashlight over the lake, searchlight style. "No sign of them. We'd see a light if they were headed back in, wouldn't we?"

"Not necessarily. They'd see the lights on shore and head for them in the dark. Keith knows the lake pretty well. Let's go back to camp and have a fire. We might as well be comfortable while we wait."

"Mark doesn't know diddly-squat about the lake," Sheila said.

Seated around the fire, they stared into the flames. Connie wanted to go to bed, to read, to have some time alone at the end of her day. The others wanted that, too. They'd all become quiet.

Dennis yawned. "All this fresh air."

Every so often one of them asked where the other two could be, more out-loud musing than a real question.

"I'm going back to the beach to wait," Linda said.

"We'll all go," Connie said. "Let's take lawn chairs. I'm going to change into something warmer. There's a chill in the air."

Dennis went to make a thermos of coffee.

After they'd changed and regrouped, they headed once again to the water and set up their chairs along the narrow lip of beach.

"Do you see anything?" Sheila leaned forward as if that might help her see farther across the water.

"No. But that doesn't mean anything," Linda said. "It doesn't mean they're not out there." Connie strained into darkness to listen for a whine to break through night's silence.

Dennis and Sheila talked about trailer repairs and Linda told about her frustration with the dealership. "You need everything in writing. Laid out in black and white. Right from the get-go."

In a while they stopped talking, then their long lapses of silence gave way to the inevitable speculations about what might have happened. All along, they had avoided any discussion of unfavorable outcomes, but Keith and Mark had been gone too long, and now they had to allow for the possibility of disaster.

"What if they're lost?"

"Keith knows the lake. I can't see that happening."

"Did they take maps?"

"I think so. At least, I'm pretty sure they did."

"They might have had engine failure. Did Keith take his tools?"

"Oh, I don't know. It was so early this morning when I saw them off, I couldn't even see straight, never mind know what they took."

"Did they have life jackets on board?"

"Keith is very strict about that."

"That's a relief."

"Maybe they stayed out late and headed back after dark and hit a shoal."

"They could have sunk the boat."

"The water's warm enough now they could last a long time. At least that works in their favor."

"They're both strong swimmers."

"Not that strong."

"Did they have oars with them, if the motor quit?"

"Yes."

"They'll be starving."

"I doubt it. I made lots of food."

Thank goodness for Linda's habit of overfeeding.

"I bet they're fine. I bet the fish were biting and they decided to stay and fish later."

Silence.

"Or not."

Connie knew they all had other ideas in mind, but no one said. In an hour or so it would be daylight. "I think we should go back to camp and make some coffee, give them until daylight to get back, and if they're not here, we'll go to phone someone."

That job was assigned to Connie and Dennis. Sheila and Linda felt certain it would be unnecessary, but they finally saw the wisdom in taking every precaution. Since the phone at the camp office was out of order, they'd head to the nearest one at Lakeland Outfitters, about ten miles up the highway. Sheila and Linda would hang back and wait.

At 4:30 they gave up their vigil.

Dennis lay down until the coffee perked and fell straightaway asleep. Connie would wake him when she was ready to go. She opened the blind on the window beside the table and watched light slowly drain into the new day.

Dennis and Connie walked Linda and Sheila down to the lake, a pewter platter heaped high with grey mist, before heading out to the phone.

At the outfitters, an employee approached them, his arms piled high with pool noodles which he dumped on the heaped-high bargain table.

"We're not quite open." He squinted at them against the rising sun, his face already greasy from heat.

"Could we use your phone, please?" Connie asked. "It's an emergency."

"Sure, I guess that's okay." He stared at them with his mouth open, then he seemed to wake up. "Come on in."

They started towards the counter at the far end of the store. Something made Connie look over to the side as she followed along behind the clerk. At first she didn't see them, planted as they were amidst the clutter. Keith and Mark sat on two wooden lawn chairs, enshrined in camping and cottage paraphernalia: bags of barbecue charcoal, lighting fluid, galvanized buckets, mosquito coils, pots of citronella candles, fish-landing gear, rubber boots, and sunflower lawn ornaments. Behind them, way up on the wall, peering down on them with a look of boredom, a scruffy moose head. They blended into the display like a pair of mannequins. They appeared to be sleeping. As she approached them, Keith opened his eyes and looked up at her.

"What kept you guys?"

Connie wanted to know straightaway what had happened.

"Motor conked. We had to row." Mark sounded disgusted. "As

if I hadn't had enough of that kind of thing already." He got up and started towards the door. "Let's get the hell out of here."

Mark had never done well without sleep.

Dennis asked about the boat. Keith said there would be a recovery mission later, once everyone rested.

In the van, Connie needed to say something, tell them how concerned they'd all been. She turned around to look at them. They looked out the windows. "We were up all night waiting for you guys. We waited at the beach. We thought you'd either got lost, had an accident, or had mechanical problems. We really didn't want to think lost or hurt, but I've heard of people missing on that lake who've never been found."

"Christ almighty." Keith looked at her. "Do you think it was the first time I've ever been out on a lake fishing?" He turned back to the window, his eyebrows pinched tighter over the bridge of his nose, and scowled.

Connie was a child again, judged, waiting for permission to speak, ashamed of herself for saying something so utterly stupid, without knowing why it was such a terrible thing for her to say. Underneath a thin layer of regret and shame, she felt a simmering anger.

"Let's just not talk about it now," Mark said. "Later, when we've had some sleep."

Without taking his eyes from the road Dennis reached over, took Connie's hand, and squeezed it. He didn't ask them anything.

The camp sites so quiet. Everyone sleeping, but Connie lay awake, bothered by the heat, alarmed by the sound of a baby crying somewhere in the distance, or was it the shriek of a blue jay? Without waking Dennis, she changed into her bathing suit and went down to the lake. A number of families occupied the beach. Children dug in the sand a few feet away from parents sprawled across blankets. Connie set up her lawn chair, then went to the water's edge. She stepped in, stood for a long time facing out across the water, her gaze focused on the islands in the distance, wondering at their impossible arrangements and the complicated paths through them. So easy to get lost. What would it be like to be lost out there, each narrow passage deceptively similar, and only one or two that would take you the right way, deliver you safely to shore?

She waded in deeper; the sting of cold made her inhale sharply. She crossed her arms over her stomach and turned to watch children playing along the shore, so preoccupied with what they were doing that nothing else existed. She walked farther out until the water came to just beneath her breasts. She opened her hands wide, placed them on the surface, and made two circular patterns on the water, without making a splash.

All through the night, as they held their lakeside vigil, she'd imagined so many outcomes for her brothers' fishing trip. Drowned, lost, or badly hurt after smashing into some rocky outcrop, clinging to the wreckage, shivering with the cold that would eventually overtake them. She imagined herself telling the horrible news to their children, their relatives; she'd felt a lump of sorrow in her throat; her eyes stung with tears. She imagined the lost looks in the eyes of Sheila and Linda as their lives fell apart. She thought about funerals.

They'd all been thinking about horrible possibilities and yet no one spoke it aloud, as if saying might somehow make it so. How do you hear or imagine an incomplete story without anticipating the ending?

Connie stilled her hands on the water's surface, her fingers spread, palms down. She made a decision.

She turned and looked towards the shoreline.

Dennis waved to her from the shore; then he started wading out, until he stood next to her. "You okay?"

"Yes," she nodded.

"You haven't told anyone," he said. "We leave soon. When are you going to tell them?"

"I've decided not to."

"No?"

Dennis looked out across the water. "Okay." He nodded, seemed to be thinking about what she'd said, weighing it in his mind. "Maybe I'd do the same."

"Who knows? Maybe it will always be just my story. It's my body, with or without breasts. What difference will telling them make?"

She would stay unexceptional, squeeze every ounce out of her ordinary life as long as she could. Hers was a story in progress; no one would guess her ending.

THE EMBRACE

So many of them Naomi had never met, the people who populated Eric's life. Each one saying how well she was holding up, especially given the suddenness of his death, as they pressed their warm, moist palms into hers and offered their condolences and encouragement.

I knew him from the Rotary, from Kinsmen. He helped with Christmas hampers. We worked out together at the gym. We curled together. We were golf buddies. We belonged to the same bike club. We were in Toastmasters. We were members of the Walk for Prostate committee. We volunteered for Habitat for Humanity. We met on Thursday nights for pub darts. We were fishing buddies. We worked together. A parade of introductions as they came to say goodbye.

They spoke of his disposition: considerate, generous, caring, giving, creative, outgoing. An amazing sense of humor, a leader, an innovative thinker, a tireless worker, generous, a community member, full of surprises, so proud of his family. Many said it was a wonder they hadn't met Naomi until today, and how regrettable under such a sad occasion. Some looked at her as if wondering if she really could be his wife. But here she was, in the flesh, solidly filling in any hazy notions they might have had of her.

This past Monday, moments after she finished her yoga class and took her phone off mute and saw a list of missed calls filling the screen, the phone rang. Eric had collapsed near the eighth hole. An ambulance was called.

She ran out of the gym, across the parking lot to the car. At a stoplight, the act of waiting stretched on, magnified by an emergency. Should she run the red light? Should she cry? Bash her fist

against the steering wheel? How should a person act? She anticipated the green light, concentrated on putting pressure on the gas
pedal. She noticed everything—the height of the light pole, the giant
X through a no-parking sign, a man leaning forward as he walked—
and somehow nothing seemed familiar. Time flexed, extended and
contracted, all at once. She didn't recognize her usual route, though
she wasn't lost.

She thrust away thoughts of how serious Eric's condition might
be, allowing them no time to fully shape. He'd be fine; the heat had
gotten to him on the course. He'd suffered a spell, a setback. He'd
be fine.

Now an older man with a fringe of white hair, pink scalp, and
a fiery complexion asked, "Was there any indication that this was
coming?"

"None at all," Naomi said. In fact, Eric had just been given the all-
clear from the family doctor.

At the hospital, as they were prepping Eric for surgery, a doctor
came out to speak to Naomi about what the procedure might entail.
Naomi nodded, but she wasn't hearing; she was thinking how the
surgeon seemed to be wrinkle-free, except in the neck. She must
have had a little nip-tuck, maybe she had a friend who did it for free.
Surgeons would have surgeon friends, wouldn't they?

After, when she came out to explain what had gone wrong, something about total blockage, Naomi laughed. This woman, this surgeon, couldn't possibly know what she was talking about; she was
lying or misinformed, or playing some hideous joke. That was it, a
joke! She could even be an imposter.

A grief counselor joined Naomi in the waiting room. Her reassuring voice explained how tragic news was processed differently and
how grieving was an individual matter—there was no right way, no
wrong way. Naomi should let her emotions out however they needed
to come; she shouldn't hold back or be embarrassed. The counselor
had one hand on Naomi's back, the other on her arm. Naomi felt
confined, trapped by the stranger with a silken voice, and oddly vul-
nerable dressed in her yoga clothes.

When Naomi first brought her yoga outfit home and held it for
Eric to see, he eyed it as if it might be a small animal that would
escape her hands and run up the curtains. "How does that help you

be more flexible?" he asked as he loosened his tie, and she repeated what she thought she'd already explained. Some moves had you practically upside down, the stretches so extended you almost fell over. "And for that you need a uniform?" he asked.

"A workout outfit, yes," she said. He wanted to know the cost, and she shaved a bit off. He never begrudged her money, that wasn't it, but he had the need to say something, to give some kind of qualifier. What she knew, and he would never say, was that he didn't want her taking on anything new, taking steps in her own life, because it altered the balance of his. It wasn't that he wanted her home either, not explicitly; he wanted her how she was, unchanging, something he could rely on. A ballast, he sometimes called her during moments of affection; she was his ballast, and a ballast must be steady.

"He was so outgoing," a woman with smooth blonde hair said. "He could always make me laugh."

"He had a great sense of humor," Naomi agreed. How easily he worked up a room, got people going, filled it with his charm and sense of timing. But when it was just the two of them, he became restless, as if being inside his own skin caused him considerable discomfort. As if he was trapped inside himself.

When the children came, she quit her job and stayed home, shutting the door on the world of business, insulating herself in their development and in domesticity. The inconsolable temper tantrums of a two-year-old became preferable to the ego-driven mood swings of her forty-something boss.

When the kids were little, Eric came home late, stepping into the mayhem of end-of-the-day crankiness, slipped into his biking costume, and headed for the trails with his buddies. Later, after the children had gone to bed, they had dinner together, though she usually only picked away at a salad, having eaten earlier.

When the kids grew older, he became more involved, their mature brains more agreeable to him. Sometimes he subbed for her and took the boys to soccer, football, and hockey, or drove Jennifer to figure skating and dance. He even managed to go to some of her recitals.

One by one the kids left home, and the house filled slowly with a crushing silence. The sound of the door closing as Eric left for one of his commitments seemed to grow louder, seemed to seal her in more tightly.

Naomi looked down the reception line at her three adult children as they received guests and condolences and felt a surge of pride. They were holding up well. After they left home, they'd been busy filling their lives with work, school, and their social schedules. They thought they knew their dad. They'd think of him often now that he was gone, sort through memories, reshape them into a workable story of how involved he was as a father, see him in a vibrant light. They wouldn't remember how, more often, he was either at the office or working on one of his many projects. Naomi was the one who could be counted on with boring predictability. When the time came, her light would not shine as brightly.

After the reception, when they went back to the house, would she tell them then, when they were sifting through the comments about how people remembered their father? Would she tell them and see their looks of disbelief and uncertainty that would challenge everything they ever knew or accepted about him—about themselves? Would they believe her?

"He gave a very moving and very funny speech at Kinsmen last year," a man with curly brown hair was saying. "He could have been a stand-up comedian."

"I'll never forget the time he showed up at my door with a Christmas hamper," an older woman with stooped shoulders and a walker said, her voice quaking with age. "I was so grateful."

Naomi planned activities against the house's stillness, after the kids moved out. Every Wednesday she watched Bollywood movies with Carla, her next-door neighbor—whom Eric called the neighborhood gossip—and that ignited a desire to take up belly dancing. Together, they signed up for classes at the university, then started their own group and met every Tuesday at Naomi's, fifteen women who came in their sweatpants, leotards, shorts, sashes, long skirts, and strapped multi-stranded beads around their hips. When Naomi put on her long Indian cotton skirt and beaded hip scarf, raised her hands above her head, began the slow undulations released by the music, heard the chatter of the beads—water gushing over loose stones in a faraway brook—she flowed out of herself.

The group became accomplished dancers. They received invitations to perform: seniors' residences, schools, the community center, the library, birthday parties. The Swivelling Hips started to have a reputation.

Naomi spotted two of them down the line, making their way towards her. They'd come for her, since they didn't know Eric. He only ever paused at the living room door to catch a quick glimpse of their gyrations, then vanished upstairs to change and head back out the door.

Eric fidgeted when people complimented her on her slimness and fitness, and she told them it was on account of the belly dancing. "They don't need to know the details," he said. Sometimes at the grocery store, someone would step up and say they'd seen her dance with the group at some event. They always said what fun the women looked like they were having. He'd walk away. He didn't mind her doing it, she didn't think, but he didn't want to hear about it.

For a long time, Naomi had trouble sleeping. She'd wake up in the night and feel distressed, with no idea of why. Worry tumbled her thoughts in the darkness, and in the light of day these same thoughts bleached away.

One night, lying awake looking up at the ceiling, she had an idea that put an end to her troubled nights. She would go to India. She would go alone. She didn't know why she settled on this, but it felt right. She kept the plan to herself, searching the internet for a travel group, and signed on for a three-week tour that would concentrate on the Ganges. At first, the only person she told was Carla. "But why alone?" Carla asked.

The night of the women's shelter auction fundraiser, for which Eric was a key organizer through his company's sponsorship, she went out with Carla to a fashion show. On the way to the car after the event, she spotted Eric across the street, walking with a tall woman, headed in the opposite direction, miles away from the women's shelter. They were laughing and talking, stepping briskly, and the woman's shoulder-length hair blew in the wind. Carla saw him too, but didn't say anything, as if she knew something Naomi didn't. Later, Naomi asked him if he went anywhere after the fundraiser and he said no, he hadn't, and turned off the bedside lamp.

She let it drop. She shifted all her thoughts to the India trip. Eric was surprised when she told him her plan. "India? Really? So far away? By yourself?" Not exactly, but with a travel group of strangers. He started to look at her differently, to pull his head back away from her, wondering perhaps who she was or who she was becoming. And what impact that would have on him.

Naomi wanted to kick off her shoes; her feet hurt from standing too long. The stories, this oral shrine to Eric, kept a steady flow past her. She looked forward to going home and stretching out on the couch, ordering in some food, taking in the sounds of her children who would disappear back to their lives in a few days, leaving her once again to face silence.

When she stepped off the plane she felt as if she was drowning in the Indian air. Spice-ridden, sweet-soured by the smell of decay, effluence, street cooking, and flower vendors, the atmosphere shook her awake after the long flight.

The tour took her to several places along the Ganges, but after two and a half weeks, when they returned to the Holy City of Varanasi, she told the Global Trekker guide she would extend her stay. He discouraged her decision, but eventually agreed after she paid him more money for the administrative costs of rearranging her return trip with another group in six weeks, and for his time. She phoned home and left a message for Eric, then she turned her cell phone off for the rest of her visit. Now she was "out there," away from him, away from everyone, on her own, suspended in an existence that people could only wonder about and not know about with any kind of certainty.

Naomi found a room in Varanasi with shared cooking facilities in a quiet building close to the Ganges. Every day she went to watch the people worship at the river. The meditative chants of their voices soothed and reassured, though she didn't understand a word. She met a man, a silver-haired man with bright eyes and an inquisitive intellect, a widower and a professor of religion at the university. He was studying ritual and came here every day to observe and interview the worshippers who prayed by the river and immersed themselves in the sacred water. She tried to explain ritual where she came from, in Canada, but it sounded more like routine, structures to prevent boredom, treatments against spiritual numbness. He said it sounded busy, perhaps not the most soothing, nothing like what the people gathered at the Ganges sought. They had long discussions about faith, belief, release, ritual, worship, what it meant to feel connected, and about the nature of time and memory. She avoided telling him anything about herself, the life she came from, rerouting his questions about her as quickly as possible. She fell into his voice, listened for its lilt and rhythms, broken often by the sound of laughter.

One night, awake in the heat and awash in the sounds coming through the window—screech owls, footsteps on the street, the shouts of late-night hawkers—she went to the window. Moonlight showered over the line of rooftops that descended down towards the water. It reminded her of a painting. She slipped light cotton pants on over her nightgown, wrapped a shawl around her shoulders, and followed the narrow stairways to the river, the same route she took every day, though now in darkness it seemed unfamiliar. It surprised her how many worshippers there were at night. As they chanted, their hands held before them in prayer, their voices sounded as natural as the drone of crickets or the whoosh of the wind as they stood with faces down to the water or upturned to the moon.

She removed her sandals, stepped down the stairs, and slipped into the river, careful not to make a splash, surprised by its warmth. A mild stink rose up; she would never dream of wading into such water at home. No one noticed her or picked her out as an interloper, drawn there by nothing more than an interest in what others held sacred. She waded out until she was up to her shoulders, held her breath, and stepped out further until the water was over her head. She stayed there, completely submerged. She opened her eyes and stared into darkness.

Panic seized her, gripped her neck, struck her heart; she wanted to leap to the surface and breathe, but resisted, as if this were some kind of test and rising too soon would leave her permanently damaged. Her eyes bulged with the pressure of holding her breath and she thought she might pass out. Through the murkiness, a ball of light floated towards her and stopped just before her. Inside its glow she saw her house. The walls of the house fell away and she peered into her kitchen, where everyone was seated around the table, talking, laughing. All of them, much younger. Calmness came over her; she could stay this way forever, suspended in time with this vision.

Her lungs were about to give. She pushed up to the water's surface and choked in the air. At the river's bank, as she started to the steps leading out, a hand came down and gripped hers and a melodic voice said, "Let me help you."

"Recreational or ritual?" the professor asked.

Naomi stared at him as he stood bathed in the blue moonlight. "I've no idea."

The professor smiled and gave a little laugh. He asked for no further explanation. He escorted her home, assisting her up the narrow stairs. She invited him in. Without saying another word, she led him to her bed. They held each other until morning came.

In the weeks that followed, he asked her to stay in Varanasi. She told him she was married, and he said he knew. "Nevertheless," he said. "I shall still miss you. I will miss our daily conversations. You have put me in touch with my life and my late wife, I believe." He held his hand affectionately over his heart. "Our conversations remind me of the ones I had with her. She was a very clever woman."

Tiredness, stifling heat inside the funeral home, and the ongoing stories about Eric made her long for this to be over, and yet, as she peered down the line she saw there were still about twenty more to pass, mostly middle-aged men, and a tall woman with shoulder-length hair she thought she should know, but couldn't place. Before she had time to think of where she'd seen her before, a fellow member of the Swivelling Hips stepped up and gave her a mighty hug.

When she came back from India, Eric met her at the airport with flowers. He brought her home, poured her wine, made her toast and jam, and tucked her into bed. He'd taken the night off from one of his activities, but the next night he was gone again, and Carla came over to hear about her trip.

After a couple glasses of wine, Carla said she had something to tell her, and she wasn't sure if she should, but the information had kept her awake at night. "Here goes," she said, taking a sip before proceeding. After Naomi left for India, the woman they'd seen on the street with Eric, the night of the fashion show, came to Naomi's house. Several times her car stayed in the driveway overnight.

Naomi had been far away in India, his ballast gone, having what she could call her own affair, though there was nothing more than the embrace. They'd clung together as an act of remembrance, a human monument of longing, desire, cherishing what each of them once had. She knew then, throughout that night, locked in the professor's arms, that she'd been as much a part of letting go, of drifting, as Eric had. Forever passive, comfortable with her resentments, her need to be present but remain in the shadows. In India she knew she must find her way out.

Naomi told Eric he had to cut back on his activities, stay at home, get to know her again, because she was someone worth knowing. She surprised him, but he went along with her, and she suspected he knew that she knew about the tall woman. With Carla as their neighbor, he should have guessed as much, should have been more discreet. They went out together on dates, he deflected phone calls. They were in the process of rebuilding and he was putting his whole heart into it. Naomi knew he'd ended his affair, wondered if it might have ended before she came back from India, but she never asked.

Before her stood the last person in line, the tall woman with the shoulder-length hair. She hesitated before extending her hand, but Naomi would not take it. Naomi held her gaze on the woman's, which seemed full of shame and sadness, and when she went to speak Naomi said, "No." She reached out with both hands and drew the woman towards her, held her. She would not tell the children, not ever.

CONTINUUM

The shoulders hunch, the broad suspender straps bunch the plaid shirt on the long slope of his back as he leans towards the window. As if he's watching an event unfold out on the sidewalk, or is about to leap from his chair; he isn't doing either. He sits. He watches. All day. Every day.

Eleanor carries the cake across the room until she stands next to him, taps him lightly on the shoulder. "Top of the afternoon, Shane." A joke, since he claims to have about as much Irish blood as a pickle.

Shane smiles, wide and welcoming, and asks, "Time for you already?" as if her appearance is a complete surprise, even though she comes here every Sunday and Wednesday at this same time.

Eleanor puts the cake down on an end table and hears Barb's mother shouting about something across the hall. Poor Barb. She is being punished by her mother for being ten minutes late. Barb had to get her three grandkids ready to be picked up by their parents, after their weekend sleepover. "Total chaos," she told Eleanor. "Herding cats. And on no sleep. But we had fun!"

Eleanor would love sleepless nights on account of grandchildren.

Shane's eyes are on the cake and his hands plunge from the armrests to his lap, his shoulders sink. "Oh my" is all he manages.

"What do you think?" Eleanor asks. "Amazing, right?" She pulls a chair up beside him. "It was a challenge, I can tell you."

His chin quivers, and he shakes his head.

"It's a daffodil cake. I made it especially for you. After hearing your story, the one you told me the other day." She waits for him to say how beautiful it looks, or how delicious, then follows his gaze to the street, to the flow of people on the sidewalk, and to the sky as a tiny silver dart, silent and dazzling under the bright sun, pierces the blue.

"Cat got your tongue today?" She can always count on him to toss out a quick retort.

"I didn't tell you the whole story." A catch in his voice chokes him.

Barb's mother shouts even louder. What now? Something about someone stealing her clothes. Once again she is the victim of some injustice. Barb will never be able to make her happy; she might just as well stop trying. "About the cake?"

"Yes."

"Do you want to tell me now?"

"No." He leans forward as the jet slips beyond the window frame and out of view. "Where will it end up?" he says.

Eleanor looks at the cake in its clear container and decides to offer him a piece later, once this mood, or whatever it is, lifts. "Did you talk to your girls today?" This snaps him out of his daydream.

"Oh yes, yes of course," he says, sky-blue eyes settling on her. "And you? Did you talk to your boys?"

No time for that this morning, not while she was making the cake, she tells him, but she'll be in touch soon. "Any news from the girls?" Eleanor feels as if she knows Kelly and Emily and their families, even though they haven't met. How could they? They live in Japan. One day, perhaps.

"I hardly had time to talk to Kelly," Shane says. "Everyone was off doing something, deadlines to meet, hurrying and scurrying, just like those folks out there. Dashing around like chickens. All in a flap." He flicks his hand towards the window, out to the sidewalk and the endless flow of pedestrians.

"What's going on with Kelly?"

His face settles into deep thinking lines as he works through something. "Kelly's upgrading her financial license, and teaching more at the university. Since Michael's heart attack she's taken on more. The kids keep her hopping, as teenagers will do. They're planning a trip to see me. I told her that's the last thing they should be doing. I told her, go off on a vacation with Michael; never mind me. I'm well taken care of."

A while back, before Michael's health turned, Shane said he worried about Kelly's marriage. He thought all Michael's travel and Kelly's heavy workload, not to mention raising two kids, was too much. "It was nice of them to offer to come and see you, wasn't it?"

"Yes, I suppose so. But I'd rather they took care of themselves. Kelly's upset about Audrey, too. She's getting tattoos and apparently gives Kelly a lot of attitude. I told her it's normal. She doesn't like Audrey's new boyfriend either, but feels if she says too much it will have the opposite effect to what she wants." He raises his hands and laces his fingers together. "I suspect she's correct."

"What did you tell her?"

"Well, it's my understanding, judging by the staff here, that tattoos are all the rage. It doesn't make them bad people. Pick your battles, I told her. It's only skin; they're only pictures. As for the boyfriend, she knows how to handle it."

"Did you talk to Emily?"

"Oh yes. She's got her problems, too. A very mouthy, sarcastic son who she thinks is smoking marijuana. She suspects her daughter is anorexic or bulimic. Maybe both. Plus, she's got a big job with her research, and her husband is flying all over the world with his work. Life is complicated these days, isn't it?" He faces Eleanor, his heavy-lidded eyes filled with longing for a simpler time. "Don't you find it complicated?"

"Very." She tells Shane about her last Skype calls to her boys a few weeks ago, even though she's already told him before. No matter. They do this often, rehash stories. It's soothing, makes them part of something. "Everyone was in a hurry, no one with time to talk. Brent was running off to swimming lessons with his kids. Ian was jumping on a plane, headed off on a business trip." A grandmother in two dimensions, half-realized. Her grandchildren could see her, hear her, but she couldn't hold them, couldn't press her nose into their silken heads and smell them. What, they might wonder, would she have to do with them, this face that popped up from time to time, detached from its body, looming at them from its iPad tent on the kitchen table, like a ghost? Grandma by title only.

"Do you know, Emily talked about visiting me, too? She and Kelly are cooking up something together. They've got a big plan to all come at once with their families. I told her the same as her sister.

Never mind jetting halfway 'round the world to see an old codger like me. I'm fine, well taken care of. I've no complaints. Emily said they might just surprise me."

Out the window, a woman walks by with a little white dog tugging on its leash, but Shane isn't watching her. He looks up into the sky, following the flight of another jet.

"Is it time for some cake?"

"Not today."

The quiver in his voice warns her against pressing him further. They visit a while longer, talk mostly about the beautiful fall weather, but Shane is not quite himself, more tired than usual. Eleanor says her goodbyes and gives the cake to a grateful staff member to take to the lunch room, requesting a piece be sent to Barb's mother. She wouldn't give up on trying to raise Shane's spirits.

At the pub, Barb leans over the table and asks why Shane refused to eat the cake, and why did Eleanor think he wouldn't tell her the whole story?

"Beats me," Eleanor says. "I thought I was doing something to free him of his pain, but I might have added to it. He seemed quite emotional when he saw the cake, I guess because of what happened."

Years ago, Shane's daughter Kelly, eight at the time, begged her mother to make her a daffodil cake for her ninth birthday party, since she'd had one at a friend's party. His wife set about to make it, an elaborate affair with angel food cake, lemon pudding, and special fluffy white frosting. For days it was all Kelly would talk about, and on her birthday, when Shane's wife produced this magnificent cake, Kelly was over the moon.

All the children were meeting in the park, which had a petting zoo they'd visit after the picnic, games, and the present opening. All Shane had to do was deliver the cake, along with some of the gifts. On the way to the park, at the first corner, he heard a terrible crash and he suddenly realized he'd left the cake on the roof of the car. He pulled over, got out to see if anything could be saved, but the cake lay in the middle of the road, a pile of white and yellow mush, the plate shattered into a thousand pieces. He could hardly speak when he arrived at the park, and never in all his years of living would he forget the look on Kelly's face when he told her what had happened.

"That's not a big deal," Barb says. "Accidents like that happen all the time. We get over it."

"There's more," Eleanor reminds her. "But he won't tell me." She knows Shane feels things deeply, perhaps more than is healthy. Even the Cedar Grove staff comment on his sensitive nature and how he is a true gentleman.

"I'm not quitting. I'm baking another cake for our Wednesday visit."

Eleanor's second daffodil cake turned out better than her first one.

"You don't give up easily, do you?" Barb says when they meet, Eleanor holding the cake aloft.

"I still think it might help him get over his sadness about that birthday party so long ago."

"It's a cake, Eleanor. It's not magic."

Shane seems agitated as she takes her seat beside him, watches his hands twist restlessly in his lap. "Look at this." He points out the window, the sky a bigger canvas than before as high winds and rain of the last two days have stripped the leaves off the trees, laying bare his view. "It's a sign," he says. "Universal restlessness. Souls criss-crossing our world, going who knows where."

Eight jet trails stripe the sky in various stages of dissipation, the earliest ones shredded into faint strands of cotton batting, the newer ones solid and thick, laid down like fresh lines of paint. She sees cloudiness in his eyes she's never seen before, hears anxiousness in his speech. It's not like him to talk in abstract terms, almost metaphysical.

"There are a lot of planes today." She hopes she can bring him back into the room with her.

He bends forward, closer to the window. "Continuum," he says, as if he might be staring into eternity, and sits like that for a long time, until the spell breaks, and his glance alights on the cake. He leans back, his head resting against the chair, and closes his eyes.

"When I pulled up at the park and Kelly learned about the cake and how it had been destroyed, she behaved like a brat. She was rude to the other children. She told one to shut up and made another one cry by kicking her. She refused to play any of the games we planned for them. When it was time to open the presents, she ripped at the paper and tossed aside the gifts as if she hated them. We made her thank her guests. She gave them the most begrudging thanks you've ever heard. Do you know what I did?"

He turns to her, his half-open eyes blazing with fierceness.

"What?" Her own boys often behaved badly at their birthday parties.

"I sent all the children home early, packed up the car, and took the family home. Kelly sat in the back, her arms crossed over her chest in defiance, kicking at the back of my seat, purposely trying to get my goat. I told her if she didn't stop right that instant she'd be going to her room as soon as we got home."

Eleanor can't imagine such harshness coming from him.

"When we got home, she called me a name. Something like, you stupid idiot, and I grabbed hold of her, pulled her to a chair, put her over my knee and spanked her.

"My wife and Emily were horrified. They clung together and cried. I told them to stop, Kelly was a brat and she was getting exactly as she deserved. I hauled her to her room and locked the door, and for the next few hours she bashed and kicked it. I even refused to let my wife give her food for the rest of the day."

Eleanor can hardly believe what he's telling her. This sweet, considerate man, so devoted to his children.

Across the hall, Barb's mother's voice rises in her usual reign of protest, engulfing the hall, murdering silence with her list of grievances.

"I will have a piece of that cake now," Shane says.

Eleanor takes a knife from her bag and cuts off a generous slab. Perhaps telling the story rids him of a heavy burden of guilt. His hand trembles as he accepts the slice she holds out for him.

"Well, it is a masterpiece," he says, appraising the cake. He rises from his chair, crosses the room, and heads out the door without so much as a word about where he might be going. Eleanor follows him into Barb's mother's room. He stands before her, a tiny wizened shape swallowed by a massive chair, her squawking voice reverberating around the room like the clatter of crows as she attacks Barb.

"Madam," he interrupts, and her head rears back to take him in.

"I am your neighbor from across the hall. I was wondering if you would do me the honor of sharing some of this fine dessert with me."

Barb's mother's face, pinched by rage, opens in astonishment at the spectacle of this plaid-shirted man, pants hoisted high by suspender straps, wearing bedroom slippers, standing before her with an offering of cake. No one, apart from Barb, ever visits her. Is it any wonder? Her voice sounds strange as she searches for a tone seldom used, and her eyes fall ravenously on the cake. "I suppose," she says.

Shane steps towards her, but does not bend to deliver the cake into her outstretched hand. "On two conditions," he says. "You need to lower your voice. I believe it's called finding your inside voice. And the other one is you must stop being so nasty."

Barb's mother is stunned, as if someone has smacked her across her cheek, or dumped cold water on her. Her head shakes in agitation and her face colors with rage. Her voice begins its climb to her usual pitch, then tumbles down to a new register. "Okay." She sounds almost sweet, and garnishes her single word with the hint of a smile.

"I will come to see you tomorrow to hear how you enjoyed it." He places the plate on the armrest of her chair, turns, and leaves the room, Eleanor in tow.

"I believe I would like a nap now," he says, sitting on the edge of his bed, then stretches out fully, one hand atop the other on his stomach, and closes his eyes.

Eleanor leaves the rest of the cake with the desk clerk. "For the staff," she says. "I'll pick up the container later. Please leave some for Shane and Barb's mom. But you are welcome to the rest."

At the pub, Barb says, "He was like an angel giving my mom a slice of sweet." She hasn't seen her mom so happy for a very long time, and they order another carafe of wine to celebrate. Even Barb seems different after today's visit, not all bruised and beat up by her mother's abrasiveness.

Friday night, the phone rings. It's Nora Wilson, Chief Administrator from Cedar Grove, regretfully informing her Shane has passed. "Peacefully," she says. "Probably of a stroke. Some of the staff mentioned he might have been experiencing some episodes this week."

Eleanor can't think of what to say. Her thoughts fly to his family, the trip they were planning. "His children, his daughters, Kelly and Emily; they'll be devastated."

Perhaps Nora Wilson hasn't heard her; she is silent on the other end of the line, then she says, "You've a cake holder to pick up, Eleanor. Could you come in tomorrow, let's say around two? I've got it in my office."

From her balcony, Eleanor stares at the Cedar Grove roof a few blocks away, sheds tears as she thinks of Shane. What will she do with her Wednesdays and Sundays?—a selfish thought, she knows.

She calls Barb and arranges to meet her at the pub around four, after her appointment with Nora Wilson. Barb will know by Eleanor's faltering voice that she needs her.

Nora offers her a seat opposite her broad desk and places the cake container in front of her. "I imagine this comes as a shock to you, and I am sorry for your loss," she says. "I heard from the staff that you and Shane were close. He was a lovely, gentle man. He was very lucky to have you as a loyal visitor. Over a year, wasn't it?"

"Almost two." Eleanor dabs at her eyes. "It's so sad because his daughters were planning on coming. He told them no, but I have a hunch they were going to show up anyway, to surprise him."

"There's something I'd like to talk to you about," Nora says, as she pulls a folder out of her desk drawer. "We found some newspaper articles he had tucked away at the back of his cupboard." She shoves the folder across the desk towards Eleanor. "Read the top clipping."

Eleanor takes a yellowed newspaper page out of the folder. Dated back thirty-five years, the headline reads: Japanese Jet Liner with 254 Passengers Disappears over the Pacific. "Yes," Eleanor says, "I remember this. They never found it, did they?"

"Look farther down the page, at the article about the Vancouver sisters, two girls who were on that flight. See their names? Kelly and Emily."

"That is a huge coincidence," Eleanor says, and thinks about it. "Did he name his daughters after them?" Even as she says this she knows it can't be, since the dates don't add up. "So what are you saying?"

"Shane imagined the daughters. You know how sensitive he was.

It's as if he couldn't bear the pain of the sisters' death in the crash so he made up a life for them. It's the only explanation we've been able to come up with." Nora removes her glasses and settles back in her chair. "Our files show that he only had a wife, and of course, she was deceased. That's not all, I'm afraid. I know this is a lot to take in, but I need you to see something else." She slides a newspaper clipping across the desk.

Eleanor picks up the brittle paper and reads aloud, "Child killed on way to birthday party." She scans the article. A child, excited about going to a birthday party, ran out into the street into the path of an oncoming car and was killed instantly. No charges were laid against the distraught driver, Shane O'Connell.

No Kelly, no Emily, no cake. Had she, by bringing the cake, not once but twice, forced him to a place he never wanted to go? A place he'd filled in long ago with a fantasy? And yet he held on to a bit of punishment, the bit about the spanking, his cruelty, unable to let go of the pain, a terrible reminder of killing a child.

By the time Eleanor leaves Cedar Grove on her way to the pub, the sky, clotted with pewter-colored storm clouds, bears down, and the wind hurries leaves through the air. The occasional raindrop strikes her face; she pulls her scarf more snuggly around her neck.

She has to tell Barb. The story about Shane and his girls, a complete fabrication, the true story about the little girl he killed. An accident. Like her, Barb will have a hard time believing it, but she will eventually, as she comes to an understanding about how the mind invents, how it protects.

As she waits at the light, she thinks of going straight home, closing the curtains on the world, curling up on the couch, and standing Barb up. Then what? Hide for the rest of her life? No, she has to meet Barb, has to tell her everything. This moment cannot pass or her deception will be concealed even from herself, become as real to her as Shane's was to him, forever locking her away in her own solitude. And after telling Barb, what then? Would Barb still be her friend? How could anyone like someone so filled with such ridiculous pride?

Down the street, the sign for the Black Sheep Pub sways impatiently in the wind. Barb will be waiting. A glass of wine first, the news about Shane, give her time to process all of that, then the story about the poinsettia, her daughter-in-law, Sylvia, and Gabe, her little grandson.

Sylvia, late as usual, the other two grandkids already there, dropped off by Eleanor's older son. Sylvia always came with a list of instructions about Gabe, her first child. Don't feed him this, give him that, we don't use those words on him, your old toys are dangerous, his nap times are at . . . as if she'd never raised two boys of her own. But even before Gabe, Eleanor found Sylvia off-putting, altogether too sure of herself. Condescending.

Sylvia started to cross the room to move the poinsettia away from the reach of the children—she'd read they could be poisonous. She wanted to put it on the counter, out of the way. Eleanor insisted no, Sylvia was running late, she should be off. She wore dress boots; she was going to tromp across the living room carpet to get the plant. Eleanor assured her she would take care of the plant straightaway, and at the same time she thought, who was Sylvia to come into her home and tell her where to put things? And dirty the carpet with her boots.

Later, she ran into the bedroom for something, gone for mere seconds, and when she came back, Gabe was chewing a leaf. The convulsions seemed like they would never stop.

An accident, Eleanor told a distraught Sylvia as they sat at the child's hospital bedside for two days. But that wasn't enough for Sylvia. She demanded an apology. An accident, Eleanor pleaded. They all stopped talking to her, her entire family. Ian said none of them would speak to her again until she owned up to her carelessness. Gabe could have died.

Eleanor spots Barb in their usual booth and makes her way across the room. After she tells her the whole story, before Barb tells her what she must do, she will tell her plans to go across town to Ian's house, then to Aurora, north of the city, to visit Brent. She will apologize to all of them and ask for their forgiveness.

Even before the incident, she hadn't welcomed her daughters-in-law into her life. She'd criticized them, questioned them. How could they know her boys better than she? But they did, and she refused to let go. So filled with jealousy, so full of pride. And then she lost them all, as if they'd disappeared on route, dropped from the sky.

KILLER CAKE

Over the sound of classmates' splashing, Brenda strained to hear Ashley shout aqua fit instructions from the pool's deck.

"Pump, pump, pump! Lift those knees. Tuck in those abs. Suck 'em in, girls!"

Brenda thought Ashley was the only "girl" present, and not that young either, probably somewhere around twenty-one. Ashley was incredibly fit, of course, and cute as a button, with a round, slightly chubby face and curly brown hair. She seemed genuinely intent on getting this group of women into shape, encouraging them with her running banter, which, all through the warmup, had been mostly about the weather, a topic that seemed uninspired. But then again, what else did Ashley have in common with these middle-aged women?

From Brenda's spot in the pool, she saw the blubbery folds of grey sky out the partially steamed-over windows.

Ashley warned them things were about to get tougher. They had better believe her. They hadn't felt anything yet. "Do you hear me?" She leaned out across the pool to hear their response.

The women looked up at her shyly. Some smiled.

"That was pathetic, absolutely pathetic. You must still be asleep. You can do better than that. Okay, raise your legs and move your arms like this." She rotated her arms in small circles and shouted, "Tight, tight, tight." She lifted a knee up high, lowered it, then raised the other one.

"Come on, go, go, go! The harder you work, the bigger the pay-off."

Not true. Maybe if you're Ashley's age, but at Brenda's the result of hard work was an injury.

"Come on, girls. Let's get moving! Lift those knees!"

Hard to say if the thirty or so women followed her instructions, concealed as they were in the water. Maybe that's why some of them took this class: to cheat or to pamper medical conditions—tendonitis, arthritis, cancer, neurological disorders, shin splints, deteriorated discs, old wounds.

A new tune came on over the pool's P.A. system. It's been a hard day's night, and I've been working like a dog.

"Yeah, baby. We're working like dogs." Ashley did a little twist, which made several ladies laugh.

It's been a hard day's night, I should be sleeping like a log.

"No way, baby. We're working like dogs." What a ham, a good-natured girl.

But when I get home to you, I find the things that you do . . .

"Oh, naughty, naughty." Ashley wagged a finger and changed her stride to jumping jacks.

Brenda was much younger than Ashley when she first heard that song. She and her best friend Jane sang every song on the album and danced around Jane's hi-fi. One night, after a high school dance when they were horsing around, dancing and singing, Jane's dad came out in his bathrobe and told them to shut the hell up. He didn't seem to notice they stank of lemon gin, consumed in the school's bathroom.

Ashley fluttered and flapped, her flushed face framing her dimpled smile. "Feel the pain, feel the strain. Hoo-wee. Come on, girls, no slacking."

Eight o'clock on a Monday morning; didn't they deserve medals for being here? And how many of them had slept well? Not Brenda, that's for sure. She would not call these women slackers.

"Work it out, girls," Ashley shouted. "Let's make cake our goal. Chocolate cake—three layers, dripping with icing and ice cream. Who here likes ice cream?" She'd given up on the Beatles, moved on to food.

A few timid hands went up; the majority held back.

"That's it, that's all? I don't believe you. I like chocolate cake and I'm not afraid to say it. Now, I'm going to ask you again, and this time I want the truth. Don't be afraid to say. I won't tell anyone." Ashley whispered this as if she were a young girl talking dirty.

"Okay, one more time. Who likes chocolate cake with ice cream?" Several hands shot into the air, but not Brenda's. She'd never been a fan of sweets.

The last time Brenda had chocolate cake was Tim's 55th. She ordered a party size from Wicked Treats, enough to serve fifty, and, as it turned out, she needed every crumb. The sparklers fizzled against the summer night, lit up his face, already aglow from wine, his cheeks rosy against his tanned skin.

Brenda's upper arms ached.

"Come on," Ashley shouted. "I want to see your pain. Two minutes. Give me everything you've got. Burn, baby, burn."

Brenda looked at the other women in the pool. So many of them had given everything they had, or had it taken from them. How eager they looked as they concentrated on Ashley's instruction, worked up a lively foam to keep their bodies in shape. Take Linda over there, for instance. Brenda last saw her at Linda's mother's funeral. And now the cancer everyone thought had gone from her sister's left breast, back again, but this time in her brain. Still, Linda told her in the locker room, just before class, she stayed optimistic. "We're lucky," she said. "The tumor's operable."

"You're slacking off." Ashley pointed at Brenda's area of the pool. "Chocolate cake. The harder you work, the bigger the piece!" Ashley strutted in a little circle on the deck. "Make sure you bring your heels all the way down on the pool floor. We don't want any injuries."

Brenda could have cake any old time she wanted, and without guilt.

They all pitched in to give Tim top-of-the-line fishing gear and a ticket for a bush plane to take him farther north. "I'm off to pickerel heaven," he said. He tested out the new rod in the swimming pool, did a couple of casts. Someone shouted, "Are you getting any?" Underwater pool lights shone up through the fish line on the surface, like a crack in glass. Around one o'clock, the cops showed up to tell them to keep the noise down. They wished Tim a happy birthday, said they thought it looked like a pretty good party.

After everyone left, Tim had another slice of cake. "This is killer cake. The best I've ever had." He sat at the kitchen table while she worked at the sink, her shoes already kicked off, summer humidity in a patch across her forehead.

They tumbled into bed as the sky leaked a trace of morning, rocked their bodies together, spun themselves over the mattress, a pair of sumo wrestlers, contoured themselves into positions gratifying to each, honed from years of practice. A petunia-scented breeze drifted through the open window, caressed Brenda's skin. Beneath them, the white cotton sheets lay twisted and damp from their sex.

"Aha," Ashley pointed at Brenda. "You're smiling. You're thinking about cake. Can you feel it? Come on, I need to hear you." Ashley cupped her hand around her ear. "Can you feel it?"

A chorus of unconvincing "Hoo-wees" went up.

"Okay, give me one minute of cross-country step, give me your best. Earn yourselves that slice of cake and ice cream. Speaking of ice cream and warm summer days, anyone going away this winter?"

A couple of hands went up.

"South?" Ashley asked. Once you got to be a certain age, it seemed you only went in one direction.

"Greece," one woman shouted.

"The Arctic," another said.

Ashley shouted, "I could use some sun right about now. Who here could use some sun?" Hands waved in the air.

Brenda looked over at Gayle, a woman she'd met in the locker room who'd had a couple of lumps removed before radiation. For the first time in seven years, she wouldn't be going to Florida for the winter.

"My boyfriend and I are planning a road trip to Montreal," Ashley explained. "I've heard it's fun, but I'm worried—my French is bad."

"Don't be," Karen shouted.

Karen, an anthropology professor at the university, had retired early to take a position with the United Nations. Now she travelled to Third World countries.

"It's a long drive to Montreal, about twelve hours. I keep telling my boyfriend, I think we should split it up into two days, then we won't arrive tired." She looked at them, wide-eyed. "Oh, I'm sorry.

Relax your arms, shake them out. I've heard there are nice restaurants in Montreal."

"There are," Karen shouted. Tomorrow, she'd told Brenda earlier as they slipped into their suits, she was flying to the Congo.

"Oh my gosh," Ashley squealed. "There we go talking about food again. Are you still thinking about cake? Come on, keep on working."

"Stop talking about cake," Wendy shouted from across the pool.

"I know," Ashley agreed. "It makes it worse, doesn't it? I've got the biggest craving."

Probably not what Wendy meant. She had caseloads, not cake, on her mind. The senior partner of a law firm, her name often ended up in the paper connected with high-profile lawsuits. It was all she could do to fit these classes in.

Tim had done fifty laps in the pool every morning that summer. He golfed, played tennis, cycled. Once, she'd gone out fishing with him, very glad she hadn't caught anything.

She should have done more with him, she thought after. He swore it was a short fling, meaningless really. They met a few times on the golf course, hit it off, joked around. It turned serious once, and he knew instantly he'd made a mistake. It took Brenda's fall, a broken leg, finding her at the foot of the stairs after she lay there all day, to put their lives back into focus. When she recovered, she took up golfing, got her membership here at the gym.

"I'm going to time you. I want you to run on the spot as fast as you can for one minute.

Starrr—tinggg—now." Ashley ran on the spot, though not vigorously.

Early in September, two months after his birthday party, Tim took his last fishing trip. He shared the fourteen-hour drive along the north shore of Superior, to meet the bush plane, with his buddies. Tim took the wheel around the eleventh hour, in the middle of the night. A zigzag of pain shot through his chest and he blanked out. The car crossed the road into a rock cut. Brenda hadn't been notified until they cut him out of the wreckage.

There was only one fatality, the police said before their parting words, "We are terribly sorry for your loss."

"Can you feel the weight sliding off you?" Ashley shouted. "Terrific. Let's slow down a bit. Keep moving, but let's end with a brisk walking pace, then ordinary walking."

Brenda wanted to keep on running.

"Okay, slow it down. Good work!" Ashley walked over to the ghetto blaster, slipped in a new CD, then dimmed the lights. "Time to change the pace. Let yourselves go. Drift on your backs."

Brenda floated with the others, arms and legs extended, a web of women, lace on the water's surface, hands and feet almost touching.

Soft music swelled through the room.

You and me and rain on the roof . . .

"Okay, let's just relax. Free fall," she said, her voice bedtime gentle.

Drying while it soaks the flowers . . .

"Feel the tension leave your body. Let it go, release it. You are drifting. You are completely free."

Maybe we'll be caught for hours . . .

They both had loved this song, said so every time they heard it. Floating on her back, looking up, the ceiling beams reminded her of a church.

Waiting out the sun . . .

Wind sifting through beach grass carrying the scent of coconut. Sweet, clumsy, furtive, exploratory sex, the hidden tenderness between the legs, spent sexual tension. Those days, before the craze to talk about everything, silence guarded something sacred.

Waiting out the sun . . .

SNOWSTORM

Only fools go out in weather like this. No one claiming to have a particle of sense would try to drive in the snow. She thinks it's enough that the television and radio have warned all day that a storm is heading north from the lakes. But still, that doesn't keep them from climbing into their cars and taking chances. Disrespect for natural forces, and God, that's what, and for the life of her she can't understand. But a lot of things don't make sense anymore.

She watches hazy globes move slower. These are lights of the city workers on their way back to the village, seventeen miles from Mary's farm. If the lights stop moving there's trouble. They fade, shrink to dots, then disappear completely as the snow and wind increase.

Mary is glad she's not out there. She's sat through many bad nights and she has no doubt she'll survive this one. When she was a girl, no one would try to go out in this weather, but they had more sense back then. Now, people with cars think there's no danger, and in a way that's true, the weather not being as severe as it used to be. Even so, Mary thinks people should know enough to stay indoors when they ought to, that's common sense, but there's a terrible lack of that these days.

Her sight is snowbound by triangles that seep from the corners and cover the window, but she doesn't notice she can't see across the fields to the concession road; she's not watching cars anymore.

She listens to the wind as it races between the house and barn. Her thoughts blow with it over an immense field that expands like a milky sea on which there are no marks or traces of definition. The flight stops as a shadow looms on the white window. The outline, obscure at first, changes to the dark figure of a man whom Mary watches with little more than idle curiosity. He stalks up and down rows of desks, swinging a pointer like a cane, stopping periodically to bounce the rubber tip off the floor. It's her primary teacher— Windbag he was nicknamed because of the way he whistled, not clear or sharp, but tuneless, the sound of air rushing through pursed lips, like the sound of the wind. When the noise stopped, everyone tensed, waiting for the smack of his pointer as he brought it down on a desk. He always came from behind, taking his victim by surprise. When the weather blew up, the students would say Old Windbag was on the loose. Mary's not surprised to see him tonight. She hears the crack of his pointer; it's enough to raise the dead.

The back door slams—Chesley come in from milking. She shouts at him to leave his boots by the door, on the newspaper, because the floor's been mopped today. He has to be told every night, in the exact words, always at the same time, after milking. Otherwise Mary knew he'd forget; that's his nature. She's long since used to his habits. She tells him Windbag's out tonight.

She outgrew her fear of Windbag after the winter of the blizzards. There were many nights like this, she recalls as she stares at the blank window. The night she spent in the attic was the worst. She watched like a sentry by the window, but it was impossible to see even to the closest house a half mile away. She'd been told, gently at first, to go to bed, and they'd insisted when she refused. Bed was the best place to be on such a night. That wasn't the real reason they wanted her to leave: it was so they could have adult talk. She disliked being treated as a child.

Upstairs, she knelt on the drafty hardwood and listened through the iron grill overlooking the kitchen. She saw the top of Uncle Albert's head, a pink, shining globe, the quick black flicks of her mother's shoes as she paced the room, and she heard her Aunt Eva's voice, soft and consoling. But she could not hear much of the conversation except the occasional lament from her mother about how they were all so helpless. They agreed the hardest part of the situation was being trapped inside. The hall was cold and airy, the wind slipping in through cracks in the window putty, and Mary, though she wasn't ready to go to bed, didn't want to stay in the chilly hall. She wanted to hide, to become a victim of the storm, to share in some of the adults' excitement. That's why she took her place by the window in the attic, under the ancient buffalo hide, where no one could find her, and where she could watch for a black figure to split through the white. But she couldn't see anything; the snow was blinding.

Mary thought she'd be dealt with severely when she was found the next morning. She felt guilt when her mother didn't scold her, knowing then that her father hadn't come home. He'd been found early that morning when the storm broke, as stiff and still as a stone carving, only a hundred yards from the house, perished in pure white.

While asleep under the buffalo hide, she had a dream she would never forget, a prophecy of her father's death. Fields of white stretched in all directions. There were no hills, nothing but bland white and one huge black tree. She was flying to the tree, carried in the beak of a snowbird twice her size in body and with an immense wing span. The two, propelled across the grey sky to the tree by a few powerful strokes. At the base of the tree was a hole with a depth of twenty feet, a width of one hundred feet, and walls and floor lined with snow. Inside the crater, a trapped horse pulling a riderless sleigh trotted around in circles, moving always in the same direction and at the same speed.

It snowed on the day of his funeral. The coffin was drawn to the graveside by a sled, followed by others containing the hunched black bodies of mourners. The procession wound its way to the graveside, an unbroken column, silently sliding over snow, its movement like a snake. Mary stood between two black coats, peering from between at the hole that was filling with snow and at the blurred vision of the minister whose white cape flapped like wings.

She can't remember if it was the wind or the mourners moaning, but there was a sound at the graveside that could have been either. The sound the wind makes tonight.

She calls out to Chesley who'd be sitting in his rocker by the kitchen window, reading this morning's paper. This night is similar to the night he was born; often she reminds him of that night. He arrived in the world during the second storm of the winter, as severe as the first. A midwife couldn't get through to assist her mother in delivery; it was lucky Aunt Eva was there. The wind blew up unexpectedly and Mary's mother went into labor, one month before her time.

The wind increased with her mother's pain. Deep, involuntary groans sounded through the house, mixing with the wind; sometimes it was the single voice of the wind. The chorus continued throughout the night, building until the first screams from a newborn were heard. The wind ebbed and by morning the storm had passed and the house stood silent, the sounds of the outside gone with the coming of light.

He certainly chose a fine time to make an appearance in the world, she reminds him. An impatient and stubborn man, until this day he has to do a thing when he makes up his mind to do it, even if it means being born a month early. He was a tough winter child; he's always been a tough man, though she never tells him that. Even tonight he'd been out in the storm—nothing could keep him from milking the herd and bedding them down for the night. Luckily, he has come to the house before the storm gets worse.

The window vibrates as the wind tries to force a way in. Mary expects the glass to give way any moment. She calls to Chesley that it will break and shouldn't if it was built like they used to be, but nowadays things are made to break easily so people spend more money replacing them.

Heavy thuds sound on the stairs leading to the bedrooms. Chesley's going to bed earlier than usual, but she can't blame him on such a night. He doesn't answer or pay attention when she calls goodnight to him.

There were times in his life when he'd have been better off paying attention to what she said. She's older than he is, he resents being younger, that's why he ignores her.

He shouldn't have ignored her the night he took Elsie, his first date, to the Moose Lodge Christmas dance. Such a fuss over a dance she'd never seen. He hitched up the mare two hours before going down to Concession Four to pick her up. After dinner, while he was getting ready, it came over the wireless that the first snowstorm of the season would hit that night. It would've been wiser for Chesley to stay home and take Elsie to the next dance, but he wouldn't hear of it. If the weather got bad he'd leave the dance early, that's what he said. He refused to take the buffalo hide because Elsie wouldn't want that smelly thing near her dress. It started to snow around nine and by eleven it was impossible to see two feet ahead. Mary and her mother waited up for Chesley until he arrived home at three in the morning. What a sight—he was as blue as his coat, his brows and hair clogged with ice, even the tiny hairs from his nostrils dripped with icy fangs. They sat up all night rubbing his hands in snow to take the sting out of the frostbite. Rarely did they talk about that night, which still pained Chesley. He felt responsible for Elsie's frost-bitten feet, which, it was said, could have been a cause of her death some years later.

Mary looks at her legs, swollen stout by poor circulation. A disease of the aged, said to affect the mind and body. But what do doctors know about old age, she asks herself. She thinks of her doctor, his young face, his detailed and patient explanations, which she ignores, for prescribing certain drugs. He's a fool to think there's a cure for old age. He tells her to exercise, to walk, that will help her blood circulate so that her body and mind won't cease. But it's difficult to move even from her chair to the stairs to warn Chesley that the window is going to blow in any moment.

Thousands of glass pieces spray through the room, a shower of diamonds. In the center of the confusion she waves her arms, a maestro conducting a runaway orchestra; she grabs at flying objects and pulls at her dress, which is hoisted to her waist. Pins are plucked from white locks, releasing them for a wind dance as snow settles in her hair, highlighting its color. She'll stop this mischief! She clutches the curtains that flap like unfurled sails, but they tear from her hands, ineffective barriers against snow and wind. Vandals sweep through the room, everywhere at once, scattering white evidence, pitching aside objects not fastened. Her mother's portrait swings on the wall as if she tries to climb out of her death; her father's is knocked face down in the snow. A mirror slides down the wall, resting on the snowy surface like an icy pool. Porcelain flowers leap from a table, sprouting like crocuses in white spring. Snowbirds flock around her head, the crackling of their paper wings sounding in her ears. She screams at them to go, for everything to go, these unwanted intruders, but the room continues to pitch in turmoil.

She fights her way to the door, struggling for sight and balance, and seals the room. Chesley will have to get up. He can't sleep while she is kept awake to listen and watch while the storm bites pieces from their house.

Her old legs protest at the strain of climbing the stairs. Why doesn't he answer her? She knows he can hear her, he's just being difficult, stubborn as usual. The hall is chilly. Air gushes from Chesley's room when she pushes open the door. He's in the bathroom, his bed is still made, but the bathroom door is open. He's not there. So he can't sleep after all, but who could on a night like this? He'll be stoking the woodstove.

By the kitchen window, Chesley's chair playfully rocks. She looks out the back door and notices his boots are missing from the newspaper. He's gone to check the cattle, to make sure they're not restless. Silly old fool going out on a night like this. She'll have to go and tell him to come back to the house, and to get the woodstove going since the house is filling with snow, and before this night is over the power will be off. It was safer when coal oil lamps were used and no one relied on power, but people today are soft.

Snow inches across the kitchen floor, stealing in through a crack made by a flying branch in the kitchen window. It's getting as bad inside as out, she thinks, as she throws on her barn coat.

She pushes against the door but the wind jams it tightly shut. When it finally gives enough for her to squeeze out, it's nearly snatched from its hinges as it swings open, smashing against the house. Her hands feel for the rails—she always uses them to ease her down the steps, but tonight she clings to them so she won't be blown off balance. Already she is snow-coated; her hat lifts and tumbles into the night. She'll find it in the morning.

It's milder now, the snow mixed with freezing rain, and when she leaves the step she is pushed along the crusty surface like a music box ballerina. She does an ice dance, feet shuffling, arms swinging, in an attempt to regain her balance, but she goes down on her belly, sliding like a seal on ice. Her breath is knocked from her; she pants. The rain and snow sting her skin, her eyes are slits, deformed by the mixture pecking at her. She buries her face in her arm. She'll wait a few moments before getting up. It's bitterly cold; she should have worn her scarf. Chesley will be sure to tell her. Standing again, without balance on the smooth surface of the snow, she brings her foot down hard on the crust to make two holes to stand in. Now she is secure, but she gets only three or four feet before she is knocked onto her back.

She's as helpless as an overturned turtle until, with some effort, she flips onto her belly, burying her face in the snow. There's no air, the wind sucks it from her; she's a seal too long underwater. Old Windbag is certainly out tonight. She's not afraid of him, she's as powerful as he is, and stronger. She feels warmer. She thinks what damn foolishness this is. Chesley will have to stay in the barn; she calls to him over the wind, and she supposes she'll have to wait up for him with her mother. What would Elsie's folks think?

The freezing rain has stopped; it's snowing again. Her father's sled will have an easier time getting home, the mare won't slide. She'll rest for a while before going back down to her bedroom. Where is her room? Never mind—she'll get back on her feet as soon as she recovers her breath; it's impossible to get lost in your own yard. She looks for the porch light; she must have forgotten to turn it on. All she sees is a thick wall of white. Again she is faced with it, the shield separating her father from his family and life from death. Chesley's fingers will be frostbitten tonight, she'll have to rub them. And Elsie's feet—she wonders about them. Her father and brother are foolish to stay out in this weather, but she'll wait for them here, in secrecy, by the attic window. Something nudges her elbow. Her mittened hand reaches out and touches the nose of a horse. Her father is home, the mare is unhitched from the sleigh, turned out to graze and wander in snowy fields. She is getting tired, her eyes heavy and strained from watching for a break in the white, watching for the bent figures of horse and man.

Snow fills in around Mary, covering her hunched body to the shoulders. She is encased in a white shroud. As she waits, she wonders why they wouldn't let her stay up and wait with them. They treat her as a child but she is old for her years. She pulls the buffalo hide around her so that she is completely covered and feels its warmth. Her eyes close. She no longer worries about her father or Chesley; she drifts with the fading sound of a snowbird's wings beating against the air as it passes far overhead.

The snowmobile people are the only ones able to get out the day after the storm, and they discover that Mary is missing. The old people, they all agree, could not survive in such a storm; it would be certain death if Mary had ventured out. Inside they find the house gutted by wind and snow, Mary's bed still made. Outside, ten feet from the back porch, crouched in a snowy tomb, they find Mary's frozen body.

The stubborn old lady, they decided, must have tried to do the milking. She couldn't be persuaded to give up doing the chores even though they were far too much for her to do. It had been different when Chesley was still alive, but after he died everyone knew it was too much for the old woman. But she wouldn't hire a hand. She said she wouldn't need one.

LITTLE OLD BABY

Ruby slumped in her rocking chair, lifted her legs to see if they looked any different. No, but how they ached. What a night she'd put in, didn't get home until after midnight. To top it all off, yesterday afternoon in the midst of the bedpan shuffle, Warren had phoned to say he and Jill would be coming from Toronto and bringing their daughter, Kyla, and her boyfriend. He asked if she'd mind terribly if they brought Noble, the dog, too. Well yes, quite frankly, she did mind. She didn't want that walking haystack drooling all over her patient. It would upset Lehla, who wouldn't let on at the time, but would take it out on Ruby after they'd gone. She'd tried to explain this to Warren. He couldn't seem to understand that his little old mommy had had two strokes and now lived in a different world.

"We'll be there around two tomorrow," he'd said. "I guess we'll leave the dog at home."

She had to keep her cool with Lehla's family. She was no spring chicken; she didn't know what she'd do if she lost this job. But taking care of Lehla was so much easier when everyone from Lehla's old life, before her strokes, stayed away. Visitors had a turbulent effect on her, like a lake in a storm. At first, water still as glass, clear enough you can see your feet on the rippled bottom. Then the waves roll in, stir up the sand, muddy the water. An undertow pulls you out, out, out. Precisely what happened to Lehla. When someone popped up, a confusion of memory swept over her and she struggled to grip the tiniest fragment of reality. It took everything Ruby had to restore her sense of calm. I am her life preserver, Ruby thought, chuckling. I don't even know how to swim.

She'd hinted broadly to Warren on the phone that it might not be the best time to come, going over the particulars of Lehla's bowels in an attempt to make him understand. But he and Jill were leaving for a Caribbean cruise in a couple of days and this was their only chance for a visit before going.

Yesterday she'd had to give Lehla a Fleet enema. No wonder Ruby's legs ached. All day long she'd shuffled bedpan after bedpan back and forth from Lehla's bedroom to the bathroom. Hard to believe that one little old lady could have so much in her. Oh, who was she trying to kid? Ruby had seen it all before with her little old ladies, her private patients over the last thirty years. She led them by the hand to this life's exit, then let go, told them to go on without her, she'd follow shortly. Don't be afraid, she reassured them, waving them on; it is beautiful. She couldn't tell Warren. He'd hired her as a nurse; he might get the wrong idea if she told him that helping people to die, without fear, was a big part of her job.

Why did the family have to come today? Tonight was her big night out with her granddaughter, their quality time. They always went together to the special matches, ever since Crystal hooked her on the sport a few years ago. They had front-row tickets for the Riot Ruckus, and her favorite wrestler Virus was challenging Sin Bad, and the winner of that match would go on to play another favorite of hers, Hell's Angel. Crystal would pick her up at Lehla's precisely at eight, and she needed to turn the reins of Lehla's care over quickly to Joan, the overnight girl. If they were too late, they wouldn't find close parking, would end up parking way out in the boonies. She sure didn't want to walk far tonight. Not with her legs feeling like this.

Ruby stood in front of the big picture window, her hands on her hips, and watched the green Jaguar slide up under the maple tree like a long sleek shark. She'd just managed to settle Lehla, after a battle to get her to take a nap.

She had herself to blame, letting the news slip last night. You need your beauty sleep, she'd said as she and Joan were putting Lehla to bed, because Warren and his family are coming. That did it! Lehla got it in her head that she needed to cook a turkey, and Joan went along with the cockeyed notion. She even encouraged it! In front of Ruby, Joan told Lehla that the next morning Ruby would help her dress the turkey and stick it in the oven.

"Why did you say that?" Ruby whispered in the hall outside Lehla's bedroom. "It gets her all worked up. Try steering her away from her fantasies. Distract her." What was the use? Joan was young, still learning, and desperate to settle Lehla so she wouldn't be up all night.

"What are you saying out there?" Lehla warbled from her bed. "I know you're talking about me." Her hearing not in the least impaired.

"We thought you were sleeping," Ruby called back.

Today when Ruby came to work, Lehla was still going on about the damn turkey as she struggled to get off the couch. "I've got to get the turkey on!"

She couldn't walk, but she sure could roll, though the chair and ottoman they pushed alongside for a barrier prevented her from going anywhere. "Get this crap out of my way," Lehla said, her eyes bugging out of her head.

Ruby sent Joan home and got working on the turkey problem.

"Let's get the turkey in the oven." Lehla had her teeth out; her words smeared together thick as peanut butter.

"What on earth would you want to have turkey for? You've got to eat it for days, and days and days. After a while you start looking like one." Lehla laughed along with Ruby, then got right back to the nonsense again.

"The family's coming. I've got to get the turkey on."

Damn her big mouth for letting the secret of Warren's visit slip—she couldn't blame it on Joan. Another rule with Lehla: don't discuss the future; it triggered a need to plan and that made her crazy; she couldn't organize the next sixty seconds, never mind a dinner party.

"Do you remember when we had to clean our own turkeys? Dip the whole works into a big tub of scalding hot water to pluck the feathers off." Ruby rerouted Lehla back to her childhood, a safe territory, a time of happy dependence.

"Oh, I hated that job."

"And the dressing. It took hours to bake the bread. Remember chucking wood in the stove?"

"Oh yes." Lehla closed her eyes and let her head relax into the pillow. "Grandma's stuffing the bird. I'm holding the twine for her. She says she's going to tie up my finger and bake it, too. That's not a very nice thing to say. Grandpa's sharpening the carving knife. He's going to give me the wing . . ." Her voice trailed off and in seconds she started snoring lightly.

Ruby waited fifteen minutes, then tiptoed towards the door. "We'd better get that turkey on," Lehla called out. "Grandma's coming, too, and she doesn't like to be kept waiting."

For two more hours the argument spun round and round, until Ruby actually felt dizzy. Somehow Lehla detoured off turkey and on to the Royal Doulton dishes, insisting that all her twelve place settings had been stolen. "Get the phone," she shouted. "I'm calling the police."

Lehla went on for so long about the Royal Doulton that Ruby found it easier to drag it all out into the family room than to argue with her. "See," she pointed at the dinner plates, the bread and butter plates, the dessert plates, the bowls, the fruit nappies, the cups and saucers, arranged in piles on the floor. "Twelve of each. Let's count them. One, two, three . . ." When she finished, she asked, "Do you believe me now?"

Lehla leaned back on her pillow, closed her eyes, and said, "I don't know who's crazier, you or me. I wouldn't drag all those dishes out for anyone." Then she fell promptly asleep.

"Why you old . . ." Ruby collapsed into a chair, started to laugh. Duped again. Lehla's idea of fun meant watching Ruby jump to her ridiculous demands. A way of being in charge, the superior one. "God have pity on your soul, old woman." Lehla's face folded softly with sleep.

Now the family had arrived. Well, they'd better not get her going again. She met them at the door with her finger pressed to her lips, signalling for them to keep quiet.

"Is she sick?" Warren whispered huskily and put a large pot of flowers on the kitchen table. Lehla wouldn't like them; she said mums made her nose run, made her think of funerals.

"Did she have a turn?" Jill asked.

"At what?" Ruby looked at her, a bit confused. "Oh, at dying you mean? No. She's just being her usual, miserable self. I don't think her bowels are clear yet."

"Let's not get into the bowel thing again," Warren said, slipping his leather jacket over the back of a chair and peeking around the corner at his mother.

True, she'd indulged herself on the phone by going into a fair amount of description about yesterday's Fleet enema event. It was his mother's bum; no one else gave a damn about it.

Kyla came through the back door, followed by a tall thin guy as hairless as a bowling ball, her flat voice registering boredom. "Hi." She shook her long, rippling hair back off her face. A deep black streak ran all down the front, looked like a giant dribble of tar against the blonde. "You've met Dirk, haven't you?"

Ruby nodded. "How many earrings you got, for heaven's sake?" Sometimes words just flew out of her mouth, all greased up, slick as buttered noodles.

"Eight. Each ear," he said, his head shining under the kitchen lights.

Not that she had anything against bald heads and earrings. Her late husband was bald by the time he was thirty. She could still see him in his casket, not quite the globe Dirk here was, and not that many years older, either.

Ruby sat in the rocking chair in the corner of the kitchen, leaned on her elbow, and eyeballed the four of them seated around the table. "Well, here we all are. The star of the show can't be bothered with any of us." Typical Lehla. Ornery to the bone. "What would we all like to do now?" She'd warned them about coming today.

"Why don't we have some tea?" Jill suggested.

Jill's hair looked freshly done, probably for the cruise. Evenly blonde, no sign of roots, turned under just a little at the chin. Must have cost a bundle. She'd look better with a little more meat on her bones. Ruby didn't have to worry about that.

Ruby looked at Jill. Jill looked at Ruby. Oh, now she got it; Jill wanted her to make the tea. She was a registered nurse, here to take care of the patient and not to serve tea to the guests, and since it was Jill's idea, let her carry on. "Tea would be lovely," Ruby said, resting her hands across her ample stomach and settling back in her rocking chair. "You might find some cookies in the cupboard. Take a look. Everything gets shoved in any old which way around here."

Warren drummed his fingers on the table while Jill prepared refreshments.

"Well," Ruby said, as they settled in with their tea and biscuits. "Usually, this time of day, Lehla and I would be fighting about something. This is certainly nicer than yesterday."

"Spare us the details." Warren looked exasperated. Today was obviously not going according to his plan. She'd warned him, don't impose your world on Lehla; she'd moved away, left no forwarding address.

They munched and sipped their way through silence, except Dirk, who seemed to be playing the drums on the table, weaving his head around to some music playing in his head.

Ruby had no intention of carrying the conversation. They'd decided to come here. Let them talk.

"Everything going all right, is it?" Warren finally asked.

"Depends what you mean by everything." A little warning bell tingled in Ruby's head, told her to watch her mouth, hold back on those greasy words. Chitchat didn't interest her. Neither did being sociable. Why should it? They didn't know each other. Ruby had nothing to prove. For Lehla's sake she did the best job she could and that's all there was to it.

"Is everything going okay with my mother? Her care. That kind of thing."

"Well now, let me think about that." Ruby put her head back and started to laugh, a big long howling gut-felt roll of laughter she capped by putting her hand over her mouth. "You don't want the details, do you? No bowels. Bowels are definitely out." Now a siren screamed in her head. Ruby, Ruby, get a hold of your tongue. "Bowels took up an awful lot of yesterday." She couldn't stop laughing.

Kyla and Dirk snickered. Jill frowned. Warren fidgeted. "I thought I made it clear about that," he said.

The whole thing—and by that she meant life—seemed like one big joke. The older she got, the funnier it got. Lehla made about as much sense as anyone, when it came right down to it. "I'm sorry," she managed to squeeze out between new rounds of laughter. "I'm just remembering what your mother had me doing before you came," she lied. "I'll be okay in a minute." She gave them the whole blooming story about the Royal Doulton, finished by expressing her most sincere wishes that they blow up all the damn dishes.

"They're Royal Doulton!" Jill gasped. "They're very expensive. They're an heirloom."

"I don't care if they're pure gold and the Queen herself ate off them," Ruby said. "Couldn't you take them with you?" She rubbed her forehead. How could she make them understand? "They're just things. Lehla has no use for them. They represent a life she can't have, and somewhere, somehow, in that funny old baked brain of hers, she knows she can't get it back. She may be crazy but she's not stupid. It would be better if all her fancy stuff wasn't around. Do you understand at all what I'm talking about? They're symbols." Around the table all the blank faces seemed to be staring at her, except for Dirk, who must have spotted a fly or something on the ceiling. "They hurt her," her last pitch.

"I can dig it," Dirk said. "Materialism sucks." He pounded on his drums, his head bobbing around.

"It's a side effect of employment," Warren said coldly.

"Well, I'm glad at least one of you understands me," Ruby said, sipping her tea, deciding that from here on, she'd keep her mouth shut. What was the use, anyway? Their ideas about what Lehla's life should be bore no resemblance to anything that took place in this house. Warren's old momma was as bad as they came, one part angel, nine parts devil. Ruby had more angel in her than Lehla had, for heaven sakes. What did that tell you?

"Who the hell's out there?"

Well, speak of the devil. Ruby jumped up, Lehla's voice jolting her into immediate action. "I'll tell you when to come," she told the others.

Ruby changed Lehla's diaper, put on a fresh nighty and house-coat, ran a brush through her white, wavy hair. "Pretty hair." She patted it lightly and watched Lehla beam. Sometimes Lehla fancied herself as the most beautiful creature on earth. Ruby thought so too. "There," she stopped to admire her work. "You look like a queen. Are you ready to receive your guests?"

"Is it my prince?"

"Your prince?" Ruby laughed. "No, it's not your prince."

"Then tell whoever it is to bugger off."

They followed Ruby into the family room, then she took her leave back to the kitchen rocking chair. Lehla didn't like to have her hang-ing around when she had company. Hired help should disappear itself, something she could do quite well, and obligingly. She needed her rest for tonight's Riot Ruckus and the big match between Virus and Sin Bad. What a time she'd have sitting ringside, jumping up and down, hollering her fool head off until she got hoarse, carrying on with all the other idiots who sat up there. Farther back you couldn't see the wrestlers' faces, couldn't tell if their pain was fake or real.

She put her head back and rocked, amused by Lehla's brand of civility she overheard coming from the family room.

"Are you eating well, Mother?"

"No. Food's awful. Half the time it's not cooked. And grey. How would you like to eat grey slop?"

"Ruby says you're doing very well." Jill's voice.

"She says things that aren't true. She's telling you that to get a raise. She's stolen my Royal Doulton dishes."

"We're going on a cruise, Mother. Jill and I." Warren cleverly changing the topic. "Three weeks on the Caribbean. The boat is supposed to be very luxurious. Swimming pool on board. A gym to work out in. A track for jogging. A nightclub. A ballroom for dancing. Huge dining rooms. Gourmet food. A library. Can you imagine that?"

"No, and I don't want to."

"Do you like my hair, Mother? I just had it done for the cruise."

"I thought it was a wig."

Ruby rocked and smiled and thought what a holy terror her star patient could be. They should know better than to come here and tell her about their wonderful life. That only reminded her. Made things worse. Didn't they know that the queen should be going off on a cruise, not stuck there on some silly couch?

When she woke up, she heard the TV. It was almost dark. She hurried into the family room where everyone seemed absorbed in whatever they were watching. Everyone except Lehla. Right away Ruby saw that something was wrong. She touched her lightly, put her face in close until Lehla's eyes found hers and a flicker of relief passed over them. She had been out there alone in the big lake, tossed about in the heavy waves, fighting the undertow. Ruby knelt down beside her and took her hand. They must swim together back to shore and to safety. "How's my little old baby? Are you tired?"

"I'm tired," she said.

"Are you hungry?"

"I'm hungry."

"Are you wet?"

"No."

Ruby knew otherwise. She put a hand on Lehla's head, massaged her hair. "Let's get you all straightened up and rearranged."

"She seemed to be getting a little tired so we put on a movie Dirk brought," Jill said, curled up beside Warren on the love seat. "You were sleeping so nicely we didn't want to wake you."

"I'll pick up Swiss Chalet for dinner," Warren said. "How's that sound?"

"Fine." She caught bits of the movie as she propped Lehla up on her pillows; it looked like the craziest darn thing she'd ever seen. "What on earth are you watching?"

"It's about the end of the world," Lehla said, her eyes closed.

"*Wayne's World*," Dirk said.

"It's hilarious." Kyla's tone registered her usual enthusiasm. "We've seen it like at least a hundred times."

It seemed to take forever for them to get on their way. Ruby kept checking her watch, hoping they'd get the hint; she had so much to do before Crystal arrived. What a night for things to screw up. Lehla had had too much company, had become overstimulated. Her nighty-night pill would have to be increased by half a tab. And why had they gone on for so long about that damn cruise?

"I want you to get my clothes ready," Lehla said, once they'd gone.

"Ready for what?"

"The boat."

"Are you going?"

"Yes. I'm going."

"Well, not tonight. Let's get you ready for bed."

"I want my two favorite sweaters. My blue one. And my other blue one. Bring me my suitcase. It's in the attic."

Ruby pulled a chair up beside the couch to take the weight off her weary legs, looked directly into Lehla's watery green eyes. "Now you listen to me. You know as well as I do you're not going anywhere but to bed."

Lehla closed her eyes to break Ruby's hold. "I'm not worthy," she said.

"What do you mean?"

"We'll be drowned in the flood waters. They'll be saved. On the boat."

"Like Noah, you mean?"

"Yes."

"Now listen here, that's nonsense. There's not going to be a flood. It's not even raining. Look, they're going to get seasick. They'll be stuck with a bunch of people they don't even know for three weeks, with nowhere to go but to their puny little cabins. That doesn't sound like fun to me." Big lie there, Ruby had wanted to go on a cruise all her life. Hard work stretching her imagination to make the whole thing sound like the most awful experience a person could have. "I think being on a tiny little boat with a bunch of crotchety old people who only want to talk about their aches and pains would be dreadful. Wouldn't that be dreadful?" Lehla thought of herself as eternally youthful, certainly not old.

"Yes. Awful."

"The food won't be fresh. Big buffets, a lot of salads sitting a long time in mayonnaise." Lehla hated mayonnaise.

"They'll all get diarrhea," Lehla said, the cruise-bashing thing catching on.

Ruby checked the time. Joan would be here in fifteen minutes, Crystal in half an hour. "You don't want to go on a silly old cruise. You've got far more important things to do."

"I'm not worthy," Lehla said.

"Of course you are."

"They kept telling me I'm not."

"That was the movie, Lehla. Not Warren, not Jill, not Kyla and what's his name."

"Then why can't I go? Why won't you pack my sweaters?"

"Because you need to go to bed." Darn Lehla's family. They should have listened to Ruby.

"I hope the boat sinks."

"That's a terrible thing to say! I'll wash your mouth out with soap, old woman! You don't mean that." Ruby shook her finger at her. "Say you don't mean it."

"I do mean it. If I can't go."

Joan came a little early. As they lifted Lehla into bed on a sheet, they rocked her a few times before plunking her down. "There, see, you're on a cruise," Ruby said.

"I'm not worthy."

Lehla wouldn't allow Joan to stay in her room. "Who's she?" She pointed at her. "I don't like her staring at me. She looks like a witch."

Joan scurried away as if a dog snapped at her heels. Poor thing. Lehla's night girl for over a year, and the old woman could still put the run on her. Lehla's meanness really frosted Ruby sometimes. She tried to explain to Joan how their sweet little old patient had a mean streak in her that you had to resist or she'd gobble you up. Joan said she could never do what Ruby did and tell Lehla to shut her damn nasty mouth. She said it went against all her professional training. Joan's problem was that she was too nice. Too nice for Lehla. Ruby fought Lehla every inch of the way when she had to, and that had gained her Lehla's respect and friendship and, well, throw in trust, too. With Ruby, Lehla had met her match.

"You stay with me tonight," Lehla said.

"Now look. I've got to go. Crystal's come to pick me up and I can't keep her waiting."

She examined Lehla's twisted body, the eroded terrain of bones and wrinkles. Behold the work of a lifetime, she thought, as her eyes rested on the old woman's face. Lehla had a way of looking at her sometimes, a look of innocence, bewilderment, and complete vulnerability; it got to Ruby every time. A crazy thing about being Lehla's nurse: when she wasn't fighting with her, she was protecting her, mostly from herself. She ran her hand over Lehla's forehead; she felt nice, just right, not chilled or too warm. "Who's my baby?"

"I am." Her eyes swam around the room, then hooked into the safety of Ruby's.

"You've had a big day." She rubbed warmth into Lehla's hand. "Now listen. I'm going. You're going to be just fine."

A tornado spun out of the black sky, twisted down and struck the lake. Huge waves spilled over Lehla and she began to drown. "You can't go. You can't go," she wailed, her face collapsing like a plastic bag, the air sucked out of it.

It took several minutes for Ruby to calm her. The only Riot

Ruckus she'd see tonight would be the one right here. Lehla had her up against the ropes. "I'll be right back. No more screaming. You hear?"

"Yes," a small voice answered. "Ruby?"

"Now what is it?" She wanted to send Crystal along. No point in her missing everything.

"I'm scared."

"Scared? Of what?"

"I don't know. I've got something in me."

"Yes, you most certainly do," Ruby laughed. "Dinner. Swiss Chalet. You ate a pig's portion."

Ruby took her time tucking Lehla in. She rubbed her knees with mentholated ointment, sprinkled baby powder on her back and tummy, massaged her feet with cream. She brushed her hair, fluffed it out around her head, washed her face with a steamy cloth. "There," she said when she finished, smoothing over the blankets. "Let's have some stories." She pulled a chair up close so Lehla could find her eyes if she got lost again. "You start," she told Lehla. "Tell me about working in your father's store when you were a little girl. Tell me about the old timers who spit their tobacco juice on the pot-belly stove."

Didn't that get a charge out of Lehla. Away she went, back to the early 1900s, back to the safest place for her to be right now, in her deep past, far, far away from all of this, a life that had no future.

Lehla rambled for another hour until, out of exhaustion, she drifted off to sleep. Ruby slumped down on the couch in the family room, told Joan she'd wait a few minutes before calling a taxi, started watching something on TV, and fell asleep.

Screams woke her up. "God almighty, what's going on?" She pushed herself off the couch and started into Lehla's room, Joan directly behind her.

"What is it?" Ruby took Lehla's wrist, pressed her fingertips into her pulse. Perhaps a little fast, but nothing that would spell real trouble.

"Something's inside me," Lehla choked out through a wheezy thickness.

"What do you mean?"

"Something's holding me down, sitting on top of me."

"There's nothing on top of you but your covers."

"It's inside on top of me."

"Oh. What could it be?" Lehla's forehead felt sticky with perspiration; she seemed to have difficulty breathing. "Do you have pain in your chest?"

"No, just weight. Something's sitting on my chest."

"I can't see anything."

"It's the devil. The devil got inside the house and now it's inside me."

Was anything about this attack physical or could it be another one of Lehla's notions? Severe anxiety could change your breathing and your heart rate. "How did the devil get inside you?"

"That bald person brought it into the house. It came out through the TV."

"Oh, I see. Was the devil wearing a baseball cap by any chance?"

"Yes."

Damn movie! The next time they tried anything like that she'd give them what for. Couldn't they have brought *Bambi* or *Snow White* or an old Cary Grant movie, something more suitable for a mixed-up little old lady instead of that piece of utter nonsense? Now look. They'd frightened her half to death.

"You've got to get the devil out of me. I can't breathe."

Left to Lehla's considerable imagination, this spell could bring on another stroke. Ruby had to think quick, not easy at this hour. "What do you think would work?" she asked.

"Water." Then she pointed at Joan, standing back behind Ruby, and shouted, "And get her out of here!"

She told Joan to get as many basins as she could find and fill them with hot, hot water. "And lots of towels, too. Little ones," she called out. "Okay," she turned to Lehla. "Now look. I'm going to get that devil out of you once and for all. He, she, it will never come back. Do you hear?"

"Yes. That would be good."

Ruby dipped towels in the basins of hot water that Joan had fetched, squeezed out the excess, and draped them over Lehla's feet. "How's that feel?"

"Good."

"Do you feel your feet getting lighter?"

"Yes."

"That's the devil leaving." Ruby had to think about what to say as she performed her first exorcism. She thought the message should have some spiritual content. "Out, devil. Come on in, God. Feel that Lehla? Your feet are filling with beautiful, happy thoughts."

"I don't think through my feet."

Ruby laughed. "Now look you, it's a wonder I'm making any sense at all. It's 3:30 a.m. Wiggle your toes." Lehla wiggled them. "See, the devil has definitely gone from there. I'll work all the way up your body until it feels light and devil-free." Working with steamy water had made her hot; she went over to the window.

"What are you doing?"

"Opening the window. To get the devil out of here."

She gave Lehla's twig-thin legs a good long rub, all the time repeating her ridiculous chant, "Out, devil, out," tossing in the odd lighthearted comment, "Get the hell out of here so I can go home to bed," to raise a laugh out of Lehla, who, at times, appeared to be enjoying herself enormously. Ruby wondered if she'd been duped once again by the old con.

She worked a long time on Lehla's chest. "Out with you, nasty devil," she said, applying pressure on the hot towels. "And don't come back. You stay away from my baby." Lehla smiled; her breathing lightened. Ruby stepped up her incantations. "That's it, go on. Get out of here. Prey upon the strong, you cowardly thing. Pick worthy opponents, not the helpless."

"I'm not helpless."

"I mean go find someone else." Lehla and her darned pride. "You've got no business here." She paused, listened to Lehla's breathing. It sounded normal. "It's gone."

"No it isn't. It's still in my chest."

Ruby sighed. She could barely move, she felt so weary. "I'll get more hot water and towels. Don't you worry, we've just about drowned it."

"Drowning," Lehla said. "Drowning."

Ruby brought back a basin full of the hottest water she could draw from the tap. "Feel that?" She held the steaming cloth close to Lehla's face. She had an idea. "What about drowning, Lehla? Are you drowning?"

"No. Someone else."

"Who?"

"Lots of people. There's dancing and singing and then there's water rushing in."

"Are the people on the boat?"

Lehla's breath was snatched away as if by a strong gust of wind.

Ruby pressed her palms against the curve of Lehla's ribs. "Feel this. The devil's drowning. How dare it come in your home, through that dreadful movie, take hold of your tongue and make you say things you'd never say." She hoped Lehla would go for this. "It is your most sincere wish that Warren and Jill have a wonderful cruise. You're glad they're going, and so am I." How true. They couldn't come back for a while and screw things up. "We wish them bon voyage and safe journey. There." She pulled her hands away from Lehla's chest. "You feel that? The devil is gone."

"Are you sure?"

"Oh yes. Look, the curtains are fluttering. The devil's leaving; the angels are coming in. They're here. Smell the air. It's sweet." Ruby walked over to the window and closed it; it was bloody freezing; it didn't help that she was wet from head to toe. "Now they'll stay here." She spread both hands out flat across Lehla's chest, the ripple of her ribs like the bars of sand on a lake bottom, and pushed down lightly. "Feel that?"

"Yes."

"Do you know what it is?"

"No."

"Angels. Inside you." Her fingers fluttered against Lehla's chest. "They're dancing. Angels do not fear to tread where the devil has once lurked." Close enough. Where'd she ever pick up that gem? "You're brimming with angels, Lehla. They're everywhere inside you, in your toes, in your nose, in your head. Everywhere. Flitting around like butterflies. Now, breathe deeply." Lehla took several breaths.

Lehla almost asleep now.

It was all Ruby could do to keep her eyes open. Morning light touched the window. "Keep breathing," she whispered. "How does that feel?"

"Excellent. Not party time." Shortly, she fell into a deep, untroubled sleep.

Ruby looked at her, smiled, and thought, you silly old bugger.

Nothing about her was simple or straightforward. Most people would simply retract a regrettable statement, apologize, admit that it had been uttered in a fit of temper, a moment of wrongness. Not Lehla. Nothing short of an exorcism would rid her of her guilt. The devil indeed! Or the whole thing could have been playacting. Her idea of fun.

Somehow she didn't think so. Not this time.

She put her head down on the bed and looked up at Lehla's face. So still, so soundly asleep she could pass for dead. She hoped that when the end finally came she would look the way she did right now. Pure calm, her belly stuffed with dancing angels.

Ruby sat up, pushed her hair back from her forehead. Joan's shift had almost finished. Not much point going home; she'd only have to turn around and come back again. She wondered who won the Riot Ruckus tonight, Virus or Sin Bad. Who had gone on to wrestle Hell's Angel?

ALL OF ME

She's left it too long. Milly doesn't know why she leaves things until the last minute. She's given up on the idea she'll ever change. It isn't all her fault. Every time she thinks to go shopping for a dress, something gets in the way. The car called it quits, one of the kids needed the money she was going to spend, all the comings and goings at the house, the help she's giving Sheila with the wedding, and at her age with her health issues, well, she only has so much energy. But never mind all that. She's here now, and Brittany, a cute little thing—oh, she wishes Ben could meet her, what a fine match they would be—is doing her best to give great service.

"I'll keep bringing you all the dresses that look right for a wedding and you can try them on, even if it's something you think you'd never wear. Why not? Now that you're here. You might just surprise yourself, you know. You don't know until you try."

Brittany evidently formed a plan of action when she heard Milly's request for a dress to wear to a friend's wedding. She got right to the task when Milly told her she was in a bit of a rush, as usual.

So sincere, so attentive, how could Milly say no to trying on everything? And just like her kids, Brittany has a little touch of she-knows-what's-best. They all know what's best when they're twenty-something.

Milly won't let Brittany into the fitting room. She is wearing her best underwear, but Brittany might be shocked by the safety pin she uses to hold her panties up, though the lace is still pretty; it's just the elastic in the waistband that's shot. Like her, stretched thin, exasperated. Her bra, well, it's her only comfortable one, and the only one that will take care of the girls, and the elastic at the back so frayed it looks like a wire-haired terrier with a fur condition. She won't be buying a new one anytime soon. A double G cup costs the earth, never mind where do you even find one?

Milly examines the layers of dresses hanging from the hooks. She'll start with the red one.

"Everything fitting okay?" Brittany calls from outside the change-room.

"Just fine." Milly wonders how she'll manage to squeeze into it, it has such a short zipper.

"No problems?"

"No problems."

Her wedding dress was red, a polyester fabric that crumpled up into nothing, with a rhinestone pin at the base of her cleavage. Diamonds to her. With her dark hair, the large fake pin, her shapely shape, Nick called her my Liz after Elizabeth Taylor, his favorite movie star.

They got married at Christmas, another reason for the red dress. Nick bought a new suit; new to him. He bought it at the Sally Ann. They thought they looked so cool in their wedding clothes that cost all of $50. Makes her laugh thinking about it. He in his too-large old-man-piss-pants suit—at least wool was appropriate for the time of year—and she in her Kmart dress, all of $24, and even then, she thought it too expensive. And after the ten-minute ceremony witnessed by two clerks, total strangers, they went for surf and turf at the Steer and Stein and got a booth at the back in the corner. To celebrate the news of their marriage, the waitress took flowers from another table and plunked them into their vase, then went to talk to the man playing piano. After they finished their dinners, still wearing their lobster bibs, the piano player announced their special occasion to the few other diners and insisted they dance. The only two on the dance floor, the disco ball sparkling overhead. He had a special song for them. What's the name of the song? It's going to drive her nuts; it's on the tip of her tongue. Oh, she hates that when she can't remember, and it was one of her favorites, too. Never mind, it'll come, eventually.

They danced the rest of the evening. Happy. In love.

Milly unzips the red dress, hoists it above her head, feels the ache in her arms and shoulders as she tries to wriggle into it.

Nick, tall, thick-chested, lots of curly black hair, big rough hands from working outside, a man's man, a glint of playfulness in his eyes, and such a capacity for fun in those days. He'd up and do anything on the spur of the moment, and Milly willing to go right along with him. He got them onto a logging truck that took them into the interior of B.C., where they ended up living for six months in a hippie commune; living off the land, they called it then. The land and the odd welfare check. They thought they lived for free. She knows better now. Nothing comes for free. Or the fishing boat, when he found temporary jobs during a herring run. She's never been sicker in her life. High swells, and though she didn't know it yet, the swell in her belly—still too early to know it was two. Spontaneous. Defines Nick to this very day.

The red dress won't do. Too clingy. Now there's a laugh. Clingy? She can't get it past her boobs. It might have fit a number of sizes ago. "I think I'm going to need a bigger size," she calls to Brittany. She honestly thought she was a sixteen, but now probably an eighteen. Maybe bigger?

"I've got something in a blue floral," Brittany calls from the other side of the door. "I think it would be lovely with your coloring. It's a cute dress."

Her coloring? What would that be? Tired blue, verging on grey? She's no beauty, not anymore. She's three times the person she was when she and Nick hooked up. Anyway, she isn't one for florals—they could either be too matronly or too girly. When was the last time she wore anything that was cute?

"Okay, I'll give it a try."

Brittany's doing her best. It's late on a Saturday afternoon, and she must have sore feet by now, this place being as busy as it is. She's so sincere and trying so hard; Milly will play along.

The blue floral sails over the top of the dressing room door. "There you go."

Ben looked more than a little blue this morning. He came in early, on his way to work, traipsing down the hall in his heavy boots, so it woke her up. He could only manage to get part of the day off.

She shouted from her bed upstairs. "Take off those boots. I just did the floors yesterday."

"I've got a Tim's coffee for you. What the hell! Can't I even do you a favor without you giving me shit?"

She looked at her watch. 6:45. So much for sleeping in. She heard Thunder on the stairs. Next thing she knew, Thunder was straddling her, running his big sloppy tongue over her face. She turned her head from side to side to avoid the dog kisses, but it was no use. Finally, she rubbed him behind the ears and gave in, her face wet with all the licks. "You big clumsy goof of a mutt."

Ben stood in the doorway smiling, holding two large double-doubles. His face looked like it had been put through a meat grinder, all scratched and bruised and puffy.

"What happened to you?"

"Someone jumped me on the way home from the bar last night."

"How drunk were you?"

"Not at all. He jumped me from behind."

"Did you say something to provoke him?"

"What the hell. Why do you always think it's my fault?"

"You need stitches."

"I'm okay. I washed the cut and put Polysporin on it."

"I can just imagine how this will look in Allison's wedding pictures." Just once, wouldn't it be nice to wake up with nothing but a normal day ahead? Without some kind of catastrophe? Sheila, the mother of the bride, will kill him, never mind how Allison, the bride, will feel. The groom won't care, he's so much like Ben. "You've got to learn to control your temper and walk away from these things."

"I haven't got time for your lecture," Ben said. "I'm out of here. I'm leaving Thunder for the day."

She shouted at him, "Get back here! I've got too much to do to take care of the dog. And I need your cell phone in case Sheila has to get in touch with me. I'm still helping her with the wedding."

He tossed his cell phone on the bed. "Don't lose it."

The red dress lies on the floor—she'll hang it up later, once she's tried on a few more outfits. Sure she will, just like the way she cleaned her room yesterday. Sweet, dear Lindsay helped as much as she could. "Mom, have you ever hung up anything in your life?" Lindsay's so efficient; Milly has no idea where she inherited the tidy gene. "Mom, you need to concentrate on one thing at a time." Lindsay sounded like the parent. "You're too easily distracted."

She had every intention of cleaning her room, but then the phone rang, and Mabel needed someone to go to a doctor's appointment with her to hear the results of her biopsy, and that meant a bus ride across town. Mabel couldn't go alone; that's no way to treat a friend. Afterwards, they stopped for a chocolate sundae at We've Got the Scoop, to take some of the sour away with a bit of sweet. She spent the rest of the day with Sheila, helping her decorate the reception hall. And in her room sat the piles of clothes, layer upon layer, settling like sediment, measuring off the phases of her life. And the other piles, mostly the stuff she got at garage sales—jewelry, shoes, purses, all waiting to be sorted. She's disgraceful; she knows it.

"You still good?" Brittany calls.

"It's going to take me at least a half hour to get through all these, dearie," Milly answers. She's already in a sweat and she has many more to go.

Allison's bridesmaids were wearing blue, so she should avoid that color, though no one would confuse her for one of them, that's for sure, since she's about 40 years older and she wishes she was only 40 pounds heavier. It's true, any bit of stress and she heads for the fridge, seeking comfort, can't seem to make herself stop. A person needs treats when stress whooshes through her house every single day like a tornado. If she could go to a spa, where people in white coats and soothing voices would commit themselves to her care, knead her knotted muscles, offer sympathy for all she must contend with, prepare healthy meals for her every day, she could stop eating. She'd become slim.

What will Thunder have done to her house? He's better than he was, but if he's left too long he starts chewing. He ate two legs off the coffee table as easily as if they were pretzels, and now she uses bricks to hold it up. A few days later, he ate the living room curtains—just the bottoms. They still provide privacy and keep the light out on days she doesn't want anything to do with the outside world, when it's all she can do to get out of bed, lie on the couch, and watch TV. And then there's the pooping. She shouldn't stay too late tonight at the wedding, though she promised Sheila she'd help with the buffet, and that meant the cleanup after. Anything to help her friend save money. Sheila has about as much of it as she has—next to nothing. But it should be a nice wedding. The reception room looked lovely, even romantic, with white streamers, paper wedding bells, and bows on all the chairs.

"The blue dress makes me look old," Milly calls to Brittany.

"Well, we definitely can't have that."

"I am old. Not much I can do about it."

"No, you are not," Brittany's voice scolds. "You're only as old as you feel."

"Oh, if you only knew. Just you wait, Brittany, someday you may understand. Hopefully not." Today, she aches in every joint. She wishes she could afford the medication to ease the inflammation.

She looks at the yellow dress with black and white stripes and thinks why not just wear a yield sign? Everyone would see her coming. She should try it on so she can report to Brittany. At least she can wriggle into it easily enough. It slides down easily over her hips; she turns to the mirror. It's way too big, and she can't really find words to describe it. A giant lemon? Oversized canary? No, Big Bird, that's who she is. She looks at the tag. She's forgot her glasses; is she reading that right? Size 24! Is that how Brittany sees her? That big? She's made a mistake, grabbed the wrong size. It shows off her hair, but that's all she can say about it. She can't hold back her laughter.

What if Nick saw her in this? What would he say? Or any of her kids? Peter, for instance, he'd have something smart to say, the connoisseur of everything that he is. She can imagine the insults.

Peter phoned last night. She was so out of it.

"Hi, Mom, how are you? Did I wake you? I hope not."

"What do you expect? It's 3 a.m. How much money do you want?"

"Hey, I never asked for money, did I? What if I was just phoning to say hi from England? Can't a son do that?"

"Yes, a son can, and you never would. How much? I'm down to my last pennies, just so you know."

"Just a couple hundred, Mom. Can you wire it in the morning?"

"I thought you said you were going to get a job."

"I tried. It's not easy. And my papers aren't in order so I have to do it illegally."

"Look, I've got a big day tomorrow. Sheila's daughter Allison is getting married, and I am helping her with the wedding, and your brother's in the wedding party. The last thing I need is to have to go traipsing off to wire you money. As if I already didn't have enough to do."

"I know, Mommy. Thank you, you're a dear. I love you. Send it to the same place as before."

"I love you too. Now piss off and goodnight."

She sent it before coming to the dress shop, after she went over to Laurie's to borrow white sling-back shoes and Susan's to borrow a white mohair shawl for the wedding.

Milly holds up the next dress. It's a soft green, fresh and summery, with a hint of yellow in the lime, and with plain lines, nothing too drastic or froufrou.

"Excuse me, ma'am," Brittany calls from outside the changeroom. "Is there something I can take away?"

"Oh, please don't call me ma'am, dearie. Makes me feel ancient. Call me Milly."

"You're not old! Have you forgotten what I told you before?"

The dresses she's tried on lie on the floor. She'll have to reach down to pick them up, then pass them over to Brittany. She doesn't want to, but Brittany has her work to do and she shouldn't hold her back. Her hips, arms, back, and knees ache as she gathers the dresses and throws them over the top of the changeroom door.

"Will there be dancing at the wedding?" Brittany asks.

"There'll be a DJ." Sheila's nephew was in charge of music.

"Don't forget to take your dancing shoes."

Once they're done in the kitchen tonight, Milly and Sheila will have a few drinks, kick off their shoes, and dance. She'll pay for it tomorrow, but she doesn't care; a person has to have a little fun. Milly does a hip wiggle and a little two-step in front of the mirror.

She feels something then, a sensation around her hips and legs. Her panties lie bunched at her bare feet. She bends down to pull them up and sees the head of the safety pin has fallen off. Was there anything else left to break? She stuffs her panties into her purse.

She'll make Ben dance with her. Oh, she could wring his neck. That face of his, all purple and blue, it'll peer out of Allison's wedding pictures forever. Unless Allison's marriage doesn't last; so many don't. Milly's not looking forward to what Sheila's going to say about

Ben's appearance; she'll be very direct about how she feels, as if Milly was the one who smashed his face in.

She lets out a moan, her hands falling to her sides, and the lime green dress slides to the floor.

Smashed face. Chrissy comes to her when she least expects it, and with her the whole incident, as if it just happened. That beautiful face, the blood matting in her blonde curls. If only Milly had paid attention. If only she hadn't gone to the church to help with Christmas hampers, something Nick's mother got her doing because it impressed the other church ladies how her family rallied around. She didn't even like Milly.

Milly wipes her tears with her T-shirt and sniffs. "If only, if only, if only. The story of my life."

"Is anything grabbing you?" Brittany calls.

Milly tries to speak, but emotion bunches in her throat. She coughs and manages a raspy, "I'm getting there."

Ten years ago, and still whenever she thinks about that night she has no resistance. It's true she thinks of her less now that Ben's out of the house. Looking at him was like looking at Chrissy, as close in appearance as fraternal twins could be.

Chrissy stayed late at the school to help with the play. As usual, Milly was running late. Her dryer broke so she went to the Laundromat, and she had a couple of other errands to run, a stop at the grocery store to buy a bag of Cheezies. She had a craving. It only took five minutes. Chrissy stood on the steps waiting for her, her shoulders hunched against the wind. It was snowing. The school doors had to be locked, Chrissy told her when she slid into the front sent, resentment in her voice at her mother's lateness.

"Chrissy, listen to this song. I love this song. This was the first song your Dad and I danced to on our wedding night."

"No, Mom, I want to tell you something. Please, never mind the radio now. I know the song."

"We were at the Steer and Stein, the only two on the dance floor. Just listen and then you can tell me what's on your mind."

The two of them fighting with the dial, pushing at each other, and Milly didn't see the truck coming. She didn't come to a complete stop. The roads were icy.

She has three other children. She had to go on, had to. But there were times when she thought she wouldn't.

Brittany's hand dangled a brown dress with splashes of leopard print over the door. "Not sure how you feel about animal prints, but I think this color is good for you, too. It matches your hair."

She's always liked browns, especially if she has a bit of a tan. Once, she practically lived in a brown bikini, when she and Nick were first married, when they had nothing and spent months at a time in the Caribbean. She baked up like a berry, though she's never understood that expression. Berries are red, mostly. They caught their own seafood, traded labor for fruit, vegetables, and meat. Nick did odd jobs, physical ones, she did housework and childcare. They looked like foreigners when they came back to Canada. Nick couldn't keep his hands off her. "My Liz, my Liz," he whispered in her hair, his breath warm on her neck.

The accident. The song whose name she can't remember. Lindsay, Ben, and Peter say she marks all time by the accident, but she has every right to, it was a turning point.

"Anything working?" Brittany calls.

"So far the green is the best. The brown reminds me of the Caribbean."

"Try this." Brittany's bracelets jangle as she waves an aqua-colored dress in the air. "Any more dresses to pass back?"

Milly hands over a couple. "These are definite nos. I'll hang on to the maybes. Two so far." She supposes she should look at the prices before she decides on one. "This aqua is the color of the Caribbean." She presses the dress into her nose, breathes in, hoping to recapture the smell of the sea, feel the warmth of the strong trade winds.

They promised to love each other forever. They leaned close for buttery lobster kisses in the booth at the back of the Steer and Stein. Before the four children came along, when all they knew to expect from each other was joy, when it seemed that was all life would bring.

After the accident, he looked at her differently. "Were you drinking coffee? Putting on makeup? Talking on the cell? Or were you just not paying attention, like you usually do, talking a mile a minute."

She'd shut up for the rest of her life if it would bring Chrissy back. The therapist said it would take a long time to heal, but there could be no healing, especially in the face of his blame. Only a slow, corrosive sense of self-hatred.

Whenever the whim took him, he left, on the spur of the moment, gave her no explanation, no notice, escaping the daily reminders of Chrissy, of all of them. Went with his buddies to golf in Florida, hunt in the north, fish on Nipissing, leaving to deliberately forget, while she was home, tending to the sorrow. And when she had a chance to go and see her mother in California, what did she find when she got back?

"Black and white is very classy." Brittany's arm waved the dress over the top of the door. "And this one has a built-in bra and a very sexy plunging back."

Milly smirks. Classy is beyond her means or position in life, but she might as well try it on. Why not? as Brittany says. "It's nice. You're a very patient, caring person, Brittany."

"I'm here to help, that's my job." The compliment put a brightness in Brittany's voice.

Milly slips off her bra, drapes it on a hook, and looks at the dress. A black and white geometric pattern on top, a solid black skirt.

Black and white. There it was when she got back from California, came home in the middle of the afternoon and a week early, expecting to find no one. And in her bedroom, the two of them. She ran downstairs and threw up in the kitchen sink. Right under her nose, he'd been carrying on with her neighbor, the woman who refused to say hello when they met on garbage night and Milly decided she just wasn't the friendly type.

Nick came into the kitchen buttoning his shirt, his feet bare, his hair dishevelled. "So, now you know. It's over, Milly. It's so over." The front door closed.

Somehow, she probably knew already, but she didn't want to admit it or face it, resisting the change that came with it. Her life had already changed so much. "Get out!"

She wouldn't bother with the black and white dress. You have to be able to strut in a dress with such a dramatic plunging back, wear it with a certain panache, with elegance, and class, and confidence; she'd feel weighed down by the pretense.

The tears well up again. She's such a jellyfish when it comes to special events, they always make her emotional, but today she is out of control. Allison and Chrissy were the same age. That's how she met Sheila—the two girls played together. It could be her daughter getting married today. Sheila and her husband Don could be Milly and Nick standing by Chrissy's side. She must snap out of it or she'll be useless to Sheila, to everyone.

She will try the lime green on again; this could well be the one. It's that spring green she likes, the color of new leaves bursting from a tree, or shoots pushing up through the earth. A color of promise, of beautiful things still to come.

A buzz comes from inside her purse. Ben's phone is ringing.

"Where are you?" Sheila asks. Milly can tell she's worked up.

"I'm getting a dress for the wedding. I won't be much longer."

"Getting a dress? Now?" Sheila sounds surprised, but she shouldn't be.

"Yes, I know, I know. But you know how I am. I didn't have anything to wear and I didn't have time before. I've been so busy, rushing around." Sheila knew she didn't go to fancy events and wouldn't have anything appropriate hanging in her closet. Or in one of her piles.

"I'm at the church, and I don't see the flowers. The service starts in twenty minutes." Sheila's voice is shrill; she's practically shouting. "Tell me you did get them! Tell me!"

"Oh my God," Milly screams. "I forgot. There's just been so much today. Money to Peter in England and Thunder underfoot, and I had to get my hair done and go to Laurie's to borrow her shoes and Susan's for a shawl. I'll go, I'll go! I'm going right now. Tell the minister to wait fifteen minutes. He won't mind. It's not a big deal."

"No, Milly, it *is* a big deal. I am not going to tell the minister to start late! This will not be on your terms. This is my daughter's wedding and you are not going to delay it one minute. You are not going to spoil it for her!"

Sheila sounds hysterical, and Milly wonders why do weddings do this to the mother of the bride? She's gone over the top. Lost control.

"You know, Sheila, I've been helping you. I'm trying to help you save money. I've decorated and I'm working in the kitchen tonight. The least you can do is give me fifteen minutes. That's all I'm asking."

"You and your confounded sense of time. You know darn well you'll be longer than fifteen minutes. Why can't you just for once be better organized? Think about someone other than yourself! Your actions have consequences. What am I supposed to tell the guests? Or Allison! This is her day!" Sheila is sobbing and seems to be talking to herself. "I don't know what to do. This is a real mess. I'll have to get Don involved, and you know what he's like.

"You know what, Milly? Don't come. Stay away. I don't want another one of your mix-ups. You are not welcome." Sheila hangs up.

Milly stares at the phone. Not welcome? How can that be? She loves weddings, and Ben is in it. They'll have a dance later tonight. Surely she should be allowed to see him? After all her help, this is what she gets? Sheila's overtired and overexcited and if anyone knows how that feels it's her.

Sheila can get awfully worked up and can be unreasonable if she doesn't get her way. Once the wedding is over, once everything settles down, she'll come to her senses and ask herself why she told Milly not to come. Sheila will remember all Milly has done for her, not just for the wedding, and be overcome with remorse. Maybe it won't be today, maybe not next week, but eventually she'll come to Milly and say that the day would have been perfect if only her dear friend had been there.

Milly must go to the wedding and spare Sheila the regret, protect her from herself, make her day perfect. Sometime tonight, once the cleanup is done and they're having a drink, shoes kicked off, feet up on a chair, Sheila will apologize, and Milly will tell her to forget it because she understands: all will be forgiven.

If she hurries, she'll slip into one of the back pews and catch the end of the service. Maybe they won't start on time—these things shouldn't, lots of people are late, not just her. She will slip away after the service and get the flowers. She'll take them to the reception hall, place them before the guests arrive, and they'll be beautiful, and no one will even notice they were missing at the church.

She must hurry. She'll tell Brittany what's happened, how as usual she's lost track of time, and she'll take the lime green dress, but she should ring it up quickly. She'll let Brittany know it wasn't her fault, this last-minute rushing; she's given great service.

She looks at the tag. Much more than what she wanted to spend, but she's left it too long and now she has no choice. She was late for her own wedding.

She pulls the latch on the changeroom door, steps out into the bright room, the store abuzz with late-afternoon shoppers.

Then it comes. The song. She closes her eyes and hears it: All of me, why not take all of me. She puts her arms out as if dancing with him. His solid arms and broad shoulders, a sturdy body that meant forever, his musky scent, the disco ball turning overhead, showering them with diamonds, a sparkling life together, feet shuffling slowly, bodies entwined as one. Why not take all of me? She gave herself to him. And he took it all.

"Ma'am!" She hears Brittany's voice. "Ma'am! I must insist you get back into the changeroom right now!"

Milly opens her eyes, her arms embracing all that she has lost as she faces the mirror on the dressing-room door and the reflection of shoppers behind her, gaping at her nakedness. Let them see her bare breasts, sagging and huge from nursing babies and age, her stomach covered in stretch marks and scars from a Caesarean birth, her darkly thicketed pubis that sent bodies out into the world, the ripple of blue veins down her legs. Tears stream down her face. Let them see what life has done.

"'All of Me,' Brittany. That was the song."

Brittany looks distraught as she moves towards Milly as if to touch her but withdraws her hands and steps back. "I have no idea what you're talking about. I am going to call security if you don't get back into the changeroom right now."

Brittany didn't know. Look at her, poor sweet lamb, somewhere in her twenties, skinny as a rail, not a wrinkle on her face, her eyes wide and bright and unknowing. She might never know.

This beaten-down old body, this spectacle, stood as a monument to life itself, and life had been taken from her until she thought there was nothing left. She must keep on giving and giving and find in that a reason to live and breathe, to try to capture moments of joy. However fleeting. Even if she didn't deserve them.

Because what Brittany didn't know, what she really could not know, is that there is no other choice.

About the Author

Catharine Leggett is the author of the novel *The Way to Go Home* (Urban Farmhouse Press, 2019); her award-winning short stories have been published in numerous journals and anthologies and broadcast on radio. She has a BA degree in English Literature from Wilfrid Laurier University in Waterloo, Canada, and she completed the long program at the Humber School for Writers. She has lived in several cities in Canada and the United States, and presently resides with her husband in her hometown city of London, Ontario. Her two grown children have long since flown the coop. She worked in the restaurant industry at all levels for years, when she was younger. More recently, she has taught Creative Writing in the Continuing Studies Program for Western University, and has been a Communications Manager, a volunteer Media Co-ordinator for a film festival, and a store owner.

www.ingramcontent.com/pod-product-compliance
Lightning Source LLC
Chambersburg PA
CBHW051342020726
47501CB00007B/2224